CANDLELIGHT KILLER

CANDLELIGHT KILLER

By James Booker

This is a work of fiction. Names, characters, places, and incidents either are the product of the author's imagination or are used fictitiously, and any resemblance to actual persons, living or dead, businesses, companies, events, or locals, is entirely coincidental, and only used to establish and bring out the historical context of the era.

ISNB 978-1-7340323-0-7

We often do good in order that we may do evil with impunity.

~ Francios De La Rochefoucauld.

CHAPTER 1

The killer stepped out of the dark. He held the little girl's hand as they walked down Mulberry Street—lower East Side of Manhattan. It was 11:00 P.M. The slum was dark. The child let out a whimper, "May I have another sucker?" The child said.

The killer pulled a sucker from his coat and handed it to her. Candy calmed her nerves, she slid into a passive state. They turned off the street into an alleyway. Men and women —slum dwellers— the newspapers called them, languished in the dark; silhouetted human bodies etched in the night like stick figures splashed onto walls.

Alcoholics and drug addicts languished in empty corridors. The killer and the girl passed unnoticed. Some glared, then turned away. A streetlamp emanated a dull and hazy light down the alleyway barely highlighting the stifling fog. Debris and rubbish decorated the gutter. Cutoff from view, they made their way deeper and deeper.

Tenement structures had lost its new look, bricks appeared to sag and zigzag. Faded mortar glistened with grease like an oil spill on a mechanic's workshop floor. They walked through piles of rotten food; rats scurried. The alleyways interconnected like spider webs. Sounds of shattered glass echoed throughout the maze.

They made another turn; more slum-dwellers. The girl coughed; her nostrils burned deep with opium, like the stench of death when the Triangle Waist Company burned in 1911, killing 146 people. The deeper they walked, the more isolated they became. Only gangs and outlaws ventured this deep.

They arrived at a secluded place; the killer found a wood crate, sat down, and placed the girl on his lap and stroked her frazzled hair. He opened his bag and pulled out some candles. He positioned them in front of both of them, creating an arch and lit them one by one. The light from the candles illuminated the surrounding area. Shadows flooded the adjacent wall. The scene morphed with occult-like features reminiscent of a high-priest ready to sacrifice a lamb or dove to Zeus or Apollo.

The killer studied the girl; checking her eyes, ears, and skin. He didn't know what he was looking for, but he was playing a part much like ancient priests would do before they sacrificed an animal. He made his decision. He pulled out a large knife; held it to the girl's throat, "This is not your fault," he said. "You were born this way. You must die so that others may live."

It was quick. The main artery in the neck was severed. The light from the candles danced and twisted like naked strippers, as if the flames were radio-active, leaving ghoulish images on the brick walls.

The child's eyes fluttered. The next moment, her life was gone. The killer placed the body beside him on the crate. He stood and hovered over it. He kissed two of his fingers and touched the child's forehead, "I fixed you." He said.

CHAPTER 2

"Ladies and gentlemen," Godfrey Goodwin, said, "Thank you for coming. As most of you know, we have rented a hall here, at City College New York to hear a lecture by Dr. Eugene Black."

The audience clapped with anticipation and eagerness; cheers and more cheers.

"Thank you. Just a few words about our lecturer. Professor Black is a well-respected eugenicist. He holds a Ph.D. in biology and two master's degrees; one in chemistry and another in mathematics – particularly in statistics. He has taught courses at Harvard, Yale, and throughout the United States, and Great Britain. Columbia University awarded him tenure when his dissertation on the *Advancement of the Human Race through Eugenics* was published in the Science Quarterly Review in 1924."

Goodwin stopped and quenched his thirst with a glass of water. He wiped his lips with his tongue, they glistened in the light. The paper he held trembled in his hands. Goodwin was in his seventies and frail. "Ladies and gentlemen," he said as his voice hit a few offbeat cords, "One of Dr. Black's famous epigrams is, 'Science is key to our survival, eugenics is the means, it's settled science.'"

The hall was packed. Approximately one hundred people in attendance— mostly students. "Now, without further ado, I wish to introduce to you our distinguished speaker; Professor Eugene Black."

The crowd stood and clapped as Dr. Black walked up to the podium. He weighed 200 pounds; five feet tall. His hair was black with a bald spot in the middle. His sideburns were cut short, revealing white streaks running down the side of his face. He had dark-beady-eyes that came close to each other like a gun cylinder.

Dr. Black cleared his throat, "Thank you for those kind words, Dr. Goodwin." And bowed to his old colleague. "Thank you for having me." He turned to the audience, "Thank you for coming." He said.

They clapped.

"Now, we will get to it. We want to thank Mr. Andrew Carnegie and many other philanthropists who have funded our cause. We've made great advancements."

The audience became enamored and cheered more.

"Evolution is great. Evolution is progress. It has brought humanity from its primordial existence to a fully functional thinking man. Charles Darwin was a great scientist." Dr. Black's double chin rolled like beer barrels rolling down a steep hill every time he spoke.

Another round of applause came from the attendees.

Dr. Black addressed the audience, "Thank you, thank you." He flipped his top paper to the side and continued to read. "Gentlemen. We must also thank another great pioneer, the honorable Sir Francis Galton. He is the founder of eugenics. All is lost, without him. He is also from a most illustrious lineage. His blood-line is pure. He is a cousin of Charles Darwin."

Dr. Black reached a high-water mark in his short introduction. The crowd clapped and cheered with higher intensity. Some stood. Others followed – like Prairie dogs sticking their heads out from holes in the ground. Electrifying; leading to a standing ovation. Most were devotes' to the cause.

Dr. Black's brain exploded with confidence. He could barely contain himself. Nor was he inclined to hide his pride.

"Thank you." He said. "Now, let us move on." He waved his arms and signaled the audience to sit. "Evolution has done its job, but now humanity is on the brink of extinction. In other words, we must save the human race from itself." Dr. Black guzzled down some water, "Some say eugenics is a fad; but it's no fad, it's settled science. Since 1900 many of its supporters have worked tirelessly to ensconce it into law and into the American Psyche. Influential people support the cause. Scientists and titans of industry have spent millions to achieve a better society and superior individuals and a perfect future."

Most of the attendees were college students and biology majors; many of the young men broke with conventional dress norms. They wore blazers and flannel trousers. Instead of ties, they wore ascots. Raccoon fur coats were favored. They preferred their pants creased in the front and back and turned up at the ankle; some even incorporated the Oxford Bags, worn by Oxford students. The cacophony of style broke with tradition.

"Yes, it is true science and technology have grown exponentially." He said, "We can build skyscrapers that reach the clouds. We have cars. We have airplanes. Now millions of people can listen to a radio. Yet, the human race is at a pivotal place in history. The world is overpopulated. There are too many inferior races. Black, brown, many white races and others are evolutionary leftovers. They are tainted. Their blood is impure. Society must stop them from procreating, or they will overtake the pure-bloods."

A silent somberness dropped over the audience like a wet blanket. They believed something had to be done. Action must be taken. Progress will save the race and the future.

Dr. Black continued, "The illustrious Dr. Herbert Spencer coined the phrase, 'Survival of the fittest.' As eugenicists, we are strong, we must aid evolution in making sure the strong survive."

Professor Black stopped reading. He pulled off his glasses and walked to the side of the podium. His appeal became personal, "My dear friends, we must answer the call. It is up to you and me to make the future safe for the pure-bloods."

Full of energy and optimism, the young men were ready to change the world, to bend it to their will. 1927 was the year all things were possible. Nothing was out of reach. And New York was the center of the world.

"Eugenics," Stated Prof. Black. "Is the idea of how the strong will continue to grow stronger and stronger. The strong are thoroughbreds."

Dr. Black's speech was in part propaganda and a rally, rather than a lecture. But he believed his words to the core of his being. The young men ate it up. They clapped, urging Dr. Black onward. Whistles punctuated through the audience.

One individual didn't clap or applaud, however. He stood out. It was apparent he shopped at the famous Brooks Brothers; a place where gentlemen went to purchase more traditional clothing. They even supplied the suit Abraham Lincoln wore for his burial after his assassination. J.P. Morgan, Charles Lindbergh, and many other famous men shopped at Brooks Brothers. They are the oldest haberdashers in the United States.

James Prescott Fox wore a black three-piece suit, pinstripe Manhattan shirt with a plain white detachable collar, and a clean looking tie. He held a walking stick. Resting on his lap was his gray Fedora hat. Just like his clothes; Fox was reserved, but he stood out nonetheless.

After the audience calmed down, Fox spoke up, "Prof. Black." Clearing his throat. "May I ask a question?"

He looked up, "Yes, go ahead." He felt a little apprehension. Rarely does anyone ask questions or dare challenge, Dr. Black.

"You mentioned 'thoroughbreds.'" Fox said. "Can you explain what you mean by 'thoroughbreds?"

"Well, you see my good man, Dr. Charles Benedict Davenport in both of his books— *Heredity, Concerning Eugenics* and *The Science of Human Improvement by Better Breeding*— proves there are fit and unfit mating. And they can either pass on good or bad traits."

"I think I'm catching on," Fox expressed, "You mean like mating two good horses to produce a better horse?"

Prof. Black's eyes lit up, "Yes. By Jove, you've got it. Right on the mark, old man."

"I see," Fox said. "So, the logic holds the other way around. If we mate two inferior horses, then that will produce more inferior horse then themselves?"

"Of course."

"Then Davenport and other eugenicists apply that same logic to the human race. If we mate unfit persons together, that will produce more inferior persons? And if we mate fit persons, that will produce superior persons?" Fox said.

"That's spot on." Said Dr. Black. "You see, according to Davenport, 'man is an organism – an animal. And the laws of improvement of corn and racehorses hold for him also.'"

"That sounds logical. But how can you implement this in real life?"

"We already have. Our team has worked hard to influence states to strengthen marriage laws, for example. These laws make sure the right people mate correctly; it will prevent inferior people of mating altogether. And thirteen states have passed forced sterilization laws. These states force sterilize inmates who are imbeciles. They will no longer inflict the world with their impurity and criminality." Dr. Black explained.

Shouts from all over the room rang out. Young men stomped their shoes; their voices created an uproar, their pride turned into sheer hubris. The frenzy tinkered on the verge of madness. After a few mintues, they calmed down.

Fox resumed his questions, "Imbeciles? What do you mean?"

"Good question." Dr. Black said, "Eugenics proved that people who are imbeciles are born that way. Low IQ individuals are the result of unfit mating. It is no fault of their own. You see, they can't learn. They can't read or write. Criminality is in their nature. And society suffers for it."

"How is this science?" Fox said.

"There is a well-known, documented case. Ada Juke was indolent and a harlot. She procreated. Her descendants produced more harlots, and they were paupers. They, in turn, interbred producing more harlots and more rude behavior. The third generation slid further into criminality. And the next generations, even more so." He said. "It's in the genes."

Fox carefully noticed the terms and definitions. He thought through the answers. "Everything I've heard sounds logical." He slowed his speech. His face was deep in thought. "But is it ethical? Is it moral to sterilize people against their will?"

Dr. Black's face turned red. His eyes narrowed. They pierced Fox's head like a knife. *If only I could lobotomize this man right here right now*, he thought. "Ethical? Moral?" Dr. Black exploded. His double cheeks rolled like Jell-O. "I'll tell you what is ethical and moral!" He thundered. "Saving the human race from extinction! We must stop unfit hordes before it's too late! The unfit are the unethical and immoral ones! They are dangerous and evil!"

The room erupted with applause. Cheers. Whistles crisscrossed from each part of the room; euphoria filled the air like helium balloons. The audience felt a rush. Euphoric— spilled over into the hallway. Boots and shoes slammed the floor. They chanted: eugenics, eugenics, is hygienic. Eugenics will purge us from people with schizophrenia.

CHAPTER 3

Two days later, on May 3, Ginger found the child's corpse. If it weren't for her, the body would have rotted and decomposed. Few cared. Skid-row was a god-forsaken place where dropouts went to escape trouble or responsibilities. Whatever the reason, it was a living hell. A place where middle-class mores stopped; where there was a clear demarcation line drawn between civility and cruelty.

Ginger was a local cocaine-addict. For three years she lived on the streets. She begged for money or sold herself to survive. Hardened by her lifestyle's choices; she nonetheless, still had a soft spot for children.

The body started to decay. When Ginger approached the scene, her nostrils flared; her neck snapped back – pungent and poignant to her senses. She covered her mouth. Flies buzzed, added to the awkward attraction. She approached like she was in a slow-moving picture. Her skin crawled with anticipation. The closer she got; fear gripped her thoughts like talons from a vulture — "Mother Mary of God!" She screamed.

She stopped. She stretched her neck out to look closer. She gasped, "My God!" She said. She recoiled. Ginger grabbed her torn overcoat out of a deep primordial fear; a subconscious force that required no forethought. She wanted to run. The need for safety was paramount. The danger was real. But a part of her wanted to protect the child, but it was too late. She knew it. But her caring instincts is what kept her connected to civilization. It kept her sane.

"Monstrous!" She said. "Who would do this to an innocent child?" Her eyes watered.

Ginger ran to the street and called out for help. Her scream was gut-wrenching. "Help! Help! A dead child!" She screamed. "Police!" She leaned her frail body against the street lamppost. Exhausted and out of breath.

A whistle went off down the block. Then another. The police emerged. Cop cars blocked the alleyway. Then the crime-scene was fenced off. They searched every corner; all the connecting alleys and abandoned buildings. They questioned every hobo and dreg of society.

"Men," Detective Savage ordered, "Go to the front street and start asking questions. You know the routine."

Detective Francis Savage was a 20-year-plus veteran. He started out as a street cop and worked his way up to homicide. He was massive; a giant of a man that could pulverize a person by one swing of his massive arm. Determined, focused, and extremely narrow-minded; for most people, this would be a handicap, but for Savage— it was a strength. He almost always got his man.

The police interviewed everyone in the proximity. No one knew anything; no one saw anything, except Ginger. But she refused to go downtown and give a statement; she feared cops. The jail was not a pleasant place, although she did enjoy two meals a day. Many only received one meal, but if an inmate was kind to the guards and didn't cause trouble, they got two.

Savage began to lose his patience, "Do you want to be arrested for obstruction?"

Ginger snapped, "You can't make me do nothing."

Savage became pushy, "There's a nice little cell downtown with your name on it if you don't cooperate. Guttersnipe!"

Her eyes were bloodshot. Tiny little veins pulsated when she glared at Savage like neon-lights flashing on Broadway in the middle of the night. "I don't care." She said. "You can even try to threaten me with your Bean-shooter; I still won't go." She stomped her foot in the gravel.

Crowds started to grow. They hovered around like bees buzzing around a hive; things began to get out of control. Cars stopped; food-carts couldn't maneuver through the street. The block clogged up like a kitchen sink.

Det. Savage moved closer, dwarfing her little frame. "Look here, sister. Talk or else—"

"Else what?" She said in anger. "Coppers are all the same. Bullies. Pushing people around like shit." She turned to walk away.

J.P. Fox emerged. He managed to work his way through the crowd just in time to catch their last words. Fox was a private detective. He was often called upon by the police department to help on high-profile cases and even low-profile cases simply to help with the backlog.

"Miss Ginger," Fox said. He took off his hat and bent his upper torso. "Please, let me introduce myself. I'm J.P. Fox. It is a pleasure meeting you."

Ginger froze, this was the first time anyone treated her with respect, at least in her recent memory. She eyeballed him; she knew the kind— neatly dressed with good manners.

"Say what you want?" She said with a curious look across her face; her lips tight with caution.

"I apologize for my colleague's rude behavior. You see, detective Savage has been under pressure. He will not threaten you again." He turned to Savage. "Will you?" He said. His voice became resolute and firm.

Savage shuffled his body. Tense and annoyed. "No." He said. But his body language said something different.

Savage and Fox worked together on many cases. They knew each other; they knew how each other ticked. They were friends, but tenuous at times.

She bent her head sideways and looked at both of them with suspicion. *Should I trust this cop and gumshoe?* She thought. After careful mental deliberation, she made her decision, "Fine. Only if you buy me a meal and give me a ciggy."

Around the corner was a local drug store. Fox, Savage, and Ginger walked in the front door. Gum, cigarettes, candy, and other assorted items were advertised on for sale signs. To their right, some of the signs hung on the walls, other signs were taped to the window casings. On the adjacent wall was a bar running the length of the store. On the walls behind the bar were full-length mirrors reflecting every person and every move in the store. Men were reading newspapers, while young boys were drinking soda pops and milkshakes. They walked to the back of the store and found an empty table.

True to her word; Ginger ordered two fried eggs, a side of bacon, bread, and a cup of coffee. She hadn't eaten a substantial meal for months; she often ate from garbage cans. Sometimes her tricks would furnish her enough money to buy a sandwich, but not much else maybe more booze. Unfortunately, most of her money went to the local drug dealer.

Ginger didn't scarf down her food like a pig. She knew from experience eating fast led to a sick stomach and regurgitation. She had to make it last. Slum-dwellers never knew when they would get their next full meal.

"Where's my ciggy?" She said.

Fox reached into his pocket and pulled out a box of Lucky Strikes. He never smoked cigarettes himself, but he carried them to give away in case he needed them to build rapport with smokers. It was one of those tricks Fox learned early in his career. It was vital. He opened the package and shook one out from the top like shaking a tree limb for low hanging fruit. "There you go." He said. Fox struck a match, a light flashed. In seconds a warm glow burned on the tip of the cigarette like a firefly.

Ginger inhaled the smoke. It was a relief, an expression of delight after what she had just seen. The more she puffed, the more her mind tried to escape the horror. She exhaled and leaned back in her chair.

"How's the meal?" Fox said.

"Fine. Just fine. I haven't eaten bacon for a long time. It's been too long." She said, running her tongue over what few teeth she had left.

"Good," Fox replied. Fox pulled out his pad and pencil. "Ginger, please start from the beginning."

"As I told the cops, I was on my way to my box. I walked by, and there she was." Ginger closed her eyes. She began to shake. "The smell was worse than anything I have ever smelled. Worse than a rat." Ginger blew smoke out of her nostrils, thinking it would clear the stench from her mind.

Fox gave her space. He wanted her to experience what she saw and felt all over again, but in a place, she felt safe. If he tried to guide and direct her, she might resist and shut down. Ginger's mind and thoughts were at war. Her emotions wanted to forget, but her rational mind knew she needed to help Fox even if it was to repay him for the meal and the cigarette.

She took another puff. The smoke was pulled deep into her overworked lungs. She crossed her legs and elevated her arm with the cigarette between two fingers. *Dignity. I must be dignified.* She thought. In reality, she was a cartoon caricature of a Hollywood actress. Ginger was once a flapper; frequented speakeasies, beautiful, and classy. Now she's a habitual slum-dweller.

"Take your time Ginger," Fox said.

He was patient. Dealing with emotional and effusive people was always a challenge. Their intellect and feelings were bruised if they felt the other person was being patronizing. Many slum-dwellers had a false sense of their intelligence. On the other hand, some homeless people were college graduates. They got caught up in drugs and alcohol, and these vices enslaved them like chains.

"You're doing fine Ginger," Fox said.

She placed her cigarette on top of the cigarette holder. Her head tilted backward. Black soot covered the ceiling like a hovering dark cloud. "There was something else. Let's see." She tapped the side of her head, trying to remember.

"Yes. Go ahead."

She squinted her eyes. She snapped her fingers, "Yes. I got it." Her eyes popped open like a cork from a champagne bottle. "There was nothing out of the ordinary the night I found the girl, but two nights ago I was walking down 10th Street. It was empty. All of a sudden, a tall man walked out of the dark and turned out of a side alley. We bumped into each other," she said. "He gave me the heebie-jeebies."

"Go ahead," Fox said.

"He was tall and wearing a cloak. The cloak was similar to what my grandfather wore."

"Can you remember anything else?" Fox said.

"Well, it was dark, you see. The street-light was dim." Ginger strained to remember. Her thoughts, however, were scattered. The drugs she had pumped into her body caused her thinking processes to be disjointed and fragmented. She could no longer think in a linear pattern. One moment she acted goofy, the next she was lucid.

Fox was forced to help her remember. "What did he look like, Ginger. Did he have any scars? Was he white or black?" He said.

Her eyes lit up like a flame. "Yes, the man I bumped into was all white. I mean white as snow. He wasn't normal, you see." Her lips quivered. "Oh my. Was that the killer?"

"Ginger," Fox said, "You mean he was an albino?"

"That's it. Yes, I think so." She wiped her lips with the towel.

"Was there anything else?"

"Yes, he was holding a case."

"What kind?"

"One of those fancy ones. It was old."

"Fancy?" Fox asked.

"The kind doctors or lawyers carry."

"Anything else?"

"That's all I can remember."

Like a light switch turned off, Ginger focused back on her food.

Fox knew that was all the information Ginger would supply him. He reached into his pocket and handed her his card, "Here's my card, Ginger. If you remember anything else, please give me a call. Thank you for your co-operation." Fox handed her the rest of the Lucky Strikes.

CHAPTER 4

After a long day, Fox arrived home at his two-bedroom one bath apartment on 91st and Broadway. It was a few blocks west of Central Park and not far from the American Museum of Natural History. Fox liked the location and the amenities that came with living there. It was a new building; had an elevator, his apartment was well furnished, and the room service was quick and served good food. The living room window faced the front street and protruded slightly outward forming a beveled arch. It allowed Fox to see between the buildings, across the street, and without much effort down both sides of the road and sidewalks.

Before going upstairs, Fox stopped at the front desk and ordered dinner, "Please bring me the soup of the day and a sandwich." He said.

"Yes, yes sir Mr. Fox, I'll have it brought up right away."

Fox's apartment was cozy. The most comfortable place in the living room was his dark-blue-leather chair. It sat close to the beveled front window and next to the fire-place. Fox was tired; he entered and hung his hat, and his jacket on the rack next to the front door, and placed his walking stick in a horizontal position in the lower rung of the stand, and sat and started to relax.

Before long, the bell rang, followed by a knock on the front door, "Room service," a small voice cried. It was the bellhop.

Fox walked over and opened the door, "Hello, come in," Fox said. A young man pushed a cart through the front door. The wheels squeaked like a flock of crows. Fox pointed, "Right over there, by the kitchen table." A dome-like silvery, shiny lid, covered the food. The silverware jangled as the bellhop pushed the cart toward the kitchen.

The young boy was in his uniform. The bellhop was spiffy looking with that natural youthful spring in his feet, "Is this the spot, Mr. Fox?"

"Yes, that's fine," Fox said.

The bellhop walked back to the door, turned, and opened his palm waiting for a tip. Fox flipped him the going rate. "Thank you kindly." The boy said. He bowed, turned, and walked out the front door.

After Fox ate, he sat in his chair by the window; he was tired, it had been a long day. His mind mulled over the events of the day. The murder, Professor Black's topic on eugenics, and the student's responses. And of course, Ginger's testimony. Each event was shocking and disturbing.

Fox had investigated murders many times before; even children's murder, but this one was different. *It appeared to be a sacrificial death. Why?* Fox pondered. Once again Fox ran through the list: Candles, the method of the crime, a possible eyewitness to the killer. Setting aside the candles and the style of the crime, this murder would be a random murder— if the killing of a child can be called arbitrary.

Fox couldn't help but think about Professor Black and eugenics. He had read about it in the newspapers but never had he listened to an expert lecture on Eugenics. *Fantastic. Why would certain institutions and individuals breed "good people"— as if good people are a matter of birth?* Fox thought. If this is true, people can't change; even God can't change them, but must be engineered.

Fox's mind drifted. He thought of his heritage; his father, his mother, their parents, and so on. In many respects, he had a prestigious background – primarily of English and Scottish stock. Many were professionals; Lawyers, doctors, and university professors. On the other hand; he had farmers, cobblers, and small business owners a part of his background as well.

Fox recalled the laundry list of diseases professor Black mentioned. Then he remembered his Aunt Gail. She suffered from mental illness. In and out of asylums. Then she committed suicide. If Professor Black was correct, *did he have her illness? Did he inherit her disease?* He thought. It was an unsettling thought.

Fox pulled out his diary and began to write, it was a family tradition. His father taught him to keep a journal to build his memories and to keep track of events so he could reflect back after he grew older and if his mind starts to fail. Besides, it helped him to focus; to arrange them methodically and logically— it was also a catharsis.

Fox stopped writing in the middle of a sentence. He didn't know why. Perhaps it was events from the last day or two. He felt lonely. His mind desired comfort; his thoughts longed for completeness, something personal and warm. Clara, Clara came to mind. His fingers flipped the pages backward like turning a clock back in time. The pages flipped from his fingertip like a silent movie moving in slow motion. There, he found it. The day he met Clara Anderson.

The day was 2 December 1924. Fox walked out the front door of Bloomingdales. Out of nowhere, a young woman appeared in front of him. Gentlemen would typically step aside for ladies, but Fox wasn't paying attention to where he was going. He was too busy counting his money. They bumped into each other. Fox looked up to say excuse me; but he froze, he was caught in a vortex. It was as if Clara was the sun, and he was pulled into her orbit. Her force was instantaneous; the hold was permanent. All he could do was stare.

Clara finally said, "well, are you a gentleman or not?"

Clara wore a long silk dress that wrapped around her body and looped in the front, imitating a goddess-like appearance. Her hair was brushed back and tucked under a wide brim hat; a large red flower donned the front side. Her red bee-stung lips accentuated her delicate white skin, and her green eyes sparkled like green gemstones. The way she dressed and carried herself – prim and proper – she was a lady through and through

Fox swallowed. Words escaped him; he reached for his hat and pulled it in front of him as if he needed to protect himself. When he did make a sound, he grunted, and his words were garbled. Then, he finally mustered a few words, "Yes. I mean – I apologize. Please forgive me."

They were inseparable from that moment on; it was a new chapter in Fox's life. He wrote down all the trips they experienced together; every dinner, every trek across New York City, upper state New York, and Long Island. Central Park was a favorite for both. By 1927 Manhattan had lost most of its natural habitat, giving way to steel skyscrapers, tenements, hotels, apartment buildings, and other structures. For those reasons and more, Central Park became an oasis for many proud Knickerbockers.

Fox read another entry. One day while visiting Central Park, it started to rain. Fox and Clara found a bench under a large tree. Some of the rain filtered through the branches; raindrops fell on Clara's hat, ran under her brim, and onto her forehead. Shiny watery beads formed on her nose like diamonds. Fox laughed. He reached over and licked the water from her nose as if licking syrup from a maple tree. She giggled. It was that moment Fox fell in love with Clara Anderson.

They were meant to be. Fox wanted to ask her to marry him at that moment on that very spot, but he was shy. He didn't have the nerve. *What if she said no.* He thought. A few minutes passed, and he was going to ask her, but his fleeting courage melted away like snow on a hot day. Chills crept up his spine at the thought of being rejected. Fox was a strong man. Intelligent and confident, but he had never faced this before. He had never loved anyone like he loved Clara; it made him weak and vulnerable. Fox began to question his self-confidence. Suddenly; he felt like Hamlet in William Shakespeare's play, he vacillated back and forth like a twig. He doubted his thoughts, motives, and actions – conflicted, to the point of madness. *Why would Clara love me? Why would she marry me?* His words exploded onto the page; *I must be mad, she's out of my league.* He thought over and over again. His obsessive thoughts almost destroyed his future relationship with Clara.

Tormented night and day, he later realized he was struggling with an inferiority complex. For unknown reasons, *Clara became his strength and his weakness.* These words haunted him; they hounded him until he was almost paralyzed.

Fox flipped through a few more pages; he landed on the page the day he asked Clara to marry him. At first; Fox struggled, but he found his backbone. He was overwhelmed by her beauty and charm. Sophisticated, intelligent, and her sex appeal captured his soul like pirates commandeering a ship. Fox heard of romances, and he remembered when his father told him of his courtship with his mother, but that seemed foreign and out of reach, until now.

He planned it all out. An excellent restaurant, a violin playing in the background. He would dress in a black and white tuxedo. Nothing could go wrong, but it did. On their way back from the theater, they got a flat tire. Fox's face turned beat-red with frustration. They got out. "I can't believe this," Fox said and kicked his tire. "Night of all nights!" He swung his arms up and down like a bird trying to take flight.

He paced back and forth. Fox fumed with anger; the more he squawked, the angrier he became. Along the side of the road was a small gully. Inadvertently, Fox slipped and fell into the muddy ditch; he was covered with dirt and slime. Sitting in filth, the blood vessels in his neck bulged and glowed like a World War I Bolt-Action Service Rifle.

Clara ran over, "Are you alright, James?"

"Yes." He said, but his obstreperous vocal cords betrayed his words. Fox had never been this angry; as if someone set his body on fire.

Clara went back to the car and retrieved a flashlight; she flipped the switched, and she couldn't contain herself. "This is why you brought me out here?" She giggled, "To see you wallow in the mud?" Her back arched, and she let out a stentorophonic laugh.

Fox tried to stand, but he just slipped back down into the mud. Covered with black mud, "This night is a disaster, this wasn't supposed to happen," Fox yelled, and he hit the dirt with his fist. More of the watery-dirt splashed on Fox's face.

Clara's dress was long, made of silk. Black silk gloves covered her arms that reached right above her elbows. Clara's sexy body was etched against the moonlight. Moon rays flashed around her frame, generating a natural silhouette that only a master painter can paint. She laughed more. Clara knew what Fox was up to. Her voice changed, "Mr. Fox." She said with a faux stern tone, but with a teasing manner, "Will you marry me?" She beat him to the punch. Clara could be calculating and mischievous at the same time.

Fox's red-face changed like a chameleon. His complexion turned white with unbelief; his blood-vessels pulsated then shrunk back under the skin like frightened poodles. Flabbergasted, he said, "Yes! Yes!"

Fox's final entry, *Clara is my strength and my weakness.*

Within seconds; Fox's head slumped forward, and fell asleep. His dreams were vivid and wild.

It was 2:30 in the morning when the wind awoke Fox. It tossed the window curtains back and forth like clothes fastened to a clothesline as if caught in a violent windstorm. Rain fell, and lightning lit up the night sky as if someone hung a million Christmas-lights around the dark clouds. Fox's head throbbed with pain. It matched the thunder. He walked to the kitchen and popped open a bottle of Ziron Iron Tonic. They helped calm his nerves and sleep. He changed into his bedclothes and nestled down in his bed for the rest of the night.

Two hours later, the front door of his apartment clicked open. It made a small creak sound, breaking the silence in the room. A triangular-shaped light from the hallway flooded into the living room. A shapely, but thin sexy leg stepped in. Her silk stockings shined. Clara was quiet. She slipped in and closed the door behind her.

Her stealth-like manner seemed to mirror her over-all etiquette— soft-spoken, polite, and cultured.

Clara made her way through the living room; down the narrow hallway, and into Fox's bedroom. She slipped off her shoes and walked to the front of the bed. A chair was in front of the vanity drawers that were against the wall. She unbuttoned her dress and laid it over the back of the chair. She unfastened her silk slip and let it gracefully fall to the floor like soft rose petals.

Clara kept her garter belt and straps on that were attached to her black stockings. She picked up a bottle of perfume and dabbed a little on her neck and wrists. Clara was a woman with desires, and Fox was the only man that could bring her sexual wants and needs to the surface. Besides, he was her betrothal— the man of her dreams.

She slipped under the covers and wrapped her arm around Fox's body. He was warm. His chest felt like soft steel. Muscular and alluring to the touch like a bodybuilder. Ever since Fox kissed her, it was difficult to control herself. Her defenses fell like the walls of Jericho to his charm and his physique. But she wasn't just attracted to his bronze construction, she was also drawn to his mind. He was intelligent with a keen sense of understanding human nature. He was attentive to her needs and wants. These and other qualities made Clara love him all the more. Over time, deep bonds had grown between them like roots from redwood trees.

It was 6:00 AM, the sun stretched through the window and lit up the adjacent room. Some of the light splashed through to the bedroom. Fox awoke to Clara's smell and the warmth of her body. He grew aroused. He turned, and she awoke. The chemistry was immediate. He wanted her, and she wanted him. Their eyes met. At first, they touched each other. It was gentle. Then, they lost all control. The next hour they experienced raw passion.

After their heated soiree; they held each other, "This is how I like my mornings," Clara said. "Right before we have to face the day." She smiled and hugged his chest.

Fox smiled, "Indeed, my love, indeed," He said; he rubbed her naked waist and ran his hand down her silk-garter belt and smooth stockings.

Clara kissed his neck and bit his earlobe. She moaned, then giggled, "My big man," she said.

Fox smiled, "My temptress."

She tapped his nose, "Remember Mr. Fox, we have wedding plans to attend too."

Fox not only desired Clara's body, but he admired her intellect. Her degree in biology sharpened her mind. A voracious reader, Clara loved to learn new things. She wasn't satisfied like many women were in just fancy clothes or to marry and have children. Clara wanted that, but more. She had a classical education and from an aristocratic background. Her family was well off financially, and they wanted her to learn to read Homer, Plato, and the Latin classics in the Latin and Greek languages. And she did.

Fox too, was well educated. He graduated from Harvard, and that meant he had to know Latin and Greek. He was an avid reader of poetry, politics, philosophy, and history. His two favorite ancient authors were Cicero and Plato. Both Clara and Fox also read modern authors. Clara enjoyed reading Jane Austen, Charles Dickens, and Edgar Allen Poe. Fox enjoyed the same authors, including T.S. Eliot, Fyodor Dostoevsky, and H.G. Wells; As for F. Scott Fitzgerald, they read him but felt he was a tad pretentious. Nonetheless, Fox felt T.S. Eliot was on the verge of becoming a committed Christian.

With her biology degree, Clara was able to gain employment at the Cold Harbor Spring Institute. The institute was located on Long Island and founded in 1890. Carnegie Institute supplied it with funds for the experimentation of evolution. The Eugenics Record Office or (ERO) is another division supported by the institute. At first, Clara did secretarial work. A short time after, she became a field-worker. Many women with biology degrees found employment at the institute.

Field-workers were sent out to insane asylums, jails, and other establishments to gain information on the physical, mental, moral, and even behavioral habits of inmates. Most were mad, sick, and criminals. The ERO recorded them into the Trait Book.

Traits were inherited. Imbeciles were imbeciles due to their family. Diseases like chorea, Bright's disease, dropsy, manic-depressives, rheumatism, gout, nervous conditions, and more. Bad traits were recorded and had to be dealt with eventually.

Fox and Clara were dressed and sitting at the kitchen table, eating breakfast. Fox became serious. He reached over and held Clara's hand, "Clara, we need to discuss something." He said.

Her bright eyes opened wide with curiosity, "Is everything alright Fox?"

"Well, I'm not sure how to say this—"

"Just say it," Clara said and squeezed his hand.

"Clara, I think we need to postpone the wedding—just for a little while."

Clara choked. She arched forward and spit coffee out of her mouth back into the cup. "What?" She exclaimed. "James Prescott Fox, what is the meaning of this? Have you got cold feet?" A fight was brewing whenever Clara called him by his full name. Her lips tightened, and she was ready to pounce like a tiger defending her cubs. It caught her off guard. She wasn't the kind of woman that got hurt and walked away crying.

Fox glared into her eyes. He knew how to cozy up to her and dispel her angsts. "Darling," he said, "It's not what you think. In the last two days, some disturbing new developments emerged."

"Like what?" She said and crossed her arms — a clear sign the door is closing.

"A new case—"

"A new case!" she blurted out loud. There will always be new cases. You've had them, and you'll have them in the future. So, what?" Clara leaned forward. "What makes this different from all the rest?" Her body expressed what was on her mind. She was firm and to the point.

Fox shifted in his seat like a schoolboy scolded for breaking a window or making up stories. His eyes dropped, and he scratched his goatee. "Well, Clara, a child, was murdered."

Clara's face changed. "How awful." She fell silent. Her eyes softened a bit, "But Fox, I understand this was a terrible crime, but children have always been mistreated and murdered. What makes this any different? And why postpone our wedding over this tragedy? Did you know the child?"

"No, I didn't know the child. But this murder is different, from other killings.

"How was the child killed?" Clara said.

"It was a ceremony. Like the child was being offered as a sacrifice."

Clara leaned back. She reached for her neck as if instinctively to guard her own life. There was also a part of her that felt her own mortality— she wanted to feel her life-blood pulsating through her body. "I understand, Fox, but I still don't understand why we must postpone the wedding."

"The way this crime was committed, it will consume all of my time." He expressed. "When we get married, I want to spend all that time focused on the wedding, our honeymoon, and only us, spending time together. I want that time for you and me." Fox looked desperate, not sure if he was doing the right thing.

Clara stared. Fox could feel Clara's eyes penetrate his skull as if she was driving an icepick through his brain. "I don't like it; it's not right, Fox. We had this planned."

Fox leaned back in his chair and thought about what she said and taking into account her feelings and concerns. "Okay, Clara. I understand. But let's make a deal. Let us postpone the wedding for six months. After six months, we get married whether the case is solved or not. Deal?"

She didn't say a word. Her arms were still closed, and her eyes penetrating. "I don't like it." She said, "I'm not –"

"Before you say another word," Fox said, interrupting her in mid-sentence, "Remember when you called off our wedding last year. Your father gave you a ticket to go and see Paris."

The frost between them melted. Clara's body loosened. The reality of the crime and Fox's desire for their future overwhelmed her. And the fact she did call off their wedding convinced her to take the deal. Clara smiled and kissed his nose. She looked into his eyes. "Alright, Mr. Fox, we can postpone our wedding— for now, but not for too long," Clara said, "And you do have a way of reminding me of my temper and my shortcomings."

Fox kissed her lips. They were fresh and soft like fresh fruit; he slid his hand into hers and smiled.

CHAPTER 5

Fox was refreshed after having breakfast and spending time with Clara. A part of him felt melancholy; they postponed the wedding, but another part of him felt relieved. The last two days disturbed Fox. First, the murder then listening to a lecture on bettering the race and what he experienced at the conference. The responses from the young college students frightened him. *Are college students being indoctrinated instead of learning to think?* He pondered. Fox knew about the campaign by colleges to expunge Latin and Greek out of their core curriculum. A generation truncated from their history and left adrift to be programmed by any new radical thought or philosophy? Was this the end result?

His thoughts were interrupted the moment he stepped outside the front door of his apartment building. Cars whizzed by; a trolley car made the usual sound, steel on steel screech as it cruised down Broadway. Pedestrians hustled in and out between the crowds like birds flying from one tree branch to another.

New York seemed to have a new smell and look to it as one of Henry Ford's new cars driven right off the assembly line. The sun fell from a clear sky, highlighting sharp-edged' skyscrapers and apartment buildings; even the old-style row-houses glistened in the fresh sun-rays. Time Square, however, didn't need the sun to accentuate its sensations. Lights on every sign and every building blinked like pulsating stars, riveting the senses. Life and action epitomized New York City.

New York's jazz life and glitzy lifestyles didn't erase the Lower East Side of Manhattan from New Yorker's memories. Squalid slums; poverty-ridden, and dangerous. It was customary for armed police officers to escort visitors through the most menacing areas—especially during the nineteenth century. Indeed, the Lower Eastside was world-renown for its poverty and treacherous conditions. Over the years, attempts were made to clean and fix some of the problems. Some of the improvements worked, but in the end, they were still loathsome places to live. Perhaps, due in part to overpopulation.

Fox needed to begin his investigation. All he had were a few facts. His first stop was to visit an old friend— a shady one at that, but it was necessary. If anyone knew anything, it would be Big Jake. Fox walked around his apartment building to the car garage. He slid into the front seat of his 1927 Falcon-Knight Roadster.

His first stop was Chumley's at 86 Bedford Street. It was almost a straight drive down Broadway into the lower Westside. Fox parked around the corner and walked up to the door. He knocked. A little door close to the top slid open. A chubby face emerged, "Beat it," the man said. The door slammed shut. Fox knew the routine. He knocked again, and once again; the little door slid open.

Fox was greeted with a pair of yellow teeth and a straight nose with pin holes on it, "Didn't I tell you to —"

"Big Jake," Fox blurted out before the man could finish his sentence and slam the little square door. Big Jake rented an area in the back. He stayed under the radar; he was a small fish compared to Al Capone, and other notorious gangsters.

The bouncer stopped and eyeballed Fox. The little door slammed, and Fox heard a metallic clang, then a bar slide across the entrance. Several chains flopped and bounced off the side. The door crept open; the hinges were rusty but manageable. There, in front of Fox, stood a giant goon. His muscles rippled like whitecaps on the surface of the sea. About 6 feet tall. Rough, not someone to pick a fight with, "Follow me," he said, with a raspy voice, eerily similar to the bucket of bolts the door was made of.

Chumley's was a pub and speakeasy. Founded by Leland Stanford Chumley. He was a socialist and activist. Many famous writers and artists frequented Chumley's. In some respects, this made it easier for someone like Big Jake to set up shop given the fact he was not on the FBI's wanted list.

They walked through a short hallway. Pictures of Karl Marx, Lenin, and other famous figures hung on the walls like cozy family members – setting aside the reality they were cold stone killers. It opened up into a large room. On the back wall was a bar. A platform was positioned on the other end. Live music played almost every night and sometimes during the day.

The room was half full. A live Jazz band played, and people danced to the Charleston. Flappers moved freely like birds of prey. Their hair was bobbed, and they dressed provocatively. Rebellion ran through their bloodstream like water. They smoked cigarettes and talked like sailors; brash, ostentatious, and immature. Round tables were scattered throughout the room. Lampshades hung low from the ceiling; dangled by wires, and a yellowish hue emanated from them like the changing color of old newspapers.

Fox followed the bouncer through the front room to another door, leading into a back room. It was smaller; somewhat similar to the front room, it had a bar and tables. This is where the real juice – illegal booze, outlawed by the Eighteenth Amendment to the U.S. Constitution – was sold. The thug led Fox up to the bar and left him there without a word.

"What's your poison, chum?" The bartender said.

"Big, Jake. I'm here to see Big Jake."

"Go chase yourself. Order, or scram." The bartender was no pushover. Deep crevices arched across his brow like cracks on the side of a granite cliff. His bushy eyebrows were a jungle. His nose was crooked, perhaps broken several times in brawls. Every time he moved his arm, the faded tattoo of a naked woman contorted itself into lewd acts.

Fox realized his mistake; gangsters played games. If someone needed something, they had to play along. "Give me some giggle water," Fox responded.

"What's your flavor, mister?"

"Rot Gut." Another coded word. Rot Gut meant alcohol was mixed with another substance. It was a deceptive code to throw off undercover cops.

The bartender placed a glass with liquor in it on the bar in front of Fox. Fox scanned the room. He was amazed at men and women drinking and playing; at how they threw away their hard-earned money. Some were dancing; others were drinking and laughing. Some of the women's makeup appeared thick as concrete in the dim light. While other women didn't need makeup at all, they were water-proof. In the far corner, a fight broke out; bottles were busted, and knives were brandished before two bouncers stepped out of nowhere, and threw the drunken men out the back door.

Fox noticed Big Jake sitting close to the back. He picked up his glass of liquor and started to walk towards Big Jake. Halfway there, Fox was stopped by a large man; another bouncer, but he seemed to be more of a personal bodyguard for Big Jake. He placed his hand on Fox's chest, "Where do you think you're going, pal?" He said in a brusque tone. His knuckles were small mountain ridges. Deep cuts on his fingers reflected his frequent fist-fights.

Fox moved quick. He took hold of the bouncer's hand and twisted his wrist up and behind him. "Don't touch me, you Gorilla." The man's knees buckled and hit the wooden floor. Fox exerted enough pressure to render him impotent.

Guns and Choppers surfaced from every angle in the room. Fox heard a thousand clicks as if a dozen typewriters pounded the same keys at the same time, "You're going down, bub!" The bartender said, pointing his Tommy sub-machine gun at Fox.

"Stop!" Big Jake yelled, "I know this Cat." The room froze; all eyes were on Big Jake. His eyes narrowed, and he adjusted his suit jacket. Always conscientious about his looks and always clean. "Put away your pieces, boys – don't burn powder. We're all friends here." He rotated his shoulders when he was ready to talk or make a speech. He snapped his fingers; the machine-guns and pistols were put away. "Fox, let go of my goon. He won't bother you anymore."

Fox looked down. The man quivered with pain; Fox let off the pressure and freed the bouncer, he stood and shook off the dirt from his trousers, turned, and eyeballed Fox. Fox eyeballed him back; the intensity mounted thick as a glacier. The bouncer felt another round of intimidation and embarrassment – his ego popped like a balloon. He turned his head away and left the room.

"Come, Fox. Let's go to my table." Big Jake said. The seats were made of leather. Worn to the point of comfort. A waitress walked over. Big Jake looked up, "We'll have the house special." She took their order and turned and walked away. Her high-heels made a tapping sound when she moved across the floor. A thick black line ran up and down the back of her stockings. Her hair wasn't bobbed like the flappers; it cascaded down to her shoulders and bounced up and down when she walked like springs on a jalopy. With her low-cut blouse with a short skirt, she was a knockout. "Just look at those stilts." Big Jake said. "Those legs will flip any man's headlights on."

Big Jake was short and thin. Perhaps the reason he named himself Big Jake was to compensate for his size. Always a neat dresser, his pinstripe suit was tailored made from Italy. His shoes came to a point and were always polished as if he was ready to meet the President of the United States at any given moment. Big Jake ate well, dressed well, and lived well. He was tough, but he wasn't cruel like Dutch Schultz— a gangster who even many of the crime bosses hated. Schultz, on occasion, tortured people who refused to buy beer when they walked into his establishment.

"It's been a long time Fox. Too long. What brings you around here?" Big Jake asked. They became friends several years back when Fox was working on another case. The cops had arrested Big Jake and was on the verge of prosecuting him for murder. Through Fox's investigative powers, he not only was able to exonerate Big Jake but was able to prove he was being framed by cops that were working in cahoots with another gangster. Big Jake never forgot. He was always in Fox's debt, but more than anything else he knew Fox was an honest man. Trust, for Big Jake, was worth more than gold.

Fox came right to the point, "I need information."

At that moment the waitress arrived with their drinks. "Information?" Big Jake said. He studied Fox's face. "Information can be dangerous; it can come with a visit to the East River wearing cement-shoes." Big Jake tilted his head toward the waitress, "Babe, hand me a ciggy." The waitress handed him a cigarette; pulled out matches, and lit it. Big Jake sucked cigarette-smoke deep into his lungs like a baby sucking milk from a bottle. He exhaled. Smoke curled up filtering through the light from the shade above the table.

"Here's the deal," Fox said, "A child was murdered. I have been hired by the police as a consultant. I need to know if you know anything."

"Children are killed all the time. What's so special about this one?"

"The child was killed like she was a sacrifice. Candles were lit during the event. It was premeditated, passion didn't seem to play a role."

Big Jakes eyes lit up like a light from a lighthouse in the middle of a foggy morning. He fidgeted in his chair; his fingers tapped the table like a nervous junkie needing a fix. He knew something. "Fox—" He said. There was equivocation in his voice.

"Jake, please, if you know something, I need to know what you know," Fox said.

A pyramid-shaped light shone down on the table. For Big Jake, it seemed to morph into an interrogation lamp. Suspense reared its head like the Sphinx on the Giza Plateau. "Fox, I don't know much. What I do know is this, get out. Step away from this case."

The overhanging lamp swung side to side; it revealed something to Fox he had never seen before – Big Jake was afraid. But why? Fox had to press him harder. "I need more than that. Give me anything." Fox said.

"The stakes are high. As I said; I know very little, but what I do know, if I'm correct, the people behind this are well connected. They not only have their own means of destroying others, but they use the Mafia as well." He said, "To put it another way, the Mafia is even afraid of them."

"If you know very little, then how can you know about the kind of power this group wields?"

"It's the candles." Big Jake was more hardened than steel, but this made him afraid. He grew up poor and fought his way through the gangs. He feared little. In and out of knife fights and fistfights. He proved his strength the hard way— his constitution was forged in fire.

Fox was confused. "The candles?" Fox asked.

"That's all I can tell you. If I tell you anymore, I could contribute to your death."

"Death?" Fox said. He was shocked. Perhaps this was Big Jake's method to scare him off the case. Confused and bewildered, Fox pushed his body back in his seat. *What do I do with this warning? What is this? Who are these people? And why is Big Jake afraid?* A chill came over Fox as if he stepped naked in the snow. Big Jake's method was starting to work. Fox became torn. He began to question his own thoughts and motives. *Why not let the police handle this one? Just call them up and tell them something came up and your too busy.* The more he thought, the more he realized he was allowing fear to take control. He shook himself. "No, my friend. There may be lives at stake. I need to carry this through."

Big Jake knew when Fox made up his mind it was made up. There was no turning back. "Just remember my warning and focus on the candles. Therein lies a wealth of clues. That's all I have, my friend." Like flipping a switch; Big Jake's face expressed instant happiness. He held up his glass, "Now, let's have a toast," Bid Jake and Fox lifted their drinks, "Here's to our friendship, to booze, women, and to your future." Their glasses touched, making a clinking sound, and they guzzled down their drinks.

CHAPTER 6

The street the killer lived on was filthy and dingy. Tenement buildings stacked next to each other like a house of cards. At any given moment, a fire could break out; burn them to the ground, killing renters. Accordion-like steps stretched up from the sidewalks up to the front doors. The skies were clear. Sun-bleached streets hummed with motor vehicles. Peddlers wheeled their hand-pushed carts; they sold fruits and vegetables. Vagrants stood on street corners asking for loose change or cigarettes. Gangs were ubiquitous and even at epidemic levels as smallpox was during the American Revolution. Thugs controlled the slums like businessmen-controlled politicians. No respectable person would venture into a slum-dwelling neighborhood.

A young lady appeared from nowhere. It was apparent she didn't belong. She was well-dressed; wore a cloche hat, and a flashy necklace dangling around her neck. Like others, she got off on the wrong side of town. Unbeknownst to her, she walked right into the Cold-Blood gang hanging out in front of a rat-infested building. They were not big-leaguers; just street thugs and thieves—who preyed on the weak and the innocent. For the most part, they wasted their days smoking cigarettes and talking nonsense about their escapades. "I beat up, Joey." One said out loud and blew smoke out from his nostrils as if to impress the others of his strength and bravado.

As the woman approached, a gang-member whistled, "Say, take a look at this, boys." He said.

They turned like a pack of hound-dogs picking up a trail. "What a dish." Another said as if his words drooled out the side of his mouth like a rapacious wolf.

The closer she approached, the more radiant she appeared. Her lips were red like a Bolshevik' banner; bold and strident, imitating her strut. She ignored their advances. But this only encouraged them to be more aggressive. When she didn't respond, Luke— the leader of the gang— grabbed her arm. "Hi-yah toots. You know who we are?" He said. "We own this block and everything and everyone on it, that means you too."

She resisted and tried to break free. "Let me go, you sap." She said.

Frank, the second in command, said, "She's a blue-nose, she thinks she's better than us." He stuck his thumb on his nose and wiggled his fingers; making a childlike sound.

The others encircled her like Indians dancing around a camp-fire – they hooped and howled like wolves. The whole scene was like watching a live skit on Broadway.

Luke pulled out a pocket-knife and flipped it open. The woman's eyes turned from agitation to fear. Luke tossed the blade from hand to hand, taunting her. She tried to run but wasn't able to. The light bounced off her necklace like white teeth. Luke's eyes widened. He held the blade close to her neck, "Listen, sister, if you want to pass, you got to hand over that ice." He said with a sadistic grin. "If not, we will have to make other arrangements." The others snickered.

The killer suddenly appeared; he grabbed the knife out of Luke's hand. The thuggish circus came to a halt. Shocked that anyone would dare challenge them, Luke shouted, "Gang, surround this wet blanket." They chuckled and taunted him more aggressively than the young lady. Their reputation was at risk.

The killer grabbed Luke by his neck. He pulled him towards himself and then tossed him into the street like a rag doll. The killer turned to the others. Dismayed, Luke screamed for them to jump him. Frank leaped toward the killer but was slammed in his stomach. It felt like an iron rod; Frank fell to the ground like dropping the curtain on a lousy performance. The others watched with disbelief. They wanted to attack, but they knew they would end up like Luke and Frank. They turned and ran like children and disappeared into an alleyway. When the killer turned, Luke and Frank were gone too.

The young lady ran up to the killer; she profusely thanked him. She noticed his eyes were dark and cold. Emotionless without pity or empathy as if a life of evil hollowed out his soul. He didn't respond to her outbursts. He tossed the blade in the trash and moved passed her like she was a shadow. Left alone, in a state of fright, she was puzzled. *Why did he help me?* She thought. But the reality was he didn't know why he helped her either. Perhaps he didn't want to help her, he just wanted to vent his rage. Fortuitous for the young lady, an opportunity or luck for the killer.

The killer walked up to his building; young men were sitting on the steps and talking about the day when they will be inaugurated into a gang. His large frame cast an indomitable shadow as he turned and started up the steps. The men were overwhelmed like facing a tiger shark. Talk ceased, and they peeled away, making a path for the killer.

The killer passed them and walked up to the steps and to his room on the fourth floor. His space was small and dirty; it was a microcosm of New York slums. The killer was a good thief and was able to afford and rent a room. Most rooms were slam-full of families living in just one place. The walls were paper-thin. Quarrels and fights were commonplace and violent.

The killer had an old mattress pushed up against the corner wall. It had lost its spring and buoyance long ago. The landlord picked it out of a trash heap. The killer crashed, falling like a stiff rod. He fell asleep. After several hours he awoke by the sound of a cockfight. It poured through his window; and came from the back-court area.

On the table were a washbasin and mirror. The killer placed his bag on the table and took out his knife and other paraphernalia. His blade was stained with blood from the child; he cleaned it and wrapped it in a clean towel and placed it back into his case. He reached under the table and took out more candles that were in a box and put them in his bag.

There was a knock at the door. The killer froze. *Was I followed?* He thought. Then, another blow, "It's Micky, from Wash & Clean. You wanted us to clean and deliver your clothes." His voice was high-pitched.

The killer relaxed and opened the door. The sixteen-year-old boy handed him his clothes tied together by hemp. The killer said, "Here." And flipped a nickel into his palm.

"Thank you kindly." He said. He lifted his hat and tilted slightly forward; a pro, who had done it a thousand times before— like a machine.

He returned to the basin of water. Washed his face and looked into the mirror. The killer glared at his reflection; intense and studying himself as if trying to find something, anything. His fixation was broken by the cockfight. He went to the back window and sat in his chair. He loved to watch two cocks go at each other. Raw and cut-throat. It not only brought out his own violent instincts but that of the crowd surrounding the pit below as if cannibals were in a crazed delirium right before they ate human flesh.

He watched until his thoughts drifted and memories of his past flicked through his mind like a silent movie. He went to a box he had in his closet, pulled it out, and took out some pictures. His mind was suddenly flooded with childhood memories. His guardians told him, "you can't go beyond this fence. You belong here, not out there." But this made him all the more curious and rebellious. One night, in a fit of rage, he sneaked out of his room and ran into the woods behind the building, he tried to run away. He never knew his father or mother—and he was different than most of the other children. He ran until he heard something whimper in pain. The plangent yelp was like a knife stabbed and cut into the darkness. He stopped and looked. There was a small dog with a broken leg standing in the rain. He felt for the sick dog. It was the only real feelings he had that came close to compassion. The dog was pathetic; it looked up for help. The boy stood for a long while studying the wretched creature. Then, he found a rock close by and crushed the dog's head in.

The night guard caught up to the child. He found him holding the bloody stone and found the dead dog at his feet. The next day his guardians sat him down, "Why did you kill that innocent animal?" They said.

"It was broken. I fixed it." He said.

The staff was flabbergasted and speechless; their hearts broke for the boy and the animal. Most boys exhibited a flux of emotions and attitudes; especially if caught doing an evil deed, they would express remorse and regret, but he didn't express normal feelings. They were concerned about the boy's future. If he continued on this course, he would eventually run afoul of police and eugenic laws. "What you did was wrong." They tried to impress upon him—trying to instill in him a sense of right and wrong.

"The dog was alone and broken. Just like me." He said. "I don't have a mommy or daddy. There must be something wrong with me too, they didn't want me. Who were they?"

"There's nothing wrong with you." They tried to reassure him.

His face was austere; his glare was empty and lifeless, "May I have a sucker?" He said.

The killer's thoughts were dragged back to the present; he lost consciousness and fell asleep.

The next morning Clara and her colleague were in front of the killer's building. At times the institute sent field-workers into the slums to gather information. Although most of their time was spent visiting insane asylums, police stations, and other establishments.

"Do you have enough pencils and paper?" Clara asked Nancy, her young and inexperienced colleague. "We have to ask a lot of questions, and it's essential we have what we need."

"I had already told you before we left the Eugenics Record Office, yes," Nancy said, a bit irritated by Clara's fastidious quality.

"Don't you dare cop an attitude with me, Nancy. We've gone through this before. Last week you said you had what we needed, then when we arrived at our destination, you had left behind the list of questionnaires."

Nancy dropped her combative stance, "You're right. I'm sorry. I think I'm just nervous about going into the slums. I recall why the institute sends us out in twos." Nancy closed her eyes; she shivered at the thought.

"Remember what they said about that poor field-worker two years ago? It was just horrible."

Clara took her by the shoulders, "Nancy, look at me." She said. "That happened to her because she was alone. We are together. Relax."

"But I can't get the thought out of my head. She was raped by a gang and was strangled. She was found dead two days later. She left behind a husband and two children. What if—"

"There are no what-ifs. We will be fine. There are two of us, and we stay on the streets and in clear view of others when we venture into the tenement buildings. Jennifer, the one you are referring to, was alone and she ventured in the back alleyways. Since then, the institute has established a clear policy. If we stick to the policy, we will be fine." Clara said with courage. "Furthermore Nancy," Clara patted the side of her purse, "I'm packing."

Nancy felt Clara's confidence. Electricity flowed through her veins; her eyes brightened, and she was apprehended by self-confidence. "Yes." She responded, "you're correct. Thank you for reminding me of the new policy and protocols."

"That's a good little soldier," Clara expressed with relief. "Are you ready to proceed into this building?"

"Yes, ma'am."

Clara and Nancy were inconspicuous. Their clothes and hair were plain without any air of panache. No jewelry. And their conserved demeanor was contrived as to not draw attention to themselves. This was part of the institutes' new policy. "We'll start on the first floor, Nancy.

We don't have to knock on every door. As we proceed, we will work our way up, and if we are lucky, we will be able to interview between two and five families."

They proceeded up the stairs and landed on the first floor. Garbage was piled along the corridors. For many, it was perhaps a better place to live rather than the flophouses where people slept on cots lined up against the walls like automatons— soulless, with their spirits ripped from their eyes. "Why don't we start here," Nancy said.

Clara shrugged her shoulders, "Sure." She knocked. Nothing. Clara knocked louder.

Someone yelled, "Coming," in broken English. There was a long wait. Finally, the door creaked open. The chain was still attached. A chubby face appeared through the narrow open slit, "What you want?" She said.

"I'm Clara Anderson, and this is my colleague Nancy Hardy. We are from the Eugenics Records Office in Long Island. We would like to ask you some questions if you have a few minutes."

The old lady turned her face so that one of the eyes could get a better look, "Questions?" She said with a scowled expression. Lines were stretched around her mouth like an old catcher's mitt, "You cops?"

"No, ma'am, we are from a private organization— Cold Spring Institute on Long Island. We are field-workers trying to gather information." Clara said.

Kids yelled and hollered in the background. The old lady turned, "Basta!" She screamed. She turned back to Clara and Nancy, "Go away." And slammed the door.

Nancy was taken back and even insulted by how the old lady treated them. "How dare— why, the audacity!" She said with her head tilted back, and her nose twitched as if she brushed the old lady aside like she was a common vagrant.

"Get over it." Clara chided her. "Don't allow yourself to cop an attitude. You won't last long if you do."

They continued down the hallway and reached the fourth floor. The tenement dwellers, who allowed Clara and Nancy to ask questions, were for the most part civil. Most didn't want to be bothered, though. The range of questions focused on family history. Point of origin, for example, but most of the items were health-related. Manic-depressive, nervous disorders, rheumatism, feeble-mindedness, and albinism were asked and written down. By building rapport, the excellent and experienced field-workers could even elicit from them if they had any criminal history. All of this was crucial. The information went to the Eugenics Records Office and into the Traits Book so a specialist can develop a statistical analysis. They turn over the report to the Eugenic committee and others. The information was used to inform health specialists, local, state, and Federal governments. Marriage licenses and even forced sterilization laws were based on what the field workers gathered and then processed.

Clara was no fan of forced sterilization laws. She was more concerned with health; healthy living, eating healthy food, and suitable and proper marriages that will produce children. Like Professor Black and members from the institute, Clara believed children ought to be bred like corn stock or racing horses. This is the only way to purge bad traits from the bloodlines.

Clara and Nancy had spent several hours knocking on doors and speaking to several families. Some of the interviews were short, some long. The end of their work-day was coming to an end. Still on the fourth floor, and they approached the last room at the end of the hall, "Why don't we make this our last interview?" Nancy expressed. "I'm tired, and my feet hurt."

"I agree, Nancy, but next time, wear better shoes."

"Let me take the lead on this one; if you don't mind, Clara. I have gained confidence by watching and listening to you deal with people."

"That's fine, but if you need my help, I'll be right by your side."

Nancy was still nervous, but she tried to hide it. She knocked. The noise startled the killer. He jumped up and listened, not realizing someone was at his door. He stood by his bed, waiting, stealth-like. Nancy knocked again. Then he realized someone was outside his room. Thinking it was the super wanting to get paid, he walked to the door and opened it. To his surprise, two women were standing there, smiling in the shape of quarter moons. Motionless, his eyes were bloodshot from the deep sleep he was just in.

Nancy felt strange; his empty eyes caused her to shake. Her knees buckled. A lump formed in her throat. Speechless. Her eyes grew wide with fright. She didn't understand why she was frightened and why she lost her nerve. But she knew intuitively something was wrong. It wasn't normal. She turned toward Clara with a helpless look.

Clara picked up on Nancy's cue and took the lead, "Hello, my name is Clara, and this is Nancy. We are from the Eugenics Record Office located in Long Island. If we may, can we ask you a few questions?"

The killer said nothing; the situation grew awkward. Clara and Nancy felt the tension mounting. To break the ice, Clara asked, "May we come in?" Clara wasn't afraid. She had a loaded gun, and Fox trained her to use it and use it well. The one thing that stopped an attacker was an equal or more powerful force. The more she practiced, the more she became confident.

Something strange came over the killer. He turned and walked to the table, leaving the door wide open for the women to go in. "Questions?" The killer said.

Clara pulled out a list of questions; small square boxes were on the left side of the page to be to checked off or left blank. "Where are you from?"

He didn't answer.

A puzzled expression came over Clara; maybe he didn't hear me? She thought. "Where are you from?" She said louder.

Nothing. The killer glared.

Clara felt a strange sensation developing. She knew this wasn't normal. *Why did he allow us in the room if he's not going to answer any questions?* She thought. Red flags went off. She sensed danger. Her defenses shot straight up like lightning highlighting the night skies. Her mind shifted and focused on her gun. She was ready.

The killer turned his back to them. He stared into the mirror and watched them. The water in the basin was still stained with blood. His knife was in his bag.

Clara realized the man was powerful and faster than herself and Nancy. If they panic, it could end badly. She had to proceed with caution. The killer reached for his bag and slowly pulled out his knife. Clara and Nancy couldn't see what the killer was doing, but they knew something was about to transpire. Clara put away her questions and opened her purse. Her hand was ready to slide inside and retrieve her pistol. Her only problem, who will be faster? — Her or the killer?

Nancy was on the verge of collapsing. Then, a hammering sound shattered the silence as if a cannon went off; they all turned towards the door, and the super was standing at the entrance. "I'm here to collect." He said. He looked at the women, "Didn't I tell you about having chippies? Whores are extra."

Clara knew this was their opportunity. Like gazelles, they lurched toward the door and pushed the super aside. In a flash, they were down the stairs and ran down the block. They reached a trolley; boarded it, and were on their way. Clara had never felt the need to resort to using her gun, but she was glad she had it. "I have never been in a situation like that before," Clara said. "Now, we're safe." The trolley took them out of danger. Their work had already taken a toll. But the adrenaline that pulsated through their veins was like strong undercurrents that ripped bodies out into the deep ocean never to be found again.

CHAPTER 7

Clara and Fox met for dinner at Keen's Steak House, located at 72 West 36th Street Manhattan. Initially, it was an all men's club. But in 1901 actress Lillie Langtry disregarded the sign "men only" and entered. She was snubbed and never served the mutton chop she ordered. She sued the restaurant and to everyone's surprise, won. This didn't sit well with Clara; she was a traditionalist. Healthy traditions were essential to maintain a civil society. Men, women, and children had roles to play. Men were to be men, women were to be women, children needed to know their place in society. Clara rejected socialism and extreme equality. She didn't appreciate the fact Langtry broke a time-honored tradition, but a part of her did admire her courage.

Keen's Steak House was elegant and ritzy. Men had to wear a coat and tie. Their food was of high quality and with top-notch cooks. Fox scanned the room. An array of ladies' hats crisscrossed the room like a parade of exotic birds waving in mid-air. They sat with their backs erected and their faces painted as if they were statuesque. A dozen little clinks were heard throughout the room; china cups clashing with saucers and silverware scraping plates. The waiter came and took their orders. Fox ordered a steak with vegetables and Clara ordered lamb chops. The waiter slightly bent forward, "Perfect choices." He said and walked away.

The wine steward came and held a bottle of one of their best wines in front of them, "This is one of our best wines, Bordeaux, Chateau-Margaux, will this do? Or we have a list of other wines?"

"What year is the Bordeaux?" Fox said.

"1900."

"That will do just fine, thank you."

The wine steward uncorked the Bordeaux and left it on the table open, to let it breathe. Clara leaned forward and touched Fox's hand, "By the way, I called the florist and canceled the order for the wedding. Sally was disappointed until I told her the wedding was simply postponed. I also called the church and the minister. They said they will work with our schedule whenever we are ready in the future."

Fox cuffed her hand into his, "You are very thorough, Clara; you'll make a great wife, and a great mother one day." His eyes were soft and gentle as he looked into her eyes; as if he was writing silent love letters onto her pupils, and it was transmitting them to her heart.

She felt them and received them; profound — and full. Clara blushed. She melted under his love. Fox was the only man that knew her intimate feelings. Then she stiffened her back, "Thank you, my love." She said. "I'm blessed to have you love me." A smile filled her face like air in a red balloon.

"Now, how was your day?" Fox asked.

Clara's eyes grew round and large, "Oh my goodness, Fox, I thought Nancy and I were doomed."

Fox became concerned, maybe even panic-stricken, "What do you mean, doomed?"

"Well, as you know we sometimes have to canvass the neighborhood slums," Clara said, "It was the end of the day, and we knocked on our last door." She stopped in mid-sentence, "Fox, I don't want to bore you with all the details, but we ran into what seemed to be a scary individual. Thank God the super showed up and we ran as fast as we could. We got away."

Fox couldn't believe what he was hearing. His emotions erupted, he couldn't control himself any longer, "I told you I didn't want you to go into the slums by yourself!" He said intensely.

"But Fox, I told you, Nancy was with me."

Fox stopped and realized his emotions got the better of him. "That's right, Nancy. Thank God for Nancy." The air in his lungs came out in short spurts. "But it's still too dangerous for even two women to venture into the slums alone."

"I agree, but I was packing. Remember, you bought me a gun and taught me how to use it?"

Fox leaned back in his seat. His diaphragm pushed out air, releasing tension like steam from a volcano. His body relaxed. His red face turned normal. "Yes, of course, you're right Clara. I momentarily forgot about the gun and the new policy you told me about." But Fox was still concerned nonetheless.

Clara tapped his hand, "There, there," she said. "Now, let's enjoy the rest of the evening.

A band began to play. A woman singer followed the tempo. Fox and Clara; along with most of the audience, turned their heads. The singer's voice had a perfect pitch. Her dress was provocative and too revealing for Clara, but she was a looker. "Who's the canary?" Fox said.

Clara stiffened her back in a show of defiance. "Really, Fox? One moment you're concerned for my life then the next moment, your salivating and gawking at another woman like some crazy dog in heat?"

Clara's laconic and sharp tongue forced Fox to realize Clara became jealous. "Clara, I'm sorry, I didn't mean to cause – well, I was just wondering who the singer was."

Clara was still a bit emotional. It took her a while to settled down after she got riled. As the night progressed, she realized how foolish she acted. "I'm sorry, James. Sometimes I overreact. It's just because I love you so much." She said, "And yes, it's part jealousy. Besides, you too became unhinged a few minutes ago." She smiled.

Fox whispered, "My emotions and love are safely locked away in my heart. You can be secure; we are one." He kissed her hand.

Clara melted. Her cheeks turned red, "By the way, the woman singing is Ruth Etting. She sings jazz and pop music." Clara said.

As usual, dinner was excellent, and the service was top-notch. After Fox and Clara ordered dessert, the waiter informed Fox, he had a phone call waiting for him in the lobby.

Clara was puzzled, "Who would know your whereabouts?" She said.

"I'm sure it's detective Savage. I told him where I would be if there were any news on the case we are working on."

Clara understood. This used to bother her, but she gradually accepted interruptions, especially when Fox is working with the police. It was par-for-the-course.

Fox entered the telephone-booth and closed the door. He picked up the receiver, "Hello, this is Fox."

"Fox, Detective Savage here. I apologize for interrupting your dinner, but new evidence has emerged."

"That's alright, what did you find out?"

"Remember no one heard or saw anything but Ginger? Also, we have candles. But we have new evidence now."

"Hold on. Let me pull out my pad." Fox retrieved his pad and pencil, "I'm ready, go on." He told Savage.

"First, the child. The child's name was Tina Roma, of Italian descent. Her parents arrived from Italy about ten years ago; they live in Little Italy. She has four brothers and two sisters. The family is dirt poor. Tina was about five years old when she was killed. The family told me she had one gift; she was a good dancer. Otherwise, she was a Dumb-Dora. Stupid as the day is long."

"You mean, she was an imbecile?" Fox scratched his scalp with his pencil. Professor Black's lecture came to him.

Detective Savage made a gargled sound, "Yes Fox," he coughed and hacked-up phlegm.

An awful revolting noise eked through the receiver, Fox jerked the receiver away from his head, as if an electrical current shocked his ear. "Are you alright? You have a cold?" He said.

"Yes." He said. He coughed and hacked some more. After Detective Savage recovered from his last bout, he told Fox the second piece of evidence, "Fox, we found something. To tell you the truth, I'm not sure if it's important, but we need to cover everything."

"What did you find?"

"We found it close to the corpse, an old newspaper. It was folded into squares."

Fox's curiosity piqued. *It might be a dead-end, or not.* He thought. "What did it say?"

The detective cleared his voice, "The title of the newspaper article is, 'Eugenic Marriage will Make Perfect Children.'"

These words splashed around in Fox's mind like a rainstorm had just uncovered a shiny object on a sandy beach. "I'm all ears, Detective." He said. He couldn't believe what he was hearing.

Detective Savage blew a fresh load into his hanky, "The article mentions there was a eugenic marriage performed. Two children were born from this marriage. It mentions how Eugenics will produce a super-race free of diseases. In fact, here's part of the exact quote, a healthier, stronger, purer, happier, and wiser race will be the outcome of the doctrine of Eugenics."

Eugenics. Eugenic marriage; super-race and the doctrine of Eugenics; all stood out like a billboard. But the term, *doctrine of Eugenics*, stood out even more in Fox's thoughts as if something sinister and clandestine was formless but full of shape and purpose behind a large curtain. *Could there be a connection between this murder and the eugenics movement?* He thought. "Thank you, detective, I'll catch up with you later. Feel better."

Fox hung up the receiver and returned to Clara, deep in thought. Clara noticed the difference like night and day. "Is everything alright?" She said. Concern dripped from her eyes like tears.

"How well do you know your employers and eugenics?"

Clara was taken back. "What's this all about?"

"The police found new evidence that points to the eugenics movement. At best, it's circumstantial."

"What did they find?"

Fox told her about the newspaper clipping and how it was found close to the body. He knew this wasn't the proper time to discuss the case, but he felt compelled, due to the fact Clara wasn't only an employee at the Cold Spring Harbor Institute, but she promoted Eugenics. "If you don't mind, I would like to discuss one part of what was written."

"Only if you promise to stop and get back to our night together." Clara was protective of their time; she didn't like unnecessary encroachments that had the potential to spoil it. She worked hard to develop their relationship; to the extent, when they looked back in time, their moments and time together would be fond memories.

"I promise," Fox said with a reassuring smile.

"What part of it do you want to discuss?"

"Part of the article emphasized, 'the doctrine of eugenics.' Have you ever heard of such a doctrine?

"Well, yes. The doctrine of Eugenics is about the betterment of the human race. Through science, we now know how diseases and traits are passed down through the bloodline. Science –" Clara stopped in mid-sentence. Her face became contorted, "Are you suggesting that one of our eugenic scientists murdered this child?"

"Well, since you mentioned it, I did listen to a lecture on eugenics by Professor Black—"

Clara threw her napkin down on the table, "I would have you know Mr. Fox; Professor Black is a distinguished professor. He has an impeccable reputation. You're barking up the wrong tree!"

"Clara, please calm down. I'm only trying to follow the evidence. I'm not suggesting Professor Black, or any other eugenicists is the murderer. When someone writes about a doctrine concerning a massive movement, I don't believe its hyperbole, I take it seriously. For all we know the newspaper clipping was there before the murder. There have always been deranged individuals who are motivated by outside influences."

Clara was still steaming, but she listened. "Yes. Like what?" She opened a little to give Fox a chance to explain himself.

"Remember a few years ago, the Leopold and Loeb case? Well, those young men were influenced by Fredrick Nietzsche's books *Above Good and Evil* and *Thus Spake Zarathustra*. They believed they were supermen and above the law. They killed Bobby Franks, a 14-year-old child."

Clara's eyelashes flickered, "Yes, I do remember that case, now. I had forgotten all about it. You're right, Fox, maybe we have something similar here." Clara crossed her arms, "But I'm still not convinced. Eugenics is the future; it's settled science – not some myth made up by a mad man."

"As I stated before, we have some evidence, and this newspaper clipping could be evidence or not." Fox explained, "Nevertheless, we need to explore everything, and that includes the eugenics movement. Everyone, at this point, is a possible suspect. We follow what we have and see where it ends. Fair enough?"

Puffy wrinkles unfurled off her forehead like a flag. Her lips thinned out and softened. *Why am I too protective of Eugenics?* She thought. Fox's words started to penetrate the barriers she erected. She looked at Fox, "Fair enough." She responded.

CHAPTER 8

The next day, Fox drove by the police department to speak with Detective Savage and pick up one of the candles used at the murder scene and the newspaper clipping about the eugenic marriage. Other than Ginger's testimony, these were the only clues he had to go on. The candle was the most obvious. Why did the killer use candles?

Fox walked through the front of the police station. Officers were conducting regular business when a person screamed, "Get off me, copper!" He and other criminals were roped off on the side of the room. Pro skirts— prostitutes— were separated in another section. Every criminal was smoking. A plume of smoke rose to the ceiling and arched over the rest of the room like a low hanging fog.

Fox knocked on Detective Savage's door, "Come in." A voice thundered from behind the door. Savage wasn't in a good mood. He still had a blistering cold. The doctor told him to stay home, rest, and eat homemade chicken soup. He refused. Savage was a workaholic with tons of open cases; this was the real reason Fox was hired to investigate the death of a poor girl. Savage had no time to waste on a slum killing.

Fox opened the door and stepped inside. "Good morning, Savage." He said. "How do you feel?" Savage's office was a wreck. Folders piled high and disjointed. The wastebasket overflowed with crunched up papers.

Savage sneezed and coughed. "As you can see, not good."

"What did the doctor say?"

"Blast that Croaker! He wants me home and eating soup." He exclaimed. "What does he know?"

"Doctor's orders, if you want to get better."

"Fiddlesticks! I'll get better doing my job." He said. He leaned back into his chair. "Let me tell you something, Fox. My parents taught me to work hard. They worked hard and lived a long life. The moment I stop working is the moment I die." His eyeballs appeared sunken like a German U—Boat that sunk below the ocean surface leaving in its wake dark rippling currents.

Savage's intractable and truculent mind matched his outward appearance. He was large and robust. Although he had a puffy belly, his arms were muscular and strong as steel. One day Fox stopped him from crushing a man's skull when he had the man pinned in his arms like a vice-grip. Savage also thought in black and white terms, he hated abstract thought and had zero college education, but he was no boob either. He learned how to read, write, and do arithmetic in high school.

Fox had known Savage long enough to know when to quit. He switched to the case, "Has your team examined the evidence? —especially the candles?"

"Yes," Savage said with a disappointed downcast. "But our research team is limited at the moment. We still have cases we are investigating from two years ago, and they keep piling up. To answer your question, however, we examined the candle and the embossed symbol: nothing, we don't know what that symbol means and why the killer used candles."

"May I take one of the candles to see what I can find?"

"Sure." Savage reached into his top desk drawer, pulled out one of the candles, and handed it to Fox. "Hopefully, you'll have better luck."

"By the way, did your team research the newspaper clipping found at the crime scene."

"We haven't had a chance. Do you want to take that, as well?"

"Yes, if you don't mind."

"Not a problem." He said. He reached back into his desk drawer, pulled out the news clipping and handed it to Fox. "Fox, I'm not sure if that article will help you."

"Why is that?"

"Eugenics has been around for several years, and it has been in the newspapers just as long."

"True, but if it was the killer's, it's a clue."

"Suit yourself," Savage said. He shrugged his shoulders with an I don't care attitude.

"Thank you, Detective. I'll be on my way." Before Fox stepped out of the door, he turned back, "Go home and get some rest." He said.

Savage's face turned red. He pointed his fat finger toward Fox and shouted, "Get out!"

Fox closed the door and smiled, but the fun was over. He pulled out the candle; it was red with a strange embossed symbol on its side. Fox retrieved his magnifying glass from his side pocket. After careful examination, he was at a loss at what it represented. He rubbed his thumb over the symbol. What does it mean?" *It's almost a secret code— of sorts— only to be understood by those who know what it means. Odd, but intriguing.* Fox thought.

Fox had a source that might be able to help him understand what he was holding, but before he drove to Brooklyn, he wanted to try a local store. On his way out, he used one of the station's phone books and found Dempsey & Carroll. It's a company that sells stationery and does engravings.

Fox arrived at Dempsey and Carroll, located at 13 East 47 Street. The company had changed its location since its opening in 1878. Well established and had a beautiful array of stationaries. People loved to write letters; even still more popular than calling someone on the telephone. Fathers, mothers, brothers and sisters, and especially lovers cherished letters. A Phone conversation ended, whereas letters were read over and over again.

The store was bubbling with life. People of all persuasions and backgrounds came and went. A well-dressed man, about twenty-eight years old, approached Fox, "Good morning. May I help you?" He said.

"Yes. I'm Mr. Fox, and I would like to speak to your engraver."

"Of course. What is this in regards to? Stationery, jewelry—?"

Fox pulled out his card, "I'm a private detective. I'm here on businesses."

"Oh, I see. Please excuse me." The gentleman turned and entered the back of the store. After a few minutes, he returned, "John will see you now, this way, please."

Fox followed and entered the back room. It was different from the floor room. Throughout, boxes were scattered all around. Machines hummed in an adjacent room. A short man was sitting in a high chair; his eyebrows bristled with upturned edges that pointed upward, to the ceiling. His back was arched, and bony ridges flared out like a stegosaurus, running up and down his spine. "Hello, Mr. Fox," John said. He wiped his hands clean with a towel and shook Fox's right hand. "How can I be of service?"

Fox pulled out the candle, "Can you help me with this? There appears to be an embossed symbol on the side. Do you know what it represents?"

John took the candle to one of his work tables. There was an oversized magnifying glass connected to a mechanical moving device; screwed into the side of the table, and a skinny arm attached to clamps. He replaced a small clamp with a large one to hold the candle. The device looked like a contrived octopus conjured up by Jules Vern from his book *Twenty Thousand Leagues Under the Sea*.

John's eyeball filled the length of the glass; it twitched back and forth like a giant cyclops. He adjusted the arm several times until a clear focus came into full view. Unintelligible sounds escaped his lips, "Hmm, hmm."

Fox waited patiently. Tension mounted; he felt John was onto something. "Did you discover anything?" Fox asked.

He pulled away from the candle, "Mr. Fox, I don't know what this represents," He scratched his head.

Fox felt this was a dead-end. "Thank—"

"Hold on." He said. John went to another table and retrieved a pencil and paper. Within minutes John sketched onto paper a larger image of the symbol. "Here you go, Mr. Fox. That's the best I can do." He handed the paper to Fox.

Fox held it up. He studied it like it was a blueprint. "Fascinating!" Fox said.

"There is one last thing I can help you with," John said. He turned the candle upside down, "Here on the back is a date, it's in Roman numerals; this is highly unusual, the date is 1900. Yes, the candle was made in 1900 and made for a specific and special purpose or reason."

It wasn't much, but it was something. Fox's eyes lit up with intellectual excitement. His left eyebrow arched – it was a dead giveaway, whenever Fox was onto something. "1900?" He said. Fox took the candle away from John and rolled the paper up and shoved it in his pocket. "Thank you, John," Fox reached for his wallet, "How much do I owe you?"

John waved his hand, "Nothing, it's on the house. Just keep us in mind if you need stationery or cards for weddings or whenever you need something engraved. Please, on your way out, have the gentleman in the front, give you one of our cards."

Fox thanked John again and took one of their cards for future reference. John wasn't able to fill in all the questions, but what he did was give specific information about the candle. The date it was made, and that it is a unique candle. Why? For what reason? The symbol or image on the candle was clear, and it was a male and female linked together with two children in front of them. He knew secret societies and spiritualism flourished during that time. *Are the candles somehow connected to a secret society or cult?* He thought.

Loaded with more information about the candle, Fox needed to go to his old source—Izzy. Fox drove through town and took the Brooklyn Bridge and made his way downtown to Grand Street. Joey owned a pawnshop, and he also held one of the largest private libraries on the occult, cults, and religion in New York. Izzy's full name was Joseph Izzy Lebronski.

Fox parked across the street. Hanging high over his shop was an extended bar, with three gold balls suspended from it like orbs descending from the sky.

Fox pushed a button, and it buzzed. A few seconds later, Izzy opened the front door. "Is that you, Fox?" He said with surprise.

"Yes, it's me. How are you doing?"

"I'm fine. Come in."

Izzy was tough but had a soft heart. He was in the great war and witnessed horrific things; men's legs, arms, and heads were blown off by tanks. Mustard gas burned men's skin; the gas caused tears and made their eyes blister with intense pain. After the war, Izzy came back shell shocked and had to spend one year in the psych-ward. He recovered and built a thriving business, but the nightmares persisted.

"Good to see you, Izzy."

"It's been a long time Fox. You're a sight for sore eyes." He said. "Is your visit personal or business."

"Business."

"What kind of business?"

Fox pulled out the sketch and showed it to Izzy, "I need to know more about this image. It's on a candle I have in my pocket."

Izzy put on his thick-rimmed glasses and held it close to his face. "Well, Fox. We are friends, but business is business. I don't run a charity."

Fox understood. He pulled out five dollars, placed it on the table in front of them, and slid it towards Izzy, "Here. That should give me entrance to your library."

Izzy recoiled, "No! Nobody enters my library and sees my books." Izzy's eyes spun with delirium, "Capeesh?" Izzy wasn't only interested in the occult and cults, but he was also a collector. He protected them like they were his children.

Fox looked into his eyes, "Izzy, this is about a killer that killed an innocent child."

That hit Izzy in the gut. The war desensitized him to death, but innocent children were something altogether.

His strident protectionism crumbled. "A child was killed?"

"Yes. Also, this candle might lead us to the killer."

Izzy shoved the five-dollar bill back to Fox. "Take your money." He said. "Follow me." He waved his arm.

They stepped onto a platform; walking down, the steps were steep. Darkness engulfed the basement. As they descended, Izzy pulled on a chain, and a flood of light flickered on. Before they reached the bottom, Izzy had turned on three lights. There was a click, and the basement transformed from darkness to light – the room was instantly changed by incandescent light. The room was immaculate. Bookshelves lined the walls with books standing up side-by-side like soldiers.

"This way." He said. "I'm always adding to my collection Fox. Besides, I have combed through these books so many times I believe I have seen that symbol before. Let me see." After a few minutes, Izzy found a few books that may hold the key to the elusive image. "Oh, here we go." He handed Fox several books, "take these to the elongated table in the middle of the room. I'll take these."

Fox started his search and was surprised by how many occultists and cults there were in the world and in antiquity. He was fully aware of the skull and bones based on Yale campus and the world's most nefarious secret society— the Illuminati. There were recently new cults established. Such as the Theosophical Society; Helena Petrovna Blavatsky founded it in 1882.

Fox flipped through the final book, scanning the images associated with each cult. Then, the image popped out. It was like he struck gold. "Eureka!" He said.

Izzy looked up, "You found it?"

"Yes. It's right here." Fox turned the book so that Izzy could see.

"Good job, Fox. Now let's see; what else can we find in relation with the image?"

They turned a few pages back, and in bold letters, it stated, Lucifer the Light Bearer. They were both shocked and looked at each other. "Listen, Izzy, it was a journal founded by Moses Harman, but the authors of this book have deemed it a cult or secret society. Harman, along with his whole family, and his followers are anarchists. They believe in the separation of church and state and promoting abortion." Fox just stared at the book. He was amazed at the radicalness of such a group, especially the killing of children.

"What else does it say?" Izzy said.

"Not much. But there were a few words under the image, wait—" Fox turned back to the image. "Written underneath in a semi-circle arched like a smile are these words, 'Keep the LifeStream Pure.'" Like a snake, a chill crawled up and down Fox's back.

"What does that mean Fox?"

"Wait." Fox flipped back to the beginning. He read further down. His face turned pale, "Izzy, listen, as stated, the journal was named, Lucifer the Light Bearer, but it was changed into The Eugenic Magazine."

A puzzled expression came over Izzy's face, "I don't know what that means Fox. Is it important?"

"Yes. It's more important than you can ever realize." Fox wrote down everything in his pad. "I want to thank you, Izzy; this was a tremendous help to me. I owe you one."

"If that helps you find the killer, you owe me nothing," Izzy said.

Fox left Izzy's pawnshop with more clues, essential ones; Lucifer the Light Bearer. The Eugenic Magazine. The image of the family and what it said underneath it, 'Keep the LifeStream Pure,' ran through Fox's mind like he was back in grad-school frantically memorizing Latin paradigms right before a test. Amazed at how the words shaped and formed into a semi-circle, Fox thought, this can't be a coincidence. The killer positioned his candles in the same way.

CHAPTER 9

A giant slum-monster crept through the iron grates like fog rising from underground on a New York street in the middle of the night. It was formless yet had tentacles. One arm was the murdered child, another limb was the words, Keep the LifeStream Pure, and another arm was the candlesticks. But something emanated from the amorphous creature. It glowed with terrifying fangs which dripped toxic saliva. Fox awoke. Sweat rolled down his face; he was terrified. Then he realized it was just a nightmare. It was 5:30 in the morning. His dream left him feeling tired and drained; coffee was the only thing on his mind.

He slipped into his robe; went to the kitchen, and started to brew White House coffee. The aroma charged his senses even before he took one sip. A new day began to take shape. After he consumed a half-cup of coffee, his mind was in full gear.

He needed to contact Detective Savage, the candle surrendered more clues. Fox called the police station, "This is Mr. Fox, please connect me with Detective Savage's office."

There were a few clicks. "Yes, is that you, Fox?" Savage said. His voice was throaty, and his nasal cavities were full and infected.

"Yes, it's me. You sound horrible Detective."

Savage hacked and coughed, his words were unintelligible and harsh as if an amateur trombone player tried, but failed miserably, to play.

"What? What did you say, Savage?" Fox said as if trying to decipher words from a walrus.

"I said," Savage cleared his throat, "We need to talk."

"That's the reason I called you, we do need to talk," Fox said. "Can we meet at Danny's Diner in two hours?"

Savage was in a daze from the whiskey he drank to help clear up his throat. "I'll be there." Detective Savage said, and he sneezed right before he hung up the phone.

Fox arrived early. The café was packed and filled with people talking and laughing. A couple just finished and left when Fox slid into the booth. The waiter came and cleared off his table and took his order. Fox pulled out the newspaper he bought. He began to read; in bold, black and white, an ad stated, *Camel Cigarettes for sale and Clear Havana Cigars in Boxes of 25 La Rosa Aromatica in 10 sizes $2.25 to $7.00 for sale. Traditional Linen for .69 cents and perfumes for sale. Peppermint Life Savers and Adam's Pepsin Gum and Clothes Wringers for purchase.*

Fox scanned through the paper. Then something on page seventeen popped out of nowhere. A small article at the bottom. It appeared insignificant, but it sucked him in. The report had between seventy-five and seventy-eight words in length. If one blinked, it disappeared; there one moment, gone the next. Shocked, Fox read the words slowly. The title stated in no uncertain terms, "UPHOLDS STERILIZATION: Law for the Feeble-minded. Supreme Court Sustains Virginia." Fox remembered reading last year about a Virginia inmate deemed an imbecile by the state and was ordered to submit to forced sterilization. The case is called *Buck v. Bell*. It appears she appealed her case to the Supreme Court and lost. Professor Black came to mind; *Now, eugenics is the method for an ideal society upheld by the highest court in the land.* Fox shook his head. *Unbelievable.* He thought.

Fox lifted his head and looked out the window. Clouds hid the sun; casting long shadows up and down the streets like an imposing, overbearing, angry tent covering the city. People all of a sudden appeared to be stick-people; born to be controlled and biologically manipulated by some hidden hand pulling a large secret lever. What disturbed Fox more than legitimizing compulsory sterilization was he understood and even agreed with their logic. Society needs to protect itself from the insane.

Fox was jarred from his thoughts; the front door swung open, and a sizeable towering figure stepped through like a Mack Truck. It blocked the street. Fox rubbed his eyes, and Detective Savage came into full view.

"Fox," Savage said. "What's wrong with you? Are you blind?"

"I'm fine, Savage. Who can't miss you coming?" Fox said with a touch of sarcasm in his tone.

"Wise guy, hey. I'm all laughs." The waiter came, and Savage ordered tea with honey to soothe his sore throat. He looked at Fox's newspaper, "What's new in the world?"

"The Supreme Court just upheld Virginia's forced sterilization of inmates. Anyone the state deems insane will face the knife. Can you believe this?"

"Good," Savage said. "Imbeciles are a menace to our society. Health boards across the country have been informing police departments across the nation; it is mostly imbeciles and their offspring that commit most of the crimes. Fewer imbeciles fewer crimes. More imbeciles more crimes."

Fox was surprised, "I had no idea you supported this form of eugenics. You are a Catholic. Catholics are against sterilization."

"So, what, I'm a Catholic—"

"So, what, you say? Surely you read one of your celebrated Catholic writers, G. K. Chesterton?"

"Yes, I've heard of him; and again, so what?" Savage said. His voice raddled and crackled under pressure from his severe cold.

"He not only wrote articles against it but one of his books— if I remember it correctly— was called *Eugenics and Other Evils*. In other words, eugenics is evil, according to Chesterton. And being a fellow Catholic, you don't see the evil of eugenics?"

"That's his opinion, and to be frank, that's the Church's position— not mine. Being a police officer, I've witnessed too much. Almost every crime is committed by bad-blood— individuals that hate society and themselves. They are scum. Low-class type animals, like snakes that don't belong in a civilized society. Society needs to control them, one way or the other." Savage coughed. "I am grateful to the Supreme Court. Maybe now we can start cleaning up the streets with more efficiency."

"But is it moral and ethical too? I mean, do we really know criminality is in the blood? Really Savage, think about it; eugenics states if someone is a thief it is something in their blood. Or if someone is a murderer, that individual has tainted-blood that was handed down to him from his parents, and so on." Fox said. "Did it ever occur to you that maybe people who commit crimes do so because of their childhood environment? And why don't we place them in an insane asylum, so they don't hurt others or themselves? Who are we to play God?"

Savage slammed his fist down on the table, everyone turned and stared. "Has it occurred to you Fox; if eugenics was fully known, understood, and on the law books—Tina Roma would be alive today?"

Savage's words stung Fox like a wasp. *Maybe Savage is correct?* He thought. *But if eugenics were developed and in full force years leading up to Tina's death, then she wouldn't have been born at all. Nor thousands of other children who grow up and have the potential of living fulfilling lives.* Fox determined to let this one go. Savage was in no mood, and his single-mindedness wouldn't allow for further discussion.

There was a long pause; Savage sipped his tea; Fox sipped his coffee. Chatter once again filled the room. Customers came and went as if nothing happened. It was just another small episode in New York, a footnote to a busy city focused on making money.

Detective Savage broke the ice, "Fox, we caught the killer. The case is closed, except for a few formalities."

"So early? Who is he, and how did you catch him?" Fox said. But he was not enthusiastic, he was reserved.

"One of my men followed up on a hunch. No sane person would commit such a crime; only a mad-man could kill a child. So, we visited Bellevue Asylum to see if they recently had an escapee. To our surprise and luck, they did. His name is Elwood B. Wade. A large man who killed his own child two years ago. His doctor and the state deemed him insane, and he was bounced between Washington Asylum and Bellevue."

"How did you catch him?"

"We went back to the crime scene, with his photo in hand, and we found him several blocks away in an abandoned building. He was all doped up."

"Did you find a bag, with candles or other paraphernalia having to do with the murder?"

"No. Wade must have ditched everything," Savage said.

"Something doesn't make sense," Fox said. "If he is our man, then where did he get the candles? And why use candles? Did he use candles when he killed his family?"

Savage felt uncomfortable by Fox's questions, "Does it matter? He killed before, and he was found in the same location. That's good enough for me."

"So, your theory is Wade escaped from Bellevue; in some miraculous happenstance got hold of some candles, killed a child— then had enough money to buy dope, get Gowed-up, and stay close to the crime scene. That's an incredible story, even for you, Savage."

Savage was starting to lose his patience again. Fox had never seen Savage this close-minded and eager to close a case this early. Maybe Savage had been at this job too long, or perhaps this case was unimportant. Or possibly he was too sick. Conceivably it was all three reasons. Whatever the reason, Savage felt the case was closed.

"At least hear what I discovered about the candle," Fox said.

"Alright. Tell me what you got." Savage said, in a begrudging way.

Fox told him everything; he hoped Savage would change, but it didn't work.

"That's all interesting, but we have our man. I don't care at this point about the candles or how Wade got a hold of them." Savage said. "You're a good sleuth Fox, but face the music— the case is closed."

Fox leaned back in his seat and examined Savage's face and his words. He ran his finger around the top rim of his coffee. "Well, the case might be closed to you, but it's still open for me. I don't believe you caught the killer, Detective. What you just said is too incredible and— to be frank—it's too easy, it's sloppy detective work." Fox stated, with firmness.

Savage slumped his head, "Alright Fox. Continue with your investigation, but you're on your own." Savage started to get up and leave, then he turned towards Fox, "Since you are continuing with the investigation, meet me at the graveyard on 25th."

Curious, Fox asked, "Why?"

"Someone reported another attempted murder. We believe the man we have in custody almost killed again."

"But if you believe you have the killer, why do you want me to tag along?"

"As I said, you're a good private detective. The more eyes we have, the faster we can wrap this case up." Savage said.

"Done. I'll be there in an hour." Fox said.

Fox arrived at the cemetery. The place was swarming with police officers. Two officers were at the entrance and prevented Fox from entering, "No one's allowed to enter, police business." A young officer snapped. "On your way." He was inexperienced and overconfident. Typical of a lot of freshmen.

"I'm here, by request. Detective Savage asked me to come. I'm J.P. Fox, a Private Investigator."

"Sorry, Sir. Step this way." The officer escorted Fox to the left and around the bend. The scene was located almost to the back of the graveyard. Sugar and pine trees dotted the area like pins sticking in a pincushion. The cemetery was unkempt; debris was strewn everywhere; against gravestones, and shrubs. Tramps and hobos slept in the overgrown sections and even on top of graves. It had been abandoned for years. They came upon the scene where Detective Savage was standing along with other officers. "Over there, Sir. Good day." The young officer tipped his hat and returned to his post.

"Hello again, Detective," Fox said. "What do we have here?"

"We received an anonymous call early this morning. The call informed us of an odd occurrence. The call was probably a local slum-dweller." Savage said. He blew into his hanky. The hanky danced a jig like the wind blew a white sheet in the air. "As I was saying, the caller told us a bizarre story of how they saw a man with a young child came in and then walked to this tombstone." Savage pointed, "The man said he was able to see and hear what happened. Well, he said he witnessed the man pull out candles and place them in a semi-circle. The man and the child leaned against the tombstone. According to the witness, the man examined the child's face as if he was a doctor. Then he pulled out a knife, but he stopped. He put the knife away and gave the child a sucker. They got up and left. What do you make of it, Fox? Sounds like our man."

"Indeed, it does sound like the same person," Fox said. "I wonder why he left the candles? And why he didn't kill the child?"

"Maybe he was in a hurry and felt he was being watched," Savage responded.

"Perhaps," Fox said and stroked his goatee. "Was there anyone here when your men arrived?"

"There were homeless people, men, and women. We interviewed two others and found out they had sex last night." Savage shook his head. "Can you believe people would desecrate a graveyard by having sex? Incredible."

"Did they hear anything or see anything?"

"Everybody we interviewed said they didn't hear anything."

"That's to be expected," Fox said. "It was dark, and people who come here want to be left alone. But I wonder, who called?" Fox scanned around, "There are no lights, so how did they see what happened?" Fox turned to Savage, "Was there a full moon last night?"

"I believe there was. Yes, in fact I know it was. My brother went fishing last night. He always goes out on a full moon."

"Then that explains the eyewitness." Fox walked over to the tombstone and squatted. "Why here? Was it convenient, or was there a reason the killer chose this spot?" Fox said out loud, "We know his methods, but what is his motive?"

"He's a lunatic. That's all we need to know. Plain and simple." Savage said. His voice was scratchy, and his throat inflamed.

"Even lunatics have motives, Detective." Fox looked at the tombstone. It was made of cheap material. Not very old, but decaying nonetheless. Fox reached into his pocket and pulled out a hanky. He brushed off the dirt. The names and dates were faded, but still readable. "Alene Houck, January 17, 1901-May 20, 1902." Fox read out loud. He pulled out his pad and pencil and scribbled it down. "Notice something here Savage, this girl died young. I wonder if or how she plays into the killer's motive or life? Could this be one of his victims? If so, he would be over fifty." Fox twisted his neck towards Savage, "I hope you are correct, and you have the killer in custody."

"Why is that?"

"If not, then I'm afraid we might have another Jack the Ripper on our hands."

Detective Savage recoiled, "You're screwy Fox. Another Jack the Ripper even an H.H. Holmes? All we have is one murder, not even close to Jack's murders. And as I told you before, we have the killer." Savage laughed; the intent was to humiliate Fox. "Fox. Don't take any wooden nickels. Wise up."

Fox stood. He waved the dirt off his hanky and placed it back into his pocket. He looked Savage squarely in the eyes. "First, you don't know you have the real murderer. There are too many holes. Second, if I'm correct, we have a deadly killer preying on innocent children. He might be psychotic, but he has a motive. Third, you may not agree with my theory, but never— I mean never, try to denigrate me again." Fox said with a firm and tenacious stare. "Do I make myself clear?"

Savage was pushed into a corner to respond. His tough-guy image didn't work with Fox. He knew he went too far. "You're right Fox. I'm not myself. This darn cold got the better of me."

"I'll take that as an apology," Fox said. He knew Savage would never say he was sorry. He had too much pride, but this was close enough.

"But I do still believe we have our man," Savage said.

"I hope your right. I will still continue the investigation just in case." Fox responded. "By the way, did it occur to you this attempted murder took place while your 'man' was in custody?"

CHAPTER 10

Fox was crestfallen when he left Detective Savage; he felt alone and isolated. Given all the new evidence, *why wouldn't Savage listen?* He thought. Nonetheless, he was determined to continue the investigation, if not for himself— at least for the victim and her family. Fox had many connections, but one of them was well connected, influential, and can possibly give him cover if push comes to shove.

Justice John Simmons is a judge on the United States District Court for the Southern District of New York. He is most known for the famous Lusitania tragedy and the Teapot Dome Scandal. His power and influence reach as far as the presidency of the United States and the Supreme Court. Fox and the Judge became acquainted at Harvard and have remained lifelong friends.

Fox called ahead and scheduled an appointment. Justice Simmons was a busy man, but occasionally he would make an exception for old class-chums. Fox arrived on time. He made his way through the building and past the opulent Greek-style columns; he walked through a set of highly polished set of oak doors. The judge's office was on the third floor.

"May I help you?" A well-dressed woman said, sitting at her desk. Her hair was stretched back and rolled into a neat-tight-bun. Fox's senses were arrested by the paralegal's pungent perfume; sharp, and alluring, but it wasn't a nickel-and-dime-store fragrance.

"Hello. I'm here to see Judge Simmons. He's expecting me."

The secretary looked on her flat calendar, "You must be Mr. Fox." She responded.

"Yes."

She pushed a button on a square device. It buzzed the next room, "Mr. Fox to see you, sir. Should I send him in?"

A muffled and crackled discordant sound filled the room that only someone close to the device understood. "He will see you now." She said. "This way, please." She knocked and opened the wood door, Fox stepped in.

"Fox!" A resonant voice echoed from the other side of the room. "Come in. How are you, old man?" He walked over; handshakes were exchanged, and the judge patted Fox on the back. "Sit, sit Fox." He said.

Judge Simmons's office was large; filled with bookcases, and books on law. His desk was elongated like a coffin but broader. Along the east wall were a fireplace, a smaller table, and two leather wingback chairs facing each other.

"I know you're a busy man, John, so, I'll cut to the chase." Fox said, "I need your help. I'm working on a strange case. A child was murdered, and Detective Savage closed it claiming he caught the killer. I don't believe he did."

John leaned forward, "I see, so, he believes he caught the culprit, and you don't think so." He said. Simmons was tall, lean, and had a keen mind. His nose protruded outward with a noticeable dip on its end like a spout on a tea-kettle. Whenever he spoke, his ghost-white-face thinned and narrowed, "Tell me more."

"You see, at first, we had little to go on, but the more I investigated, the more clues surfaced," Fox said. "I'm not sure at this point, but I believe – call it more of a hunch, this case is bigger than what I originally thought, even sinister."

"Sinister?" John said, "What do you mean?"

"Eugenics. I believe eugenics may play a part."

The judge leaned back in his seat, crossed his legs, and placed his forefinger across the bottom of his cheek. Deep in thought, "Eugenics, you say. Fascinating." John expressed, "But I don't see how I can help you, Fox. I'm not a scientist, I'm a judge. What can I do?"

"Do you know anything about eugenics? And the recent Supreme Court decision in *Buck v. Bell?*" Fox said.

"Yes, who hasn't heard of eugenics. And I am well aware of *Buck v. Bell.*"

"Do you recall what Justice Oliver Wendell Holmes stated in his final opinion?"

"Yes, he determined three generations of imbeciles are enough." John said, "But what has all of this to do with me?"

"I understand many powerful and influential people are connected with eugenics. Do you know anything more about the movement – given the fact you are in a powerful position?" Fox said. "I guess what I mean, have you been approached to join the cause?"

"No, no one has approached me to join, or for that matter to contribute time or money. But the eugenics crowd aren't exactly hiding; the movement and its members are in plain sight. In fact, anyone can find a list of its members by simply reading the newspaper." Judge Simmons said. Hard work and long hours displayed itself as dark circles around his eyes. "Eugenics is evil; I'm against it, Fox. But I don't see how I can help you. I even have friends who support it. What can I do? But I understand even your fiancé works for the movement? Correct?"

"Yes."

"It would seem she knows more about eugenics than myself."

"Indeed, and I have tried to gain more information from Clara, but she throws up walls, and becomes defensive," Fox said. "At this point, what I really need from you is cover if I get in trouble with Detective Savage. I need your weight and influence to overshadow this case."

"I'll do what I can, but you have to understand I'm limited."

"I do understand, but one call from you can make people think twice."

Judge Simmons folded his fingers together like fingers slid into a glove. He tapped two of his fingers and bounced his leg up and down. The more he thought, the more his thoughts submerged deep into his consciousness like a lead weight falling to the bottom of the ocean. "Fox, we have been friends for a long time. I know you. You wouldn't be asking a request like this if it wasn't serious. I'll do what I can. You have my word." He said. "But let me caution you. Find your man, don't get too sidetracked with eugenics. Just find your man."

Fox left with a good feeling. Now he had an influential person guarding his back, at least in part.

Fox arrived back at his apartment. He nestled down in his chair; pulled out his pad, and read over what he had written up to that point in his investigation. Like a sponge, he took everything in. The candles; Ginger's testimony, Big Jakes warning, Savage ending the probe and judge Simmons – all congealed, forming a stream of loose connections. He mulled over each part as if they were pieces to a jigsaw puzzle.

He got up and walked to the window. People walked up and down the streets. Cars hummed by like hummingbirds attracted to flowers. There was a sudden bang, then a puff of smoke. It was an old Ford chugging along the road. Dusk was near. Far in the distance were artificial structures etched along the horizon in a reddish glow. Only in the big city; skyscrapers took the place of mountains and fields of grass where the sun crowned the earth with a halo.

Shadows fell. Fox glanced across the street and noticed a mysterious figure between two buildings. At first, it didn't register in his conscious mind. Then something jumped out as if it was a latent response; subliminal, and visceral. His eyes reverted back. There it was again. Fox felt watched; as if a dozen eyeballs were glued to his body. The shadowy figure lit a cigarette. The light revealed a stoic-silhouette; and a beleaguered form. His square jaws were ridged like a rocky cliff. Ominous, without a shred of fear. Fox backed away from the window so as not to alarm the individual. *Who is that? Is he a police officer or another private dick?* He thought. Fox decided he needed to confront the sap.

Fox slipped out the back of his building and made his way down the block. He crossed the intersection and disappeared behind the adjacent buildings. Fox made his way up the alleyway, he hoped to surprise him from behind. He emerged from the back, but the dark figure was gone. Fox examined the area; he found the cigarette still lit on the ground, odd. Most people rub it flat to extinguish the fire. Fox ran to the sidewalk to see if the man run away. His heart raced; his adrenalin pumped through his veins at record speed. Calm down. He told himself. It's probably nobody.

He crossed the street and headed back to his apartment. When he reached his floor, his door was wide open. His heart started to beat fast again like a horse on a race-track. He pulled out his revolver and slowly made his way to the open door. *On three*, he told himself. He jumped in front of the door and waved his gun. The front room was empty. He made his way to the other bedrooms and bathroom; nothing. *I know I closed that door on the way out. Why was it open? Was I robbed?* He thought.

He must have been robbed, was the logical conclusion. He looked for anything that might have been stolen.

Everything appeared to be in its place. Even the three hundred dollars he had in his drawer beside his bed was still there. He bolted his door and sat in his chair. Confused, maybe the thief didn't have enough time to take anything. He tried but failed.

CHAPTER 11

That evening Fox and Clara arranged to meet and have dinner at her apartment. On the way there, Fox couldn't shake the feeling he was being watched and followed as if a hound-dog had his scent. Maybe it was just one person; if so, Fox felt he or she was omnipresent. Overall, Fox never experienced it before, and it was plain creepy.

Fox arrived, and Clara was dressed in her usual manner. Posh frock. Straps exposed her shoulders. Her silk dress flared with ruffles below her waist. Tied off in the middle was a turquoise embroidered ribbon. Fox knocked; Clara opened the front door, and they kissed. When she turned, her ruffled dress fanned out like a parasol.

"Come in, I've made one of your favorites." She said.

"Fried Chicken?" Fox said. His mouth started to salivate. Clara was a good cook. She especially loved to cook southern food.

"Of course."

The evening was a typical night. After they ate, they settled down for their evening activities together. Clara enjoyed word puzzles; it was the new fad. Fox enjoyed reading. At times they would listen to the radio, but Fox was restless. He couldn't take his mind off the case and shake off the feeling he was being followed. Nor did it help matters Clara had several candles lit throughout the apartment. His eyes were drawn by one particular candle sitting on an end table in the corner in front of him. The flames contorted and twisted out of control, but still was regulated. Fox became mesmerized. Almost in a trance-like state, the crime scene came to mind; vivid, as if he was actually there. Fox followed the killer into the ally. He watched him sit on a crate and position candles around himself in a semi-circle. He visualized the knife. Fox re-coiled. He reached for his throat. A faint voice called out to him, "*Fox. Fox. Fox.*" It was Clara's voice.

He was jolted back into reality. "It's the candles." He said. His voice filled with anxiety.

"What about the candles?" Clara asked. She was surprised by Fox's laps of consciousness. "What is it?"

"Extinguish the candles, please." Fox was surprised at himself in how he reacted. This has never happened before. "What's happing to me, Clara?" Fox rubbed his throat as if a part of his subconscious mind told him he had a slash.

Clara snuffed out the flames. "There, it's all gone. Do you feel better?" She asked.

"Yes. Yes, thank you." Fox started to relax.

"What happened Fox?"

"I'm under a lot of pressure; this case has me preoc-cupied. I suppose I had a momentary lapse and lost con-trol of my thoughts. It's all over now. Nothing to worry about." Fox explained. He didn't want to tell Clara the whole truth about his feeling of being watched and fol-lowed, and the break-in at his apartment. He didn't want to alarm her.

"I'll turn on the phonograph. It will help you relax." Clara put on soft music. She returned with a small pillow. "Lift your head." She said, "Now, relax." She pulled up a stool, took his shoes off, and placed his feet on it. "Now, just relax and forget about the last few days."

"Thank you, Clara. That will help. But I need to call Savage after I rest."

After Fox rested, he went to the kitchen to call Detective Savage; he made sure Clara couldn't hear their conversation. It was after 8:00 PM.

"Hello, Savage here."

"Savage, this is Fox."

"What's the meaning of this Fox? It's after 8:00 in the evening." Savage said, his voice was hoarse and harsh.

"Sorry to bother you, but we need to talk about the case," Fox said, "It's important."

"Case? What case—?"

"The one where the child was murdered—"

"I told you, Fox, the case is closed."

"Did you put a tail on me?" Fox blurted.

"Tail? What in blazes are you talking about? Have you been drinking?"

"Someone is following me, and they broke into my apartment."

"It was probably a thief. Did they take anything?"

"Not that I can see. Everything seems to be in place."

"I didn't put a tail on you; and if nobody took nothing, then you're delusional," Savage said. "I told you this case is closed. Get a grip. Wise up and let it go."

"I can't."

"Damn-it Fox! For God sakes, why not?"

"The evidence doesn't point to your man. The evidence goes toward a different direction." Fox was beginning to tire of having to repeat himself. "Sometimes, Savage, you can be thick in the head."

"Thick?" Savage screamed. "Listen to me, gumshoe, enough! If you don't drop this case, you're going to be all alone. The more you're alone, the more it will drive you crazy. Then we will have to throw your sorry ass in the asylum, for your own good!" Savage roared. He slammed the phone down. The line was dead.

Savage's tone struck Fox like thunder. Fox realized; perhaps for the first time, Savage was not only close-minded, but he was daft. *But why?* Fox thought. *Could it be something else causing Savage to be obtuse and act in a child-like manner?*

After Fox returned to the living room, Clara saw frustration written all over his face, it prompted her to ask, "Is everything alright?"

"He's insufferable!" Exclaimed Fox. "He is one of the most irritating persons I have ever known!" Fox threw up his arms in disgust. "If he was here right now, I—I, could strangle him!" His arms shook with violence like a wind in a hurricane.

"Settle down Fox," Clara said, "you're going to give yourself a heart attack. "I'll get you some tea." She left, and a few minutes later, she returned with a cup of brewed tea. "Here, sit down and relax."

"But—" Fox started on a round of expletives.

"No buts, sit," Clara ordered and pointed her finger to the chair.

"Fine, but do you know he hates our President, President Calvin Coolidge?" Fox shook his finger in the air as if he was beating Savage.

"What? You mean, he's a Democrat?" Clara said with surprise.

"That's right Clara—"

"Well, I never." She flopped down in the adjacent chair and crossed her arms with a defiant look. Politics and religion are what Fox and Clara agreed on.

They sat for a long while. Clara calmed down. "He has been your friend for a long time, and I have been friends with him as well. Nobody is perfect, Fox; we can overlook some of his shortcomings."

"Yes, Clara. You're right, as usual, he still is our friend. He will be the best man at the wedding." Fox said. "But he can be infuriating at times."

Fox left Clara, his mind was relaxed and tranquil, but he still had that feeling he was being watched and followed.

He couldn't shake it. He pulled up to a red-light; looked into the rear-mirror, and noticed the car behind him. To his chagrin, it was the same car behind him ten minutes ago. The hood ornament was unmistakable, it was of a winged lady. He was being followed.

The light turned green; Fox slammed on the peddle. The engine roared like a lion. He swerved between cars. Buildings on either side were blurs as he sped down the freeway at high speed. His tail kept the same pace. Fox even ran red-lights, almost causing several accidents. But his shadow kept approaching. He tapped the outside of his jacket to make sure his pistol was there. He was relieved, it gave him some comfort. Fox had to think quick and fast. He decided to turn the tables around. Instead of being chased, he would do the chasing.

Ahead was a small wooded section with a dirt road. It led to a deep ravine and a dumping area. Fox slammed on the brakes, made a sudden turn, and his lights disappeared behind trees. His shadow followed. The dirt road was bumpy. Both vehicles threw up dust, causing their head-lights to appear dim like light from a lighthouse on a foggy night. They were tossed and cavorted about like rag dolls. Car to car. Bumper to bumper. Fox managed to get ahead of his pursuer. He killed his lights, but before he was able to turn off the road, his pursuer rammed the back of his car and was thrust forward like a rocket. His head hit the steering wheel. Blood gushed out from the gash on his forehead. Between the sudden blow and the blood, Fox was dazed and slumped forward.

After several moments Fox regained consciousness. He retrieved his pistol and pushed the car door open and stepped out. Steam billowed out from the radiator like a volcanic cloud spewing puffs of white air; his car was totaled. The engine was still on when Fox approached the stranger. The windows were dark. All he could see was a silhouette. Fox cocked his gun and held it up to the window, "Get out!" He yelled. There was no movement. Fox tapped the window and screamed again, "Out! Now!" Nothing. *Maybe he is unconscious?* Fox thought. He tried to open the door, but it was locked. Fox knocked on the window to try to wake him up and get his attention. He stepped back. The car suddenly roared and tried to pull away from Fox's car. The car broke free after several gyrations. "Stop!" Fox yelled.

Fox stepped behind a rock in case the man tried to run him over. He shot at his tires but missed. His pursuer slammed down on his accelerator and sped forward. Fox yelled, "Stop man, there's a ravine just ahead!" Fox's words were muffled by the car's engine. Fox knew he was headed for his death. He was powerless. In the next moment, his tail-lights disappeared. There was a sudden crashing sound, then a massive fireball shot straight up like fireworks on the fourth of July. The flames outlined the ravine and the surrounding area in a hellish haze.

Nearby homes heard the sound, and some could see the glow from the fire a mile away. The police and fire trucks arrived. They found Fox sitting on the side of the road and pulled out hoses to put out the flames. Fox's car was towed, and he was questioned by the police on what had happened. Afterward, he was driven to his apartment and informed he needed to speak to Detective Savage in the morning.

CHAPTER 12

Fox arrived at the police station the next morning; he knocked on Detective Savage's office door, and walked in, "Good morning, Savage."

Savage's eyes were wild; animated like a wide-eyed nocturnal animal hunting for prey. "Fox, you're insufferable! I told you the case was closed! Period!" Savage said. His voice was hoarse and throaty.

"But I was—"

Savage slammed his fist down; everything on his desk seemed to jump and jerk as if an earthquake jolted the building. "Damn it to Hell Fox! Now there is a dead body and a jalopy at the bottom of a ravine. It will cost the city tons of bucks to examine the corpse and retrieve the car." Savage laid his head in his hands and muffled incoherent sounds.

"Let me explain—"

"Damn straight. You better explain Fox, and you better have a good explanation. If you don't, I'm tempted to throw your ass in the Can."

"I was leaving Clara's apartment, and someone followed me. I decided to turn off onto a side road and either try to lose or catch him. All I wanted to do is see who it was and why he was tailing me." Fox said.

"Then, why is he dead?" Savage glared at Fox like he pointed a double-barrel shotgun right at Fox's head.

"It was an accident; his car rammed into mine, and I ordered him out of the vehicle. Instead, he broke loose and drove straight into the ravine. I don't believe he knew it was there, his headlights were damaged, and he was driving blind. I never meant for him to die; honest, it just happened."

Savage was exhausted. His cold was worse and had taken a toll; his face was drained and flushed. Puffy and swollen like a blow-fish. His nerves were shot. Overall, however, his indomitable will compensated and fought back his body's desire to go home and crash. "Go home," Savage said. "I'm telling you once again; it's over, case closed. If another body turns up dead and you're linked to it over this case; I swear, I'll lock you up for obstruction. If I can't find a legal reason, I'll do it to keep you out of trouble." He sighed. "Now get out of my sight." Fox turned to leave, "By the way," Savage said, "you got a nasty cut over your eye, better get it taken care of."

Fox was drained as well. He still felt a residue of adrenalin from last night; it soared through his veins like poison. Fox hadn't eaten; ravished, he felt an animalistic craving began to seize his thoughts and take control. His body needed to be satiated, he wanted food. But Fox was more determined than ever to find the killer and find who put a tail on him. The more Fox thought about the case, the more he was convinced the killer was connected to eugenics; to what degree, he didn't know, but he needed to talk with Dr. Eugene Black— privately.

After he stopped for a quick bite, Fox visited Professor Black at his office at the university. He didn't call ahead, he wanted to catch him off guard and surprise him. He located his office on the first floor of Building B, office number 51. The door was slightly ajar, Dr. Black was alone.

Fox prepared himself; he wanted to stun Dr. Black and frighten him to his core. He shifted his jacket and tightened his tie. On the count of three, Fox slammed the door wide open and rushed in like it was one of Palmer's Raids. "Listen up, miscreant!" Fox exclaimed; he was past playing nice.

Shocked and confused, Professor Black jumped straight out of his seat like exploding popcorn. "What, what?" He screamed. "What's the meaning of this?" He stammered. "Who are you?"

Fox grabbed his lapels and drew him close to his face, "Recognize me now?" Then he shoved him down into his chair like he was a sack of dirt.

"You?" Professor Black said; surprised and overwhelmed.

"That's right, me."

Dr. Black's arms started to shake, "What do you want?" His lips quivered like a leaf in the wind.

"A child has been murdered; I'm trying to find the killer."

"I didn't do it. What does that have to do with me?"

"Eugenics played a part, and you know something," Fox said. "Does that jolt anything in that brain of yours?" Fox tapped the side of his skull as if he tried to knock some sense into his brain.

"I don't understand." Dr. Black responded.

Fox reached into his pocket and showed him the candle. "Recognize it?"

He put his glasses on and looked at it, "No," He said.

Fox turned the candle, so the embossed side could be seen by the professor, "What about now?"

His eyes widened; his face contorted, Fox frightened him, but this created a new fear— something deep and profound. He remained silent.

Fox hit a nerve, "So, you do recognize this symbol?" Fox grabbed him again and shook his body, trying to force him to spill his guts. "Talk, or you'll go to the hospital in a body bag.

"No, I can't. They'll—"

"If you don't talk, you'll be dead before they – whoever they are – have the opportunity to take you out."

Fox continued to brow-beat the professor until he realized the professor wasn't going to talk. His fear was thick as molasses; it dripped and oozed out of every pore in his body. He left the professor's office with the reassurance he was on the right track. *But what exactly did Dr. Black know? And why did he fear it?*

Fox caught a taxi and went to his apartment. After he changed, he went to bed for some needed sleep. But, Morpheus, the god of dreams, wouldn't allow him to have a peaceful night. Images of the killer flashed in and out of sight. He could see him, but he couldn't recognize who he was. He was always there, just out of reach. The image eluded him as if he was trying to catch a shadow.

Clara arrived, and Fox was still asleep. It was 3:00 in the afternoon. This wasn't normal for Fox to sleep like this. She bent down and kissed him, leaving a red stain on his cheek. He awoke and found Clara looking at him. Her perfume seduced his senses and his sexual drive into gear, "Fox, wake up. Do you know what time it is?"

He looked at his clock and rolled out of bed. "No. I've had a rough couple of days." Fox slipped on his robe, "Let's go into the kitchen, I need some coffee."

"You look awful, James, that cut looks bad, it needs a new dressing, it's bleeding."

Fox touched his gash, "Oh, yes, I taped a make-shift bandage over the cut last night. I must have accidentally agitated it during my sleep."

The coffee percolated until it was done; Clara poured both of them a cup, and they sat at the kitchen table. "Fox, we need to talk," Clara said. A serious look came over her. She was tense.

He knew that tone; he was reluctant to ask what it was about, but he did, "About what?"

"I'm concerned about you and this case."

"Clara, I'm fine. There have been a few hiccups, but I'm getting somewhere."

"Just look at you. I'm afraid you're in over your head. Please stop this investigation."

"I've been in many dangerous cases before, what makes this different?"

Clara wasn't responsive to his question. "Just stop. End this investigation before—"

"Before what?"

"Alright. You want to know why I want you to quit, fine, here it is. Word has come to me; you were involved in a man's death."

Fox shot up from his seat, "That darn Savage. He had no right—"

"He had every right; he's your friend, I'm your fiancé, and we care for your wellbeing. Don't be angry at him. He has informed me the case was closed. If you don't stop, you'll force him to do something he doesn't want to do."

"Clara, I can't stop," Fox said, "You don't understand, he's got the wrong man. If I don't find the killer, the wrong man will go to the chair." Fox held her hands, "Please, try to understand what I'm doing."

She slid her hand out of Fox's grip. This was the first time she had ever turned cold and against him. "There is another matter. You made a visit to Dr. Black's office. He went to the police. If Savage didn't intervene, you would be charged with assault and battery." Clara stood. "Fox, we are concerned with your health."

"My health? What does that mean?"

"What that means, we are concerned with your state of mind. You are alone, but you still defy everyone's advice. A man died. You're obsessing over this case. If you don't stop what you're doing— well, you know where that will lead."

"But Clara, please listen—"

"No, Fox, you listen." She pulled off her engagement ring and laid it on the table. "The wedding is off. At least till you come to your senses and stop what you're doing."

She turned to walk away. Fox reached out and stopped her, "Please don't leave, not like this." Fox said.

"It's for your own good Fox. Goodbye." She walked out the door.

The room seemed to twist around. Pain gripped his heart like it was run through the teeth of an old fashion washing machine. His life came to a grinding halt. He moved to the window. Images of his life flashed before him. *Should I run after her? Or not?* Fox thought. *Should I stop trying to find the killer?* Across the street, tall trees shot straight up and aligned themselves along the side of the buildings. Leaves were falling; a light breeze swirled them around into a little twist. Rejected, he could almost hear waves of pain crashing against his heart. Clara appeared from out of the building below. He watched her walked away; his heart sunk deeper. But Fox realized he had to let her go. If he was correct; the more he investigated, the more dangerous it will become. At least now Clara is not in the picture—she's out of danger. This, in some odd way, gave Fox comfort.

CHAPTER 13

Depression descended on Fox like a cold, lonely, winter's night. Now; with the investigation shut down, Clara walked away from him – Savage was correct, he was all alone – he made sure of it. The only person he could count on was his old classmate, Judge John Simmons. But Fox was still being followed; this made him more convinced than ever, he was on the right path, no matter what, the killer had to be found. Savage had the wrong man. What troubled him was Clara. She didn't want to listen and support him. But this was for the best, as he concluded earlier, it might be too dangerous for her.

He needed a plan. The next logical step was to find more about the cult, Lucifer the Light Bearer. This could lead to the killer. He showered, dressed, ate, and called for a taxi. The taxi was waiting by the time Fox stepped out of his apartment building and onto the sidewalk.

"Where, too, Mac?" The driver said.

"New York Public Library."

"Ab-so-lute-ly!" The car jumped into gear. Churning and throwing debris against the street lamp post. "Say, Mac, did you read about what happened last night in the newspaper?"

"No, I haven't had a chance to read the paper yet."

The vehicle bounced from side to side like a boxer pounding a punching bag. "Yeah, a man drove off that steep ravine; you know where the old dumping ground is?"

Fox's eyes lit up, "Yes. What did the papers say?"

"That a man drove a car right over the cliff." He said. "What a dope."

"What else did it say?" Fox said.

"The cops showed up and found a gumshoe sitting in the road." The driver clenched his fingers around the steering wheel and smacked his lips. "If you ask me, I think the Dick killed that man; I don't trust them, never did, they are always snooping around in other people's business like a dog sniffing through garbage." The driver said, his face wrinkled with disgust. "You know the type? They dress dirty, lie, and will cheat to make a buck." The taxi driver's head bounced side to side in lockstep with the car's shocks.

Yes, I know the type," Fox said, "Did the papers mention anything about the dead man?"

"Nope." The driver noticed Fox's eyes were bloodshot. His veins displayed a puffy web-like shape in the white of his eyeballs. "Hitting too much of the Hooch? I've been there myself. What you need is some Java. I'll stop, so you can get some coffee."

"No thank you, I already had some. Just straight to the library."

The driver pushed his shoulders up and back, and tightened his jaws, "Suit yourself," He said.

The taxi driver dropped Fox off at the entrance of the New York Public Library. It was a large building with thousands of volumes and growing. What he needed to find out was if the library had anything on the occult, cults, and eugenics. The front desk directed him to the last room at the back of building on the right side. There was a small wood-framed table. Nobody was there. He noticed a bell sitting on the table and tapped it. Within seconds, a young woman came from the back. She smiled, "May I help you?" She asked. The name on her name-tag said, Helen.

Fox immediately noticed her short black hair. It wasn't quite an Eton style, but more like the Orchid crop where the sides were slightly frazzled with some bounce and curl to it. Helen appeared to be five feet, seven or eight inches, with a curvy body; she was somewhat thin with a solid frame. Her glasses didn't take away from her natural beauty, in fact, it added to it. Fox was drawn to her smile like a moth to a flame. "Yes, is this the section on the occult and other odd topics?" Fox asked.

"Yes, it is," She said, in a spirited tone. Helen was elegant, but she also had a tomboyish spunk about her.

"I'm looking for information on a cult. Its name is Lucifer the Light Bearer. Have you heard of it or maybe it's in another section?"

Helen tapped her finger on her chin, "I don't think I've heard of it, but— well, follow me. We might be able to find something."

Fox followed Helen down and between bookshelves. She wore a black skirt and white blouse. Conservative in dress, perhaps due to her position. The library frowned on provocative clothes. She wore a dark blue sweater over her shirt. Enamored by her body and the way her hair bounced, Fox couldn't take his eyes off the way she moved.

"By the way," Fox expressed, "I'm J.P. Fox. Nice to meet you, Helen."

She turned her head, "Nice to meet you as well, Mr. Fox." Her white teeth glistened from ear to ear. They arrived at the area; loose journals and newspapers were lying on tables ready to be placed on racks or bookshelves. "What was that name again?" She asked.

"Lucifer the Light Bearer. And anything related to eugenics."

"Oh, yes, eugenics. That's always in the newspapers." She responded. "You search this stack," She placed a load of journals on the table, "I'll search these. It should be easy to find if we have it—skim through, and the name will stick out."

After a few minutes, Helen found a 1901 journal, named Lucifer the Light Bearer, "I found it." She said and handed to Fox.

"Thank you," Fox said. He sat and flipped through it.

After a few minutes, Helen asked, "Found anything interesting?"

"Well, yes, and no. It's just more radical ideas."

"Like what?"

"They are anarchists. Moses Harman was the publisher, and his daughter believes and advocates for the same beliefs. They advocate for abortion, and they are against religion." Fox said. "Listen to this, 'Lucifer the Light Bearer stands for light against darkness, freedom against slavery, free thought, free speech."

"Wow! That's some wild stuff. What else does it say?"

"Apparently, they believe marriage laws are evil. They support free love. In other words, a woman should be free to have sex in or outside of marriage."

"Why would they advocate for that?" Helen said a puzzled look crept over her face. "Don't they realize marriage is a good thing? It helps keep men responsible, and it gives children a name and lineage."

Fox thought about what Helen stated, "You're correct, Helen, but at the moment, I need to focus on how this group is connected with the candle."

"What candle?"

Fox pulled out the candle and showed it to Helen. "Notice the emblem and inscription?" He said, "Better yet, here's an enlarged sketch of it." He handed her the paper that the engraver had sketched a copy of.

"Yes, I see it." She said, "Wait a minute," She turned the journal over, "It's a match." She said. "See." And handed the journal to Fox.

"By Jove, Helen, you're a lifesaver!" Fox looked up into her eyes, "Can you think of a link between this cult and eugenics?"

Something clicked. "I think so. We have a selection of silent films, and a place you can play them." She looked at Fox, "Follow me, it's this way."

Fox followed Helen into a small room with a projector in the back. "Why are we here?" Fox asked.

"Have you ever heard of the Black Stork?"

"I don't think so."

"Sit here. In a few minutes, I'll play it for you. Just prepare yourself. You may not like what you see."

The film started to flicker images on the screen. A child was born with defects. The eugenic doctor informed the family and nurse the compassionate thing to do is to let the baby die, and it was the moral thing to do. Withhold food, milk, and love; if the unfit child were allowed to live, it would live a life of misery and be a burden on the family or the state. Fox felt his conscience assaulted and even terrorized like a thousand knives were being plunged into his senses; tears formed in his eyes and rolled down his face. Powerless, he couldn't help the child. *How could anyone do this to a baby?* He thought. The film ended. Fox's pain turned into anger. *If I ever get a hold of these people.* His thoughts raced on like wind toppling buildings and tossing vehicles over like sand.

Helen flipped the lights on and walked up to Fox. She saw pain and anger mixed in his expressions and eyes. "Mr. Fox. Are you alright?"

He slowly stood, but he was weak. He almost fell to the ground before Helen caught him. She swung his left arm around her neck and walked him out of the projector room and helped him sit in a chair. "Sit here while I get you some water." She returned, "Here, drink this."

Fox sipped the water and slowly regained his composure. "Please forgive my loss of control. It's just—"

"It's the film, I know. I couldn't sleep for two days when I watched it." Helen said.

Fox stood to leave, "I want to thank you for all of your help. I'm sorry I almost fainted on you."

By now, Helen was infatuated with Fox. She loved his physique, his intellect, and his compassion. She was drawn to him. Something inside her didn't want him to leave. She was afraid of never seeing him again. "Mr. Fox!" She blurted out. "How can I get in touch with you? —I mean, what if I come across more material that could help you?" She was both excited and cautious, but she only allowed him to see her contrived outward appearance – calm and collective.

Fox smiled. There was chemistry. He could feel her hidden desire to see him again. He reached in his pocket, "Here, this is my card. Please call if you find anything. I would appreciate the help. And by the way, you may call for any reason, if you like."

She blushed. Her cheeks turned red like fire, "Thank you, Mr. Fox." She felt shy as if she was back in school, and she experienced a crush on a boy. "Yes, I will—I mean, here's my card as well." Helen handed him her card, "Please call if you need anything." She stumbled over her own words. She became nervous and started to giggle.

Fox walked away, and she held his card tight to her breast. She beamed with delight. *Please look back. Please, please.* She said to herself, jumping up and down inside.

Fox looked back just before he turned around the corner. "Yes!" She said out loud. And twirled around on her feet like a ballerina.

CHAPTER 14

Fox was refreshed after he had a good night's sleep. The itchy spider-veins were gone from his eyes. His gaunt facial appearance had disappeared, but his bandage had a red blot on it from the deep gash on his forehead. He cleaned it and applied a new bandage. After a quick breakfast, he sat in his chair to contemplate his next move.

As he flipped through his pad, a sudden feeling of dread seized his mind. *If my suspicions are correct, this is much bigger than one lunatic on the loose.* Big Jake's warning started to sink in like quicksand. But the film the Black Stork clinched the deal. The connections are uncanny.

T.S. Eliot's poem *The Hollow Men* came to mind. He retrieved a copy from his bookshelf and began to read,

> We are the hollow men
> We are the stuffed men
> Leaning together . . .
> Those who have crossed
> With direct eyes, to death's other kingdom
> Remember us—if at all— not as lost
> Violent souls, but only
> As the hollow men
> The stuffed men.

These words seared into Fox's consciousness like a hot iron. The poem, Hollow Men, was about the horrors of the Great War— a war to end all wars, so they say. But there was something more universal about this poem. It reflects the condition of the human heart. It speaks of treachery. Instead of peace and harmony, it's about a culture devaluing human life to the extent, even the victims see themselves merely as a caricature in a lifeless silent film. Stick-figures, whose only shape is formed by heartless men and a callous culture. The murdered child, victims of eugenics, and the child in the Black Stork illuminates the reality they are nothing more than hollowed out manmade constructs— stuffed with humanities' contrived notions of inhumanity.

Fox needed feedback, he needed someone to talk to— if not just to air things out in the open. He called Justice Simmons and arranged to have another meeting. A taxi drove Fox to his office. He arrived and was escorted in after Judge Simmons finished with a meeting.

The judge smiled, "My good friend, Fox. I'm glad to see you, but your call sounded urgent. What's wrong?"

"The last few days have been horrific. I am still working on the same case. Detective Savage not only has shut down the investigation, but he is also threatening to put me in jail or place me in a psych ward if I don't stop investigating."

"So, this has become serious," John said, his face turned from jocular to sincere.

"Not only that, I'm being followed. My pursuer accidentally killed himself when he tried to escape. And Detective Savage turned Clara against me. She called off our engagement when I refused to comply with Savage's order and her wishes."

"You mean Clara won't stand by you?" Rows of wrinkles puffed out over his eyebrows.

Fox's eyes drifted to the floor, "It's probably for the best. This has become dangerous, and I want her to be far removed and safe." He said.

"What can I do?" Judge Simmons said.

"I'm not sure, but I just need someone to talk too. Isolation isn't a good thing when under this sort of stress. Ears. Ears are what I need. And you have them, you always did. I remember while in college, you had a way of listening to your teachers, then reframing their arguments and viewed it in another perspective. There was a reason why you were the debate team's star back in college." A small crack formed between Fox's lips, indicating he was trying to be funny.

"That's true. I loved debating."

"Your ears, the way you debated, along with your analytical mind— has made you a great judge. I think you'll be tapped to sit on the Supreme Court one day."

Judge Simmons laughed, "That means something, coming from you." He said, "One day Fox, flattery will get you through the Pearly Gates."

"When it comes to this case, I need something other than flattery."

"Is your focus still on finding the killer?"

"Yes, but it has expanded."

"Why?"

"Clues. Clues have opened the case like a fishing net. The more I found, the larger the net grew. There are more connections here than rabbit holes. I believe eugenics is central."

"How so?"

"I don't know yet. But I'm getting closer."

"Well, my advice is, forget eugenics and just focus on the killer."

"Your advice is well taken, but it's not that simple anymore. And I don't have time, and you don't have time for me to show you everything, at least not right now."

Judge Simmons was silent and took in every word, but he was somber. The silence was broken when he said, "Fox, my friend. I have your back, and I support you. But there's very little I can do."

"That's all I need to hear. Thank you." Fox said. "I'll be leaving now. Have a good day."

"Same to you, old friend." He smiled as Fox walked out of his office. "By the way, Fox, have my secretary validate your parking."

"No need. I have a taxi waiting. Thanks, anyway."

Fox stepped out of the courthouse and approached the taxi. He opened the door, and a goon was waiting for him in the backseat; he was pointing a gun right at Fox, "Get in." He said.

Fox slid into the seat, "What's this?" He said.

"Shut your, puss." The boob turned to the driver, "Drive." He said. "Slowly give me your Bean-shooter." He ordered Fox.

He was a large muscular man. His jaws were square; his elephant-sized ears dominated both sides of his face, and his nose was straight steel. Cheap suit and cheap cologne that would gag a maggot. Fox surmised he was all bronze and no brains. A want-a-be Al Capone—perhaps. The taxi driver never looked in the rearview mirror. He, too, remained silent. They reached a destitute section in the Lower East Side. Fox knew this was not a good sign; the taxi came to a full stop between two abandoned buildings. The buildings were gutted; with ghost-like impressions of a bygone past where people worked, laughed, and made plans. Now, it's a dive for slum-dwellers and gangs.

The goon shoved his pistol into Fox's side, "Get out or I'll pop you right here."

Fox stepped out. A gang stepped out of the shadows; they fanned out and surrounded Fox. They wielded lead pipes and brandished knives. The taxi sped off, left dust and rocks in mid-air in the tire's wake.

Fox looked for an exit; there was none, he was boxed in and unarmed. He scanned the ground for a weapon. There, on the ground, was a pipe. He lurched and grabbed it. The gang closed in around him. A young man jumped towards him; Fox was able to fight him off, he went down. Another one ran towards him; he, too, ate dirt, but Fox was out of luck. The first two were just decoys. Someone wearing brass knuckles punched him in the back. The pipe fell from his hand; his back arched in excruciating pain, then another one hit him in the head. He hit the ground. The gang surrounded him. "Don't kill him!" A voice yelled. "Just rough him up a bit." They kicked his stomach a few times; he tried to get up, but another person rammed his fist into his face. Fox fell back to the ground, unconscious.

"Stop!" The voice yelled again.

The next day Fox awoke in a hospital bed. One of his eyes was swollen shut. He had bandages wrapped around his ribcage. Tubes were hanging from a pole and connected to his arm. His breathing was shallow. He scanned his surroundings and tried to get out of bed, he couldn't move. A nurse walked in. "Hello there. Are we thirsty? I know you must be hungry too." She said.

With a raspy voice, Fox managed a few words, "Where—am," Was all he could muster.

The nurse patted his arm, "There, there, don't try to talk. I'll feed you." She said. "The doctor will be in later. Just relax."

The next day Fox was better. His vocal cords were back. The doctor arrived, "You're a lucky man Mr. Fox. You have a fractured rib, multiple lacerations, and have a dislocated shoulder." Doctor Ashton expressed.

"How did I get here?" Fox asked.

"We don't know. A taxi dropped you off, then left without leaving any information."

"When will I be ready to go home?"

"I would advise you to stay another day unless of course, you have someone to take care of you. He said. "Mr. Fox, there is something else. We found a note pinned to your lapel." He reached in his pocket and retrieved it and handed it to Fox. "Can you shed some light on this?"

Fox read it out loud, "We are watching." It stated. It was an encrypted note that only Fox and his pursuers understood. The game just turned into a blood-sport. "Doctor," Fox said, "All I know at the moment is a gang beat the hell out of me and then I woke up here. I don't have a clue who brought me here or why. As for the note, I don't know who wrote it. I'm a private investigator, and I am getting close to something, and that is making some-body uncomfortable."

Doctor Ashton placed his hands in his white sterile jacket, "I understand. In the meantime, is there anyone who we can call? A wife, family, friend?"

"Yes. In my coat jacket, you'll find a card. The name on the card is Helen Carlyle. She works for the New York Public Library. Please give her a call, I would appreciate it." Fox had a hunch Helen would be more than willing to help him. Besides, he had no one else to turn to except the judge.

CHAPTER 15

The next day Fox opened his eyes; the room had a strong, pungent smell about it, redolent of a garden filled with flowers. Sitting on an open windowsill was a vase full of daisies and myriad of flora. Fox heard water, then he noticed steam rising from a crack from the floor of the bathroom door like fog rolling off the lagoon. A cheerful, high-pitched voice was singing; Helen's sweet voice added to the cozy atmosphere. Between the smell, the tranquil song, and the soft bed, Fox experienced a much-needed respite from the stark last few days. Fox yawned.

The water stopped; Helen popped her head around the corner, "Good morning." She said.

"Good morning." As he stretched his arms in the air.

"Give me a moment, and I'll be right out."

Fox watched her get dressed through the mirror hanging on the bathroom door. *What a looker.* He said to himself. "Helen, I don't remember you picking me up and how I got here."

"You were pretty out of it."

Fox looked around. "Nice setup."

"Helen walked out of the bathroom. "Thanks." She said. She approached Fox and sat on his side. "How are you feeling?" She touched his forehead to see if he was running a fever.

"I think I'm doing much better. Thanks for helping me."

Helen smiled, "My pleasure, Mr. Fox."

"Please, call me Fox. Just Fox. That's what all my friends call me, but my full name is James Prescott Fox."

"Okay, Mr. Fox," she smiled again, "You mean the animal – Fox?"

Fox chuckled, "Sure." He said, amused by her light jest.

"Now, Fox, what would you like to eat?" She said, touching his nose with her finger.

"Coffee and toast will suit me fine."

"Your wish is my command. While I'm getting things ready, why don't you get dressed, if you can? If you need my help, just call." Helen left the room and started the coffee.

Bruises covered his whole body. A large white bandage wrapped around his ribcage to protect his fractured rib and help it to heal. Remarkably, his body was pliable enough to walk and take a shower. Helen came in after he was done and helped him re-bandage his ribcage and dressed the gash on his forehead. "Thank you, I feel much better now after taking that hot shower," Fox said.

"Good, now you can get dressed; then come to the kitchen, and have your coffee, and toast."

"I can't thank you enough, Helen. You have been so helpful, but I have a request. I understand if you say no."

"What is it?"

"May I stay here for a while? I can sleep on your couch?"

"Of course, but don't you have a place to stay?"

"Yes, I do, but the case I'm working on is too dangerous for me to work from home." Fox pointed to his ribcage, "They know where I live."

Helen leaned back in her chair; crossed her arms, "Hmm, I see," she said, she crossed her legs and bounced the loose one up and down. "So, you think you can take advantage of a single woman?"

"No. That's not it at all—"

Helen cracked a smile, "Just kidding. Of course, you can stay here, silly, but on one condition."

"Anything."

"I get to help you with your investigation."

"Out of the question. Helen, it's too dangerous."

"Then, we don't have a deal." She puckered her lips and tilted her head backward.

Fox thought for a moment. "Fine," He said, "but I'm the boss. You do what I say. I don't want to put you in any danger. Understand?"

Helen thrust her body in a forward motion and rested her head on her clasped fingers on the table. A big grin crept over her face, "Great!" She said. "Yes, Fox, you're the boss?" She smiled, "When do I get my gun?"

"Gun?" He said. "Now wait a minute, do you know how to handle a pistol? Have you ever shot a gun?"

"No. But so what. I saw gangsters and cops in the movies use them. Just point and pull the trigger."

"No, you will not get a gun."

Fox was uneasy, not sure what to make of her forwardness. But she made him smile; in part, she was kind of cute. Nonetheless, he felt strange that he brokered a deal with a beautiful and alluring woman. "I must warn you, Helen, I'm all alone. The police believe they have caught their man and the case is closed. People are watching me, perhaps the same ones who roughed me up. And my fiancé left me as well, she called off our wedding over this case. Does any of this alarm you?"

Without hesitation, she said, "No." She grabbed his hand. "I believe I'm a good judge of character. I trust you."

Amazed by her bubbly optimism, Fox was enchanted. *She's either incredulous, a thrill-seeker, or the real thing. Time will tell.* He thought. One thing Fox did know; Helen didn't know what she was in for, and he had to protect her at all cost—without her knowing it. "What about your job?" He asked.

"I've worked there for four years without taking time off. I have already called and told them I'm taking my vacation time."

Fox blinked, "So, you had this planned all along, even before we talked about it?"

She grinned. A glow emanated off her face like she had suckered some poor sap out of his lunch money, "What's the plan, handsome."

Fox couldn't stop himself; he was taken in as if he wanted to be duped, "Well, I left my notes at my apartment. I need it."

"We'll just drive over and get it."

"We can't, they are watching. If I show up, I will be followed every step of the way."

"Then I'll drive over. Give me your key?"

"It's not that simple. You'll be putting yourself in danger."

Her elbows landed on the table again with her hands perched up under her chin, "Then what can we do?"

"We'll go together; park down the street, and you can walk to my apartment. I'll be the lookout; I know that neighborhood like the back of my hand."

Helen drove and parked two blocks down the street. "Where is your pad?" She asked.

"It's on the table, but before you go, here are some instructions. I want you to walk and act normal. If you feel nervous; think happy thoughts, if that doesn't work, abandon the plan, turn and walk back to the car. Got it?"

"Sure. I'll think about you." She smiled.

"Yes, if that takes your mind off the situation. Now, walk down the street and into my building as if you live there." Fox looked to see if any suspicious people were hanging around, "Remember, act normal."

"Yes, Fox, piece of cake. I got this."

"But it's not that simple. Stick to the plan."

"Act like an actress in a silent film?"

"Yes, now when you walk to my floor, look around and make sure nobody is hanging around. Then use the key, and my pad should be on the table by the winged-back chair."

Helen nodded her head and counting on her fingers like she was walking through each step in her mind before she did anything. "Got it."

"One last thing, in my bedroom in the closet there is a shoebox with a pistol and knife; retrieve both of them."

She shook her head. "Will do." She said.

She opened the car door and got out. Fox couldn't help but notice light refracted off her hair like it was silk. It created a harmonious symmetry within his eyes. "Are you forgetting something, Miss Helen." He expressed.

She turned, "What?"

He dangled his keys in mid-air. "Like these?"

She reached back in and grabbed them. "Which one?"

"It's the one with tape wrapped around the top."

The street was crowded. Cars flew; haberdashers were busy, all together created a discordant noise. Fox had to get in front of her. He knew there would be one or more persons watching. Fox dashed behind the nearest building and made his way around to the back streets. He rushed, dodged behind garbage cans, and looked for anyone suspicious.

Helen became nervous. She started to whistle and began to swing her arms like she was walking through a graveyard by herself. Then, a goon spotted her; but before he could follow, Fox hit him on the back of the head with a two-by-four. He lost consciousness and went down. *There's probably one more thug waiting under the stairs in my building.* He thought. Fox dashed across the street and entered the back of his building through the back entrance. There, Fox spotted him. He stood with a lit cigarette dressed in a black suit and bolder hat. Fox's instincts told him the clown didn't belong. He sneaked up behind him; lightly tapped his shoulder – he turned – and Fox swung his fist across his jaw, he fell to the ground unconscious. Instant pain ripped through his midsection. In anguish, Fox forgot about his fractured rib.

By the time Helen came back to the car, Fox was sitting in the passenger seat. "Here you go." She pulled his pad, the pistol, and knife out from her purse. "I told you I can do the job. Nobody noticed me." She beamed with self-confidence.

Fox glared into her eyes and caught a glimpse of her innocent soul. Untouched and unsullied by the harsh realities of a vile and wicked world. Fox wanted to protect that innocence. Her light-hearted expression exhibited a child-like quality that made her all the more attractive. She was both outwardly and inwardly beautiful.

CHAPTER 16

"That was exhilarating!" Helen said. "When can we do it again?" Her heart was beating fast. She didn't realize, but adrenaline pumped through her body as if the racehorse – Superman – competed in the Kentucky Derby. The wind tossed her hair around in a crazed, disheveled twirl. "What else is on the list? I mean, wow!" She said, "I was so nervous—"

"Keep your eyes on the road, Helen. You want to get us killed?"

Helen ignored Fox's words; in a raptured state of euphoria, "I like this Fox. I mean, I have read Sherlock Holmes and other detective stories, but doing detective work, well, it's better, much better."

"Try to calm down. Focus. We need to stop at the city morgue."

Helen turned her nose upward in disgust, "Where? Why the morgue? Yuck!"

"We need to speak to the coroner; maybe he can shed more light on the person who fatally drove off the cliff and into the ravine."

She shrugged her shoulders, "On my way." She made a left turn and sped down four blocks and made a right. Within minutes they were at the city morgue. Dr. Edward Nash was the Chief Medical Examiner. He and Fox were long-time acquittances; Dr. Nash has helped Fox on other cases in the past. Of course; Fox paid for information, but that was how New York City functioned, a little Jack got someone what they needed.

They walked through the building; Dr. Nash was on duty and busy performing an autopsy. Cadavers were stretched out on gurneys; white sheets covered them. Tags hung from their big toes like price-tags dangling from meat in a meat market. Dr. Nash wore a pair of clear glasses and a surgical mask. He was bent over; drilling a hole on the right side of a skull, when interrupted, "Nash!" Fox yelled.

The grinding of bone stopped. Nash looked around and spotted Fox and Helen. "Fox!" He said. "What has brought you here. And it's good to see you."

"Good to see you too, Nash." He pointed to Helen, "This is my friend, Miss Helen Carlyle."

He put the drill on the table and approached Helen and Fox. He reached out his hand, "Nice to meet you, Miss Carlyle."

She recoiled from his bloody hand, "Nice to meet you too."

"Oh, my apologies." He said, and snapped the gloves off his hands, "Let me wash up." After scrubbing his hands with soap and water, "There we go, all clean now." He said. "What can I do for you today?"

"Recently, a man drove his car off a cliff and was killed. I need to know more about him."

"Oh, yes. Come this way." Nash walked like a duck; feet pointed out, and his body swayed back and forth like a live rock formation on their way to the gurney. They surrounded the body. "Not much to work with Fox. His body was pretty much burnt to a crisp." He reached to the top of the sheet and pulled it off the dead body; black and chard, like he had been fried in hot oil. Helen grabbed her stomach. Fox caught her before she fainted. "Women." Nash rolled his eyes.

Fox walked Helen to the hallway and placed her on a sofa. "Wait here. I'll be right back." Fox walked back in, "Do you know who he was?"

"No, his identification was destroyed by the fire."

"Were there any marks or tattoos?" Fox said.

"Well, there is something, but I'm not sure what to make of it."

"What is it?"

"There was a tattoo on his right arm," Nash said, "Follow me." They walked to the other side, "See." He pointed.

"Yes, but part of it was burned."

Dr. Nash lifted an oversized magnifying glass over it, "See? You can barely make it out, but it spells Ubermensch. And below that is the number 12." Nash put down the magnifying glass. "I can't make heads or tails of it." He said.

"Ubermensch is a German word, but I'm not sure about the number," Fox said.

"Ubermensch?" Nash questioned. "That's odd, very odd. What is that all about Fox?"

"I'm not completely sure, but I have no time to waist." Fox reached into his pocket, "How much do I owe you?"

"Nothing. There wasn't much I could help you with this time. Put your money away; save it until next time." Nash said.

"Thanks, Nash. Until next time."

"Take care of yourself, Fox. Goodbye."

Sitting in the car, Fox turned to Helen and informed her, "we need to make one more stop."

"Where, too, now?"

"The New York City Library."

"You mean where I work? Why?"

"Yes, the word Ubermensch is tattooed on the corpse's shoulder and the number twelve underneath. I need to do some research."

Helen squinted her eyes, she struggled to say the word, "Uber—, how do you pronounce it?" She said.

"It's a German word. Say it like this, Uber - mensch. Ubermensch."

She slowly repeated the sounds, "Uber -mensch." Then she said it quicker, "Ubermensch. Ah, I think I've got it." Helen turned the car on, the engine revved. "Do you believe eugenics and this term are connected to the killer?" Helen asked.

"At this point, Helen, they appear to be connected. But I'm not sure how they fit together. All we have are disjointed pieces to a puzzle. With luck and good old fashion work, the more we can start piecing the parts together, an image will come into focus."

They arrived at the library, "this way, Fox, I know a secluded area where we can do our research," Helen said.

Fox pulled out a piece of paper and scribbled down a list. He handed it to Helen, "Do you know where we can find these books?" He said.

She read out loud, "*Thus Spake Zarathustra, Beyond Good and Evil, Ecce Homo, The Birth of Tragedy, Human, all too Human,*" Helen thought for a few minutes. "Are these books by the same person, and what type of books are they?"

"They are all written by Friedrich Nietzsche. They will be in the philosophy section," Fox said.

"Wait, right here." Helen left; rows of books lined up like neat stacks of refined wood, ornate and elaborate. They stood in silence like soldiers guarding a national treasure; in this case, information. After several minutes Helen reappeared. "Here we go. These are new books, just arrived."

They sat. Fox pulled out his pad and fountain pen. He began to skim through the pages, not really sure what he was looking for. But Fox needed to learn more about Nietzsche and his beliefs. For years, the newspapers ran articles about Nietzsche; Fox didn't pay too much attention to them—he thought it was a fad, here today and gone tomorrow like clothing. "Here." He handed Helen a book, "You can start with this one."

"Fox, I don't know what I'm looking for."

It never occurred to Fox Helen had no college education. He treated her like he treated Clara, "I'm sorry,

Helen." He said. "Before we start, can you get us some coffee? – I need to plan on how to proceed."

"Sure." She said, and left. After a short time, Helen returned, "Here's yours, and this one is mine." Steam from the cups twirled and curled like smoke from a cigarette.

"Helen, while I read why don't you take notes. Sounds fair?"

"Yes." She grabbed the pen and pad. Her body shifted in an upright position like a professional secretary. "Ready." She said. Her voice changed. It was almost baritone, contrived, but efficient.

Fox marveled; it was like watching someone copy another person, but this was her style – light and cheerful. Fox focused on his reading and began to dictate, "Friedrich Wilhelm Nietzsche. Born 15 October 1844 at Rocken in Prussian Saxony. His father was a Lutheran minister but died when Friedrich was young. During his childhood, he was raised by women; men didn't have any influence on him. He appeared to be classically trained." Fox stopped dictating. "Why don't you stop, I need to read more."

"Of course." Helen relaxed and sipped her coffee.

Time lapsed. "Ready?" Fox said.

She squared her shoulders and positioned her body, "Ready. Shoot."

"Nietzsche's beliefs: He rejected absolute morality. Values were trans-valued or can be adjusted to suit the situation. At one point he believed only in aesthetic values. Reality is Apollo v. Dionysus. Apollo represents order; Dionysus represents the wild, untamed nature of man.

There are two sets of morality: one for the masters and the other for slaves. He hated Christianity. Christian morality was a slave morality or herd-morality." Fox stopped. "Did you get all that, Helen?"

"Yes, I believe so."

Fox continued, "In his book, *Thus Spake Zarathustra,* is the word Ubermensch found."

Helen's eyes lit up. "Really?"

"Yes. The word was translated into the term superman, by the playwright George Bernard Shaw."

"Superman?" Helen Expressed. "That's all in the newspapers. "I never realized that is where it came from, but what does it mean?"

"Well, according to Nietzsche's writings, the Ubermensch or Superman is a person that rises beyond the concepts of good and evil. In other words; traditional right and wrong must be rejected; it belongs to the herd— not fit for a master."

Helen's lips flattened, then folded up like an accordion "What a strange statement, I still don't understand Fox."

"Look at it this way. If a person has the courage, according to Nietzsche, to reject universal morality— then that person can make their own rules. And they are not subject to the slave-morality, the superman is free. They are masters of their own thoughts and actions. No force outside of their will could make a claim on their actions or conscience – if, in fact, they have any conscience left. They are masters in every way possible. That is why he named one of his books, *Beyond Good and Evil.* A master makes their own morality—according to their own will, or what he calls: Will to Power."

Helen flashed her eyes in disbelief. "You mean this man rejects Christian morality and traditional morals? Is he a mad-man?"

"Funny, you should say that. Nietzsche died insane. He was also a militant atheist."

"Didn't you mention, Fox, or did I read in your notes, that the cult, Lucifer the Light Bearers, are atheists?"

"Yes, they are, but for the moment Nietzsche's word, Ubermensch is tattooed to that dead man's shoulder. And, it would appear the cult Lucifer the Light Bearer is influenced by Nietzsche. How much?" Fox looked at Helen, "I believe we have a dangerous cult running around in New York, and maybe other places." Fox stopped talking and started to ponder.

"What are you thinking?" Helen asked. She began to feel a dark force; this was beyond anything she had ever experienced.

Fox repeated out-loud, "Masters. Transvaluation of morals. Ubermensch. Superman." He paused. Then said, "If all this is mixed with eugenics; I'm afraid this is darkness the world has never seen before — a recipe for death."

CHAPTER 17

The next day Fox sat in Helen's living room; he mulled over the new information they uncovered the previous day: Nietzsche, Ubermensch, eugenics, and a cult, all seemed far-fetched. *Can there be such a conspiracy in this modern age?* Fox thought. *Needless to say, facts are facts, nefarious people are at the center. But where is the center?*

Helen entered the room. She smelled like a bouquet of flowers; fresh, and pristine. Her smile drove away Fox's dark musings. "Good morning, Fox." She said and kissed his forehead.

Fox returned a smile, "Good morning, Helen."

"Fox—" The phone rang. Helen was caught off guard, "I wonder who that could be?" She went to the kitchen and answered the phone, "Hello?" Nothing, not a sound. "Hello?" She said. Again, there was no voice, no hello. "It must be a prank call." She said to Fox.

"Wait, don't hang up," Fox walked over and took the receiver out of Helen's hand and placed it to his ear. He didn't say anything; first, he just listened, there was a long pause, then he said, "Who's this?" No words, only deep breathing, "This is Mr. Carlyle. Who is this?" He said, hoping it was just some kids playing around. Still no words, just raspy sound. Fox waited, then there was a click, and the line went dead.

A flash of concern furled itself across Helen's forehead, "Who was it? Did they say anything?" Helen asked.

"Nothing. Whoever it was, I think the caller just wanted to scare us." Fox explained.

"How do they know where you are?"

"I'm not sure, but everything will be fine," Fox said. But this is what he wanted to avoid. He didn't want Helen to be in any danger, "I think I need to leave—"

"I don't think so." She exclaimed. "I know where you're going with this Mr. Fox. The answer is no. I will not be scared off. I'm with you no matter what. I can take care of myself." She said with defiance.

"Helen, I've been thinking about our next move." He said. His abrupt change of topic caused Helen to forget about the phone call, at least for the moment.

"And what's that?"

"Do you remember reading in the newspapers about Leopold and Loeb; how they kidnapped Bobby Franks and murdered him?"

Helen strained her eyes, "A little, when did it happen?"

"1924."

"Oh, yes, it happened about three years ago. Yes, now it's starting to come back. But I really didn't keep track of the case, it was too horrific. How could two wealthy young men kill an innocent boy and throw their lives away? But what about them? And what do they have to with your case, Fox?"

"Leopold and Loeb were influenced by Nietzsche's Superman."

Helen's eyes lit up, "Great, Scott!" She expressed with surprise, "I can't believe it; it's too incredible."

"At the time, it was an interesting case. I didn't understand why two wealthy young men would be so duped into believing they were supermen. But now, it's starting to make sense." Fox said.

"Where are they? Are they still alive, or did they go to the chair?"

"They are in prison."

"Are we going to interview them?" Helen said.

"Yes, we need to speak to at least one of them."

"Where too?"

"Statesville Penitentiary at Crest Hill, Illinois."

"When do we leave?"

"Tomorrow morning. Pack light. We'll stay no longer than a day."

The train ride to Chicago was bumpy. The rhythm of the locomotive's wheels, steel against steel, evoked an emotional feeling in Fox; as if a deep plangent wave crashed against jagged rocks on the seashore. The more he dug; the darker secrets came to light. Mystifying, on the one hand, terrifying on the other.

Statesville prison was new, built-in 1925, and a state-of-the-art facility. Nathan Freudenthal Leopold was recently transferred there from Joliet Prison. Fox and Helen arrived. The floors were clean, and fresh paint was still lingering in the air like a sterilized hospital. Two guards stopped them, "May we help you?" One of them said.

"Yes, hello, I'm Mr. Fox, and this is Miss Helen Carlyle. We called ahead and were given permission to see Nathan Leopold, one of your inmates."

"Oh, yes. Newspaper reporters are always coming to see him. I don't know why. He and his partner are cold-blooded killers; they murdered a boy . . . I hope he rots in here." The guard stated.

"We aren't reporters, I'm a private investigator. I just want to ask him a few questions."

"Why? They confessed to the crime." The guard shrugged his shoulders, "It's your time. Go right over there and see that person sitting at the desk." The guard pointed. "Don't go anywhere else unless you have a pass." He looked at several other guards holding rifles. "Do as you're told, and you'll be just fine."

They walked away and toward the desk, "That was creepy." Helen said to Fox. "I don't like him. He's rude and nasty."

"He's just doing his job. He's been hardened; criminals will make anyone churlish. Didn't you notice the long scar across the side of his face?"

"Sure."

"That's not a normal scar. I surmise he was cut by a prisoner."

Helen looked back, "Maybe, poor guy, but I still don't like him." She said.

Sitting at the desk was a man who appeared to be both a guard and a bureaucrat. A pencil pusher. Someone who did a lot of paperwork and wasn't happy about it. He was huddled over filling out forms. Fox said, "Excuse me."

He didn't say a word, he picked up a rubber-stamp and slammed it down onto a piece of paper. Every guard was alive and alert; except for the pencil pusher, he was oblivious to his surroundings.

Fox cleared his voice, "Excuse me," Fox said with a sharp tone.

The guard looked up; his glasses hung on the end of his nose like it was a hook, but he kept stamping papers. "What?" He said. His voice strained with frustration and annoyed someone bothered him.

"My name is Mr. Fox, and this is Miss Carlyle, we—"

"Can't you see I'm busy?" His voice crackled like the static on the radio.

"Yes, but we called ahead and have permission to see one of the prisoners."

"Who do you want to see?"

"Nathan Leopold."

"For God sake! Not another reporter? I've had enough —"

"No," Fox quickly replied, "We are not reporters. I'm a private detective, and Miss Carlyle is my assistant. We simply want to interview Nathan Leopold to see if he has any knowledge about another case."

The guard's name tag slipped out from behind his jacket when he shifted in his seat. Alfred Kline was his name. He pushed his glasses back onto the back of his hooked nose. His eyes were large and round like a pitcher's mound. "So, you're a private dick? You might have permission, but I'm the gate-keeper." He tilted his chair backward, "What do you say about that?"

"I say you're an important person." Fox reached for his wallet—"

"None of that." The guard waved his hand, "What's the magic word?"

Helen spoke up, "Open sesame!" She chuckled.

The guard jumped, "What? What did you say?" Said the guard. His eyes glared at Helen as if she was a criminal and he was ready to hit the buzzer to call the other guards to take both of them into custody.

Fox pushed Helen behind his back, "She was just joking. She didn't mean anything. What she meant was, please, please would you allow us to see Leopold. We would appreciate it."

Kline said nothing; instead, a scowl expression filled his face like an exclamation point. After a few minutes, he scribbled their names on a name tag, "Here, pin this to your clothes. Keep it on you at all times or else." Kline turned towards the guard holding a rifle and titled his head, to signal for him to escort Fox and Helen to their destination.

They walked down a long corridor; bright lights everywhere, no shadows for anyone to hide. At the far end, a metal door stood closed and locked. It separated the outside world from locked up criminals. It was sealed from the inside. The guard on the outside knocked. An elongated metallic small door slid open. Eyeballs peered through the slate. "Yeah?" A voice said. They exchanged words. Suddenly, the narrow corridor filled with a rattling sound; a rotation of wheels clicked and churned, then chains in the thick walls vibrated until the door sprang open. They were waved in. Another lever was pulled; chains vibrated and the door shut. This was all controlled from the middle of the room. It was the central nervous system to a large round complex. Three levels with cells connected to each other like a honeycomb. Every cell could be seen at any given moment from the central control center. Between the control center and the cells; was a flat, smooth concrete floor. Any prisoner caught within the circle without permission was shot.

"Follow me." The guard said. "Leopold's cell is number 604."

All the cell doors were closed; inmates were in their brick-walled cubicles. As they passed each unit, Helen noticed the tired look plastered on their faces. Haggard and dirty, too tired to even whistle at a beautiful woman. "Why are they dirty and exhausted?" Helen asked.

"We just brought them in from working in the pit."

"The Pit? What's the pit?"

"The pit is where we take them to dig ditches and split rocks. Sometimes we take them to clean up roads. We put chains on their legs and chain them to each other. Today, they worked at the pit."

One inmate was lying on the floor, his leg was bleeding. Helen ran up to the bars, "This man's bleeding, he needs help." She said.

The guard shoved his Billy-stick between Helen and the bars; and pushed her away, "Lady, these men are killers. If you get too close, they'll either grab you between the legs or snap your neck." He turned to Fox, "Keep your woman on a leash." Even though it was a small incident, it spread to every cell like wildfire. Prisoners hit their tin cups against the bars. They screamed and yelled; the noise grew until it reached a bad-chorus of buffoonery.

Helen covered her ears. She grabbed Fox's arm, "I'm scared." She said.

"They can't hurt us; keep calm, and stay close to me," Fox said. "It'll stop shortly."

"Just keep moving and do as I say, you'll be fine." The guard said.

Several prisoners, had their hands and arms hanging through and between the bars, and chained, "Why are some of these men manacled to the bars?" Fox asked.

"Oh, well, they are trouble-makers. When inmates fight with each other or with the guards, we chain their arms and legs to their cell bars to teach them a lesson. We keep them there all day, sometimes two days."

"That seems cruel. How do prisoners eat or use the bathroom facilities?" Helen said.

The guard started to laugh, "Cruel? What about the people they killed and tortured? — please, spare me, cry me a river, sister."

They arrived at cell 604. The guard hit the bars with his stick, "Hey, Leopold, got some visitors."

Leopold was lying on his cot reading *Thus Spake Zarathustra*. He closed his book; looked up, and eyeballed them— he studied the way they were dressed and their mannerisms. "You're not reporters." He said.

"How do you know?" Fox said.

"You're well dressed. Newspaper reporters dress boorish; they have manners like a toad, they are churlish— when they stand, walk, and speak. You, I can tell, have been trained to be a gentleman, they are wan-a-bees." He looked at Helen, "You're nice, but you are low class."

Helen didn't speak, she was afraid, she moved closer to Fox.

The guard slammed his stick against the bars, "Watch yourself." He said.

"My name is J.P. Fox, this is Helen, if you don't mind, we would like to ask you some questions?"

"If you're not news reporters, why?"

"I'm a private investigator, and I'm working a case," Fox said. He inched closer to the bar, "You see, a child was killed."

"So?" Leopold spoke with an air of defiance.

"Eugenics played a part."

"Again, so what? We killed our own kid."

"Nietzsche also played a role."

Leopold's eyebrow raised, "Now that's interesting." He said, "Are you saying there is a copycat out there?" Leopold laughed. "Finally, someone appreciates our work."

"Rub that cocky expression off your face, or—"

"Or what?" His grin was sinister; even extremely confident.

"Look, Leopold, we came to ask you some questions, that's all."

"I can't see how I can help. Do you think I might know the killer?"

"Not exactly. But here's my question: You killed an innocent child, without remorse; what did it feel like?"

"Do you eat meat?" Leopold asked.

"Yes."

"Do you feel guilty about the death of a cow or fish?"

"No."

"Why not?"

"Animals aren't humans; they have no souls, no conscience."

"But that's where you're wrong, Mr. Fox."

"But animals do not feel guilty," Fox said, "when an ant walks by a dead ant, it feels no guilt. It just keeps going. It doesn't stop and bury the other ant and doesn't erect a marker. No Leopold, they aren't made in God's image; on the other hand, human beings are, and we feel guilt and shame when we do wrong."

"Ah! What you just expressed is what Nietzsche called slave morality. Supermen are above all that; he or she creates their own morals or values."

"So, you honestly believe in what Nietzsche wrote? Why?" Fox asked.

"Why not?" Leopold leaned against the bars. "Why should I choose to be a slave? — I am above that; Nietzsche has shown the way to a life without guilt and chains of despair."

Fox studied Leopold. *Did he really believe what was coming out of his mouth?* He thought. Killers have ways of obfuscating and embellishing their own self-importance. But Leopold was not the normal killer, he didn't fit the profile. He wasn't hardened by life or years behind bars.

Leopold was intelligent. He scored 210 on an IQ test, whereas most people scored between 90-110. A score of 210 places him on the genius level. He graduated from the University of Chicago and was planning to study law at Harvard before he killed Bobby Franks. With a firm tone, "Why did you kill Bobby Franks?" Fox said. He wanted to see his reaction.

Leopold wasn't moved by Fox's sudden jab. He was stoic. "You know the answer to that, Mr. Fox. I'm a superman. I have no guilt; I don't care if Bobby Franks is dead, I'm a master. Supermen are of the master class— the master race if you will."

Leopold's coldness sent chills up and down Helen's back. She gripped Fox's arm.

Fox didn't notice any shame in Leopold's eyes. They were precise and deadly. "But you're Jewish. I'm sure you were taught not to kill. It's found in the Ten Commandments." Fox said.

"Once again, Mr. Fox, that's slave morality. Moses set them free only to put them back into slavery. Moses wanted to control a bunch of slaves, but he remained the master." Leopold pointed at Fox, "Can't you understand? You too can be a superman, just try."

"I'm beginning to understand."

"A superman rises above good and evil. Good and evil are mere constructs, they are chains."

"Is that why you killed Bobby Franks?"

"To be frank with you, Mr. Fox, I didn't kill anyone. To kill or not to kill is also a construct. It puts them in chains and binds their minds."

Fox was almost finished, but there was one last thing, "If you're beyond good and evil; and you're not a slave like the rest of us— then tell me this, why are you behind bars—unlike the rest of us?" Fox quipped.

Leopold became enraged, "You're a son-of-a-bitch; I'll kill you—" He reached through the bars and tried to grab Fox.

The guard's Billy-club smashed down on the bars, "Back!" He yelled. Leopold jumped, "Superman! Yeah, sure!" The guard said, mocking Leopold.

In an instant, Leopold was calm. "I think we're finished here, Mr. Fox."

Fox wasn't done. He had one more card up his sleeve. All the questions led up to his last statement, "Lucifer the Light Bearer." Fox said without equivocation. There was no weakness in his voice or tone. He watched Leopold's reactions.

Leopold turned white; his knees began to buckle, and his eyes grew round as if in a state of shock.

Fox leaned closer to drive his statement deeper. He knew he hit a nerve. "Lucifer the Light Bearer." He stated again, "You know this group, I can see it in your eyes. Who are they? Spill your guts."

Leopold's lips quivered with fear. Fox witnessed a strong; arrogant, young man change into a frightened little boy. The mention of Lucifer the Light Bearer drained Superman from his veins, and his ego shrunk like a prune. "I—I—" He began to stutter.

Fox had him pinned. "Who are they? Are you part of this group?"

Leopold didn't know what to say or how to respond. He then refused to talk.

"What are you hiding? What are you afraid of?"

"You don't understand." Leopold's breathing became erratic. "I can't tell you anything."

"Why?" Fox pressed harder. "Why, Leopold? Why are you afraid to talk?"

"They— they— they could be listening. Stop with the questions!" He screamed. "Stop!"

Fox turned to the guard, "We're done here." They turned and walked away, leaving Leopold drowning in fear and self-doubt.

Helen asked Fox, during their drive to the train station, "We didn't learn anything new— did we?"

"Indeed, Helen. We did learn something new. We learned Leopold is fully aware of this cult, and it scares him. He was or still is part of the cult, and the cult is more powerful than we thought." Fox said. "Very powerful. So powerful it can even reach into prison and scare supermen types like Leopold and Loeb."

CHAPTER 18

It had been a long day. Helen felt dirty after they visited Statesville Prison, especially after their talk with Nathan Leopold. The train bounced and rambled along on the tracks. Helen looked out the window of their compartment. The sun faded and melted into the horizon. But the skies still had a remnant of itself as it twinkled away to shine elsewhere.

Helen reached out and slipped her hand into Fox's, "What does all this mean?" Her light-heartedness began to fade with the fading sunlight.

Fox felt her confusion, "I don't know, yet." He said, "We have more investigating to do. That's part of the job."

"How do you do it, Fox?" Helen squeezed his hand tighter.

"Do what?"

"How do you continue? I mean; it seems everything we learn is a surprise, and they're not good surprises. Everything we know is really, really awful. If people knew what happens in the dark— well, I'm not sure what would happen. It's not good."

Fox sensed her vulnerability. Reality clashed with her positive and bubbly personality. Her world started to be altered; a crisis was at hand. He knew he had to handle her in such a way as to help keep her from falling apart. He took his left arm and wrapped it around her like a big soft blanket. "Relax. You're not alone. I'm here, and you're protected." He said. Fox sensed, moments like this, Helen needed both affirmation and support.

An hour had passed. Helen began to forget about the harsh world, about the murdered child, the killer, Leopold, Superman, and the cult. Somehow, she was able to regain her composure. She pushed her body away from Fox's warm embrace, "I'm famished." She said. A smile sprung across her face like the sun rising above dark hills. "Let's go get something to eat."

They hopped from one car to another until they reached the dining section. The seats were plush; tables and chairs were comfortable but pragmatic. Spiral-shaped curtain rods displayed evenly folded curtains, spiral ropes holding the ends in place so passengers could look out the windows. Most passengers had eaten and were in their compartments, but Fox and Helen weren't alone. Some were still eating and chatting. Fox ordered a turkey sandwich, and Helen ordered the house salad.

Out of habit, Fox scanned the dining area. He noticed faces, scars, hair color, mannerisms, and the way people were dressed. He learned to be observant; it paid off in the end. Then, a short man came into focus. He was at the other end of the car, acting suspiciously. Part of his hat was tilted over his face, and he was studying Fox and Helen. He didn't want to alarm Helen, "Please excuse me, I need to use the men's room." He said.

Fox walked to the back of the boxcar; he opened the door and stepped onto the landing that connected another car. He moved to the right; just enough to stay hidden, ready to pounce when the door opened. His heart raced, staying in lock-step with the passenger train barreling down on the tracks. Then the door opened; it was the short man. Without a thought, Fox pounced, it was a trained reaction. He grabbed the man and slammed him back against the back of the iron wall. He struggled, but Fox was strong enough to pin him tight.

"What do you want?" He yelled. "Take my wallet, there's not much in it, but it's yours." He said.

Fox punched him in his stomach, "I don't want your dough," Fox said. "Who are you, and why are you following us?"

"What—what are you talking about?" The man said. His mouth quivered and sweat formed over his eyebrows and dripped off the tip of his nose.

Fox pulled out his knife and held it against his face, "Spill! Now!"

"I'm nobody. I was hired by a man to follow you and keep tabs on you; that's all, I swear."

"Who hired you? — What's his name?"

"Fields . . . Damien Fields is his name. That's it, please, please let me go. Look. You can search me; I'm not carrying a weapon. I swear I was hired to follow you and take notes, not to hurt you or the lady."

"Who's Damien Fields?"

"I don't know."

Fox tightened his coat around his neck, "Talk."

"What I mean, I think he's the Fuzz."

A surprised look came over Fox, "Policeman?" Fox retorted. "Explain."

"He was too clean-cut to be a Goon or a Dropper— you know what I mean, a hired killer." He said. "That's all I know, please let me go."

Fox hung the man's head out the side of the train. The wind tossed his hair around. "I promise you," Fox said, "If I see you again, I'll throw you off the train— get it?" Fox was emphatic.

"Yeah. Got it." He said, desperate to be free.

Fox pulled the short man's body back onto the landing, "Now scram, before I change my mind." Fox said.

"Are you alright?" Helen asked Fox. The laceration on his forehead was bleeding again. His breathing was short and sporadic. "Did something happen?"

"I'm fine, no need to worry."

"I'm not; I'm concerned, and something did happen. Did you fall?"

Fox looked away like he was guilty of something, "No, I didn't fall. Everything is fine."

Helen leaned back, "You're lying, Fox. Something did happen. You won't look me in the eyes, and you act like you're hiding something." She grabbed his arm.

When she touched him, she felt his jittery nerves, "Fine." He said, "Something did happen. A man was following us, but not to worry— he didn't mean us any harm. He was hired by a man named Damien Fields. The man didn't know who he was, but he believes he is a copper or someone working for the government— I suspect."

"What did he want?"

"He was to follow us around and take notes," Fox said. "Someone is keeping tabs on us."

"Who do you think it is?"

"I'm not sure, but when we get back, we need to take a visit to our good friend Detective Savage."

"I know you'll get to the bottom of it; now, let's eat, we should be arriving home soon."

It was past 9:00 PM when Detective Savage arrived home. He opened the door; switched the lights on, and was shocked – he blurted out, "What the devil?" After realizing he wasn't in danger, "Fox," He said, "What in blazes are you doing here?"

Fox and Helen were sitting on the couch. "Come in, my good friend. We have things to talk about."

Savage's surprise turned to anger, "What's this? How dare you come to my home, unwelcomed!" He gritted his teeth, "I'll run you in for breaking—"

"Shut up!" Fox said, "I have a mind to bust you up. Now, close the door and sit down."

Savage flopped into his chair, "You're in big trouble, Fox, don't make it worse on yourself."

"Too late for that. By the way, this is Helen."

"We already know who she is."

Helen quipped, "How?"

"We just know, sister. We know." Savage said.

"Look, Savage, I need your help."

"My help? Are you living on the same planet the rest of us are? You got a lot of nerve, and you have some loose wires in that skull of yours."

"Who is Damien Fields? And why are the police following me?"

"Fox," Savage said, "you're making quite a name for yourself. You're sticking your nose where it doesn't belong."

"Maybe." Fox said, "But, I hit someone's nerve, and they are striking back."

"Fox. Why don't you stop? We already caught the killer."

"No, you haven't, he's still on the loose and if this was a simple case of a poor child murdered, then why am I being followed and chased? Why are you and others trying to stop me?" Fox leaned forward, "Now, who is Damien Fields, and why are the cops following me?"

Savage's face turned red, "Fine! Damien Fields is someone important, but he's not a cop. I don't know who he works for. I got a call from the top, and they told me to work with him and assist him in anything he needs. That's all I know. Now, one last time Fox, stop before it's too late. This case is an obsession of yours."

"I can't stop, given the knowledge and information we have discovered."

Something snapped in Savage's mind. Pride rose up like a beast from the dark regions of a lost swamp. His body lurched from the chair, "Listen to me!" The veins in his neck bulged like a fortified bulwark protecting a fort, "I'm taking you in!"

Fox reacted with equal force, "No! You listen to me!" They were face to face. Fox's rib was pounding, his face turned red with anger. "If you caught your guy, then tell me why I have been chased, beaten up, followed, and warned."

Savage's nostrils flared like a pig, but he started to take in what Fox said. He backed off, slightly, "Fox. I'm only trying to help you."

Fox backed away from Savage. He was haggard; pain flooded his body. His head throbbed, and his rib ached. He grabbed Helen's hand, "We need to go. Right now."

"What's the matter, Fox?" Helen said.

Lack of sleep and his injuries had caught up with him. His body screamed for rest. "We just need to go, Helen." He said. He didn't want to divulge his condition in front of Detective Savage.

"Go. You can't hide, no matter where you go." Savage said.

After Fox and Helen left, Savage sat down and began to question his own actions. *Fox is a friend of mine.* He thought. *Our friendship may be in jeopardy. Is it my fault? And Fox is in deep trouble. Is that my fault as well?* The more Savage pondered, he rationalized it away. *No.* He said to himself. *No, Fox is the stubborn one. He will not listen to reason; he's intractable, thick, and bullheaded. Why can't he see this case is beyond him and me?*

CHAPTER 19

Tommy, a seven-year-old boy, was standing in front of a knickknack store playing kick-the-can on 4th Street in the Bowery. He was wearing torn knickers. The dirt had faded into the fabric like black soot from an oil lamp. Smudged coal stains marked his cheeks like a cheap cosmetic product; it shined when the light reflected off them.

On the other side of the street, the killer watched Tommy play. Without thinking, he stepped off the sidewalk into the road. A horn honked, "Are you an imbecile? Watch where you're going!" A delivery man shouted.

The killer paid no attention; he was in a trance-like state. He made it to the other side and walked up to the boy, "You want a sucker?" He said.

The boy's eyes brightened up, "Sure, Mister." He grabbed the sucker from the killer's hand. The only time he got candy was on Christmas day. Even then, he was lucky if he got any, his poor family lived and scraped for food from day to day.

"May I sit here on the bench and talk with you for a few minutes?" The killer said.

The boy looked up and squinted his eyes, "Sure, why not," He said and shrugged his bony shoulders.

They sat. Tommy dangled his skinny legs off the end of the bench, he looked up at the killer with a gnarled expression, "You're white." He said, "I mean, you look queer, mister."

The killer didn't flinch, nor was he offended; he had become accustomed to others starring at him. When he was young other children called him names and poked fun at him; it used to make him cry, but over time, it made him hard. He had only contempt toward other orphans. "Do you like the sucker?" He asked.

Tommy was licking away, "Ab-so-lute-ly!" The boy answered.

"What's your name?"

"Tommy, Tommy is my name."

"Where are you from?"

"Here, the Bowery." The boy said. "What about you, mister, where do you live?"

"Someplace, you never heard of before." He said. The killer slid close to him, "Say, look it," He hunched close to Tommy and looked around, "I know about a place—you see; it's nice, and you can have all the candy you can eat. Want to see it?"

Tommy became animated, "Wow! You mean, I can have all the suckers I want?"

"Yes, that's right."

Tommy took another lick. Euphoria spilled across his face like he was talking to Santa Claus at the local drug store. He gulped, "Sure!"

A high-pitched voice called from the end of the street, "Tommy! Tommy! Time to go." Tommy and the killer both turned their heads towards the sound. The killer became irritated that someone would disturb him.

"Yes, Grandma."

"Come along. Leave that man alone."

Tommy cocked his head back toward him. "Thanks, mister, for the sucker." He hopped off the seat and ran towards his grandmother.

Bent over and leaning on a stick, Tommy's grandmother couldn't help but notice the killer's white skin; it stuck out as though a moose walked down Times Square in midday light. She also thought it strange the odd-looking man wore a peculiar looking cloak on a hot sunny day. But the killer's ring sparkled; it was colorful and bright. It had a particular brilliance about it; the way it was structured as if it spoke of wealth and affluence.

The grandmother reached out her hand, "Spit," she ordered Tommy. She took her hand with the spit in it and brushed Tommy's disheveled hair back. "We need to wash your face when we get home, Tommy. Where did you get that candy?"

He pulled the sucker out of his mouth and pointed his little finger, "That man gave it to me." He said.

The killer had disappeared by the time Tommy's grandmother looked back up.

The killer felt cheated. Dismayed, he made his way back to his apartment. The slum he thrived in was a cesspool of crime and human depravity. Even the smog from nearby factories blotted the sky. Feeling shaky, he reached in his cabinet and took down a large cross. It appeared to be made of solid metal. He flicked the top part open, but the cross was hollow – not solid, but it contained hero-in. He grabbed a chair and went to the back window; a crowd was building, locals gathered for a cockfight. As he administered the heroin, his body relaxed. The pain in his head disappeared.

A strange light emanated from the pit below. Images cavorted, twisted, and cast distorted shadows. Civilized manners caved to lost inhibitions; tribal dances, bonfire, rapacious shouts sent chills throughout the back court-yard. Wild and ravenous sounds, dissonance language as if it was a taboo warning for nonbelievers to stay away, or else.

All the raucous caused the killer's thoughts to drift to a point in history he hated; a place he grew up as a boy: The New York Foundling Asylum. He was put there at a young age. *Who and why did they put me there,* He thought? Children came and went, but he stayed. *Why didn't any-one want to adopt me?* The sisters told him to be patient, his day would come. It never did. He eventually stopped desiring, and he wouldn't even show up at the interview room where parents would size up the children.

All the hullabaloo from below yanked his thoughts back to the present. The noise rose like a puff of black sulfur. The violent acts from the pit gave him a sense of power.

Then, another memory surfaced like a submarine. *I was young and playing in the playground, I heard a loud bang. I didn't know what it was, but the sisters and children rushed out of the orphanage afraid and confused. Pandemonium was everywhere. After a few seconds, a man waving a gun ran out. He jumped the bushes; right before he shot himself, he yelled, 'You can send me to the electric chair for this. I don't care. There's no use living without a father or mother and without knowing who they were.' It was Henry J. King, a former orphan.*

Henry J. King's last words, 'There's no use living without a father and mother and without knowing who they are were,' left an indelible impression; those words lingered in the killer's mind like cement. It haunted his thoughts night and day. It grew like a disease. He, too, wanted to know his father and mother.

CHAPTER 20

Damien Fields stood in Detective Savage's office; he tapped his shoe on the floor in an agitated mood, his spats were white and clean; his arms crossed. Savage arrived late. After he walked through the door, the air tensed up and tightened; they said nothing, a wall of silence spoke words of disdain. With his narrow eyes, Fields threw silent-daggers at Savage as he crossed the room and sat in his chair. Damien became even more enraged when Savage ignored him.

"Well?" Damien said, in a huff.

"Stop that confounding tapping!" Savage shouted. "Are you trying to pound a hole in my floor?"

Damien shifted his body, "What about Fox? Did you find him yet? — well, I'm waiting?" He uttered in a condescending tone.

"Blast! Blast you, Damien! I can't get any work done with you breathing down my neck every minute."

"You were ordered to work with me, and that means keeping me informed of your progress."

"I'm a good cop. I'll do what it takes to get the job done. I don't need you to tell me what to do and how to do my job."

Damien laughed and began to tap his shoe again like the sound of a typewriter, "Then what is the latest news?" He said, his harsh words dripped from his lips like a salivating dog.

Savage reached his boiling point. He looked deep into Damien's eyes, with a brusque cast, "Just who are you?" He said.

Damien had a queer look on his face, "What do you mean? You got the memo. I'm from the district attorney's office." Damien was insulted, he had never been questioned before.

"I know what the memo states," Savage said. "But what I want to know is why the state is interested in James P. Fox and this case? And why did they send you?" Savage stood. His eyes were ablaze with fury. "Who are you, Damien?" Savage asked with a claw-like resolve.

"You got your orders," Damien said. His voice quivered. Some of his arrogance dissipated, and he started to back away from Savage. Then, he felt he needed to regain control. He cocked his limped head forward like he attached an invisible splint. "That's right. You got your orders, and I'm here to make sure you perform your duties." He tilted his chin in the air, "Besides, you're just a paid cop— you're not paid to think."

Savage leaped forward like a lion. He grabbed Damien's thin body and rammed it up against the wall. His legs flapped about like two wet noodles hanging on a wire. Fear gripped his mind and body. "Let me tell you something little man; I'm a good cop, someone you don't want to mess with. I can take you out anytime." He said. "As for the memo, I've had just about enough of you and where you came from. In fact, you can crawl back from under the rock you crawled out from." An odd, but familiar noise interrupted Savage. He looked down and saw a stream of piss shooting down from Damien's pants. He looked back up, "Really?" He said, "Really?" Savage had a disgusted expression on his face. Then he dropped Damien's frail body to the ground.

"You'll pay for this!" Damien said as he scrambled out the door. His pants soaking wet, and his spats faded yellow. With a puckered face and ruddy cheeks, "I'll get you—" then he slipped, falling face down on the floor. He tried to get up but fell again like a schoolboy who slid off a wet rock trying to cross a river.

CHAPTER 21

By the next day, Fox felt better; except for his cracked rib, and the bruises covering his body, but he had to go deeper; he and Helen had to go undercover. An armchair sleuth and research would never take the place of old-fashion – nose to the ground – detective work; following up on leads, search, track, and observe, yields good fruit to solve cases. Going undercover is like playing a part; an actor acts, he or she dresses for the role and learns the words and mannerisms to imitate and to fool others.

Fox dressed in an old dirty pair of overalls; a faded coat, holes in the front and the back, and a splotchy shirt. He donned his feet was a pair of dirty shoes; the bottoms flapped when he walked, he tied strings around the soles and the top; and to top it off he wore a straw hat.

Before they arrived at their location, Helen needed to dress the part; they stopped at a nickel and dime store. Fox bought Helen a tattered dress; it reached to her ankles. Helen picked a stylish cloche hat, "I like this one," She said, "It's bright."

"No, Helen," And he placed the hat back on the rack. He looked around, "Let's see, oh, yes, this will do." He said. It was a cheap hat; no bright colors, with a crooked brim.

"Fox," Helen said, "That's ugly. I'll look like a tramp."

"That's the point we need to blend in."

Helen fumed, but she relinquished, "Oh, alright, if you say so, Fox."

Helen drove, but Fox gave directions to a location where they can park her car without it being molested. She parked in front of an abandoned building. "This part of town isn't too bad," Fox said. "But in a few blocks; well, just stay close to me."

Helen slipped her arm under his, "This is the first time I've been to a slum, but what do you mean stay close to you?" She said.

"The streets are full of pickpockets and gangs."

Helen smiled; she bounced alongside Fox as if she was a schoolgirl playing hop-scotch. "Alright." She said.

Fox stopped, "Let's go-between these two buildings." He said.

Helen was puzzled, "Why?" Then it dawned on her, Fox wanted to smooch. She smiled and licked her lips with anticipation. *All of a sudden Fox wants to be romantic, here in the slums? I feel a little bad. Hmm.* Passion filled her thoughts.

They turned, walked between the buildings, and stopped behind some trash cans. Helen positioned her body against the wall, closed her eyes, and puckered her lips. She ran her hands up and down her body— she felt her sexuality and prepared herself for Fox's embrace. Instead, Fox stooped to the ground; scooped up dirt, rose, and smudged it all over her cheeks. Helen's eyes flashed open, "What—what are you doing Fox?"

"I'm plastering dirt on your face and mine."

Helen pushed his hands away; she tried to brush the dirt from her face, but it only made it worse; she trembled with rage, "I thought—"

"Thought what?"

Angered and embarrassed, Helen spoke incoherently, "Just look at me! I'm . . .. I look and feel like a rat. My God, Fox, what do you take me for?"

"That's too much dirt," Fox said, and tried to brush some off, "There, perfect."

Helen marched out to the sidewalk, in a huff, and positioned her fist on her hips, "Perfect? You call this perfect? I'll let you know, I'm not some chick – a Chippy, you can push around."

"What's wrong? What did I do?" Fox said, bewildered.

"If you don't know, well—" Helen turned her head up and away. "Let's just get on with it." She said.

Fox's father's advice came to mind, "Don't argue with an angry woman; don't try to figure them out; many have tried, but ended up in an asylum, strapped in a straight-jacket, and drool leaking out the side of their mouth. Fox let it go.

After several hours of canvassing the neighborhood, Fox and Helen felt pangs of hunger when they smelled hot-dogs. "Get your hot-dogs. One hot-dog and a drink for a nickel." A sidewalk vendor yelled.

Helen yanked Fox's arm, "I'm hungry, can we eat?"

They walked over to the pushcart. A scrawny little man stood, "Hot-dogs! Get your hot-dogs," He repeated again.

"Two dogs and two drinks," Fox said.

They ate and took a break. A mass of people hobbled about; throngs pushed, maneuvered, clashed until individuality lost itself to a collective; all seemed unified, all seemed one and the same. Fox watched like watching a parade. Across the street, scruffy-looking young men dart into a building; *must be a gang*, Fox determined. Women of ill-repute converged around lampposts; all showcasing their wares. Beggars begged for money. Kids played in front of an open fire hydrant. The city would open them to cool off pedestrians. The stench smelled like smutty bedsheets.

Fox looked at Helen, "It's quite another world." Fox said.

Helen looked around, "Yeah." She said, and pulled out a hanky and covered her nose, "It stinks – so, what's next?"

Fox spotted an old lady across the street, leaning on a stick and holding onto a little boy's hand. "Let's start with her." Fox pointed toward the haggard-looking woman.

"Okay."

They crossed the street and approached the woman; the old lady pushed Tommy behind her, instinctive, as to shield him from harm; suspicious, she studied Fox and Helen, "I'm just an old lady; what do you want?" She said, teeth girded.

"We just want to talk," Helen said.

Still cautious, "About what?"

"We need some information, we mean you no harm," Fox said.

The old lady had a good reason not to trust them; Fox and Helen looked like swamp-rats that just got off a boat at Ellis Island. "Information? Does it look like we have information?" She said. She gripped her walking stick tight; bare white knuckles flared like mountain peaks.

Fox sensed her fear, "Please," he said, "let me explain; excuse our attire, but we are undercover; I'm a private detective, and we are looking for a suspect. We don't mean to alarm you, but he may be connected to a murder; all we need to know is have you seen him?" Fox reached into his pocket and pulled out two dollars, "Here, take it, in exchange for what you know."

The edgy grandmother didn't lower her defenses, but Fox's offer was sweet, too sweet to pass up, "Who are you looking for? But mind you, I don't know anybody." She said, her eyes squinted still suspicious.

"That's fine," Fox said, "We are looking for a rather large man; he usually wears an old cloak, and he's an albino."

"Al-bin-o?" The old lady said. She tried to mimic the word, but she didn't know what it meant.

"Albino," Fox repeated. "That means he is white— very white, whiter than you or me. Have you seen such a person; you would know, he stands out like a toad crossing a busy road."

Tommy jerked his grandmothers' arm. "Grandma, don't you remember?"

"Yes, Tommy, I do."

"Here," Fox said. He placed the two dollars in her hand. "That's yours." And he closed her fingers.

"You mean this is mine?" Tears welled up in her eye ducks. "Nobody has given me anything before." She stiffened her lip and wiped her eyes, "Yes, we did. He was sitting on a bench with my Tommy; they were chatting."

"Do you know what they talked about?" Fox said.

Tommy tugged on his grandma's arm again, "Let me, let me."

"Go ahead, Tommy."

Fox squatted, "Hi Tommy. How are you?"

"I'm fine."

"Can you tell me what you two talked about?"

"Sure. I was playing kick the can; a large man walked up to me and wanted to talk. Wait, he gave me a sucker."

"A sucker?"

"Sure. I took it. The man said I could have all I wanted if I went with him. I think that's what he said." Tommy scratched his head.

"Did he say his name?"

"I don't think he did, mister."

"What else did he say?"

"That's all I can remember; then my grandma called for me."

Fox patted the boys head, "Thank you, Tommy." He looked at the boy's grandmother, "Is there anything you can remember about the man?"

"I don't think so—wait, yes, he was wearing a ring. It sparkled in the light. Nobody wears a ring like that around here without being mugged if you know what I mean." She said.

"Do you remember where all this took place?" Fox asked the grandmother.

"Yes." She lifted her skinny finger in the direction behind Fox and Helen, "Right over there."

Fox and Helen turned and saw the bench. Then they looked at each other.

They turned back to the woman and boy, "Thank you for your time and help." Fox pulled out a nickel from his pocket and flipped it in the air towards the boy, "There, that's for you."

Tommy caught it, "Wow! Thanks, mister! A sucker and a nickel." He bit down on the metallic object and shoved it in his pants. He smiled and squared his shoulders like a little man on top of the world.

Fox and Helen watched Tommy, and his grandmother walked away; they blended into the crowd like shadows. "The killer is close; I can feel it in my bones like gout," Fox said.

Helen felt creepy all of a sudden; the thought of the killer nearby made her all the more self-conscious. "What do we do, Fox?" She asked; as though a clump of hair got caught in her throat.

"We continue; our goal is still the same – we find the killer. That means we need to stakeout this location." Fox looked around and spotted a church. "What time is it, Helen?"

"It's around 12:00 PM. Why?"

"We'll start there, at the church across the street. They should be holding mass right about now. Besides, we need to sit and rest for a little while. Ready?"

"Yes." Helen said, "Resting my feet sounds good."

St. Joseph's Anglican Church had been at this location for over a hundred years. At one time, only the middle class and well-to-do were members, but its wealthy members gave way to the poor, as the community turned into slums. Now it is a mission church; even the locals weren't able to pay tithes, least of all offer offerings.

When Fox and Helen walked in, a priest officiated the service. His flowing black robe stood in stark contrast with the parishioner's appearances; dressed in drab clothes; many of whom were gaunt-looking from lack of nutrition – overall, they matched the gutter they lived in.

The altar— with all of its shiny objects— appeared to many, to be another world. The Eucharist is the central focus of worship. With the wine holding flagon, the breadbox, the lavabo or finger dish, finger towels, holy water, and the cruets. And, of course, the Chalice, brought people into a special relationship with God and each other; all done in the light of the Eucharistic candles – a reminder of the Light of the world.

The usher started at the front, and moved backward, from pew to pew, motioning parishioners to walk to the front and take communion. Fox and Helen followed and participated as well. They returned to their seats; after the service came to an end, Fox nudged Helen, "Let's question the priest."

By the time they walked to the priest's office, church members were gone, and the door was ajar, Fox knocked and opened the door farther, "Hello." Fox said.

"Yes." The priest said. "May I help you?" Sitting in a beige, overworked chair, sat a fat, round, bald, little man.

Fox walked and a jolt of surprise registered on his face; he couldn't believe his eyes, beside the priest; a framed newspaper-article stood in plain view exulting eugenic marriages. "Does the church promote eugenics?" Fox blurted; he couldn't control his emotions.

"Oh, yes." The priest said. "The church, now, requires a blood test before we marry anyone. The science of eugenics proved crime and diseases are carried through the blood-line. It's settled science."

Flabbergasted, Fox didn't know how at first to respond, "What changed? Since I was a youth, I, along with everyone else, was taught marriage is the church's domain. If the state gets involved, then it will eventually take over and take it out of the church's hands. I'm shocked."

"Rightly so." The priest's whitish complexion revealed years of sunless exposure; stuffed away in an office or library. "But we live in a modern age. With the help of science; the church can be used by the state to purify the race, thus making it healthier for people to live."

The priest's logic seemed sound, Fox thought. "Is it not a slippery slope if we allow the state to dictate what the church can and cannot do? When will it end, or is there an end?" Fox said.

"Nonsense. If we stick with science, the state will stay in its place. We are only helping the state to create a better society."

"With all due respect, sir, the church has always played a vital role in the health of the state; by promoting basic morality, charity, and promoting strong families." Fox said, "In my opinion, the church shouldn't try to perfect society – that is playing God."

Helen tapped on Fox's shoulder, "We are here about the killer, remember?" She said with a low voice.

"You're correct." Fox cleared his throat. "My name is Mr. Fox, and this is Helen Carlyle. I know I don't look the part, but I'm a private detective." Fox pulled out his wallet and showed the priest his credentials. "May we ask you some questions about a case I'm working on?"

The jolly priest grabbed his belly, "Of course you may."

"Well, we are investigating a murder case; a murdered child, to be exact, and we are looking for the killer."

"How awful. I will help if I can."

"He's a rather large man. He wears an old cloak, and he's an albino. Have you seen such a person here or maybe on the streets?"

The priest balled up one hand into a fist, and then covered it with the other hand, and rested his chin on both of them, "Let me see, if he's an albino, then he would stick out." Thinking . . . A long pause; then, the priest shot his head up, "By Jove! I think I have seen an albino and recently. In fact, he came to one of our services, but he wouldn't participate in the communion."

"What did he do?" Fox asked.

"He sat and observed."

"Did you notice anything else?"

"Let me see; he was alone, but he seemed to be smiling— yes, it was odd. He had this grin slapped across his face as if he knew something everyone else didn't know."

"When was this?"

The priest scratched his bald head, "Well, I was here," he started to count on his fingers, "Okay, yes, two days ago."

Fox looked at Helen, "You know what this suggests?"

"What?" She said, eyes full of curiosity.

"He— the killer— lives around here; or comes to this location often," Fox said.

Fox looked at the priest, "Thank you for your time and for the information."

"Anything I can do to help catch a killer." The priest said.

They stepped onto the sidewalk. Fox felt the killer close; closer, in some respects, than his own thoughts; he didn't like it; a strange and funny emotion, "Helen," Fox said. "The information we garnished from the old lady, Tommy, and the priest; we are close."

Helen's body shivered; nervous, she worked herself up into a tizzy. She began to babble incoherent words, "What do we do now?" She said nervously, "Where do we—" Others noticed and turned, but they moved on.

Fox grabbed her arms, "Helen, look at me. Look into my eyes and get a grip." He turned her and began to walk. After a few minutes, she was calm.

"I'm sorry, Fox. When I get nervous, I tend to talk fast. It's just nerves, that's all, nothing to worry about." She padded his shoulders. "I'm fine now."

"Good; the day is still young, I think we need to continue, but this time, we will be on the lookout for an albino."

It was about 1:30 PM. The sun blazed down like a supersized heater. Two hours passed; they walked from store to store; flophouse to flophouse, and strutted past tenement buildings; more people interviewed; the Lower East Side magnified the lowest of the low, from common thugs to scratchers – forgers; one big metropolis of hell on earth. Fox and Helen felt out of place; if it weren't for their disguises, they'd stick out like the albino; the only difference – he belonged.

"This is how the other half lives," Fox said, to Helen.

"I've seen enough, Fox." Helen's conscious awareness grew tenfold. As she mused over the whole experience, she noticed something out the side of her eye, "Fox!" She said and grabbed his arm. "Look, wait. I mean, the killer is across the street." Her body shook like a tree-branch caught by a gust of wind.

Fox moved slow and cocked his head; there, the killer was walking perpendicular to them, going in the same direction. "Yes, Helen, I believe that's our man. Stay calm and do what I say."

Helen nodded her head; too frightened to speak. The killer walked like he and the slums were one and the same; oozing human depravity. But the way he swaggered his body was as if Bram Stoker's Dracula stalked the streets of New York City in broad daylight. A bloodsucker; capable of killing without remorse and conscience.

"Yes, Fox," Helen said. "Please, be careful."

They waited till the killer was ahead of them, and they crossed the intersection. They walked a few paces behind, they stopped, and stopped again; Fox and Helen looked into stores, dodged behind buildings, they did not want to alarm the killer to their presences; the killer made a sudden right turn, Fox and Helen rushed and slowed their approach, Fox peeked around the side of the building – the killer was gone. Fox turned back to Helen, "He's gone. I don't see him."

"Did he pick up on our scent and dodge into a building?" Helen said.

"I'm not sure," Fox said. "Let's keep moving, slow." They turned the corner; then, out of nowhere, Fox spotted the killer ahead of them. The killer moved fast; he weaved in and out of crowds like a machine. For the most part, slum-dwellers ignored each other, the killer was no different, except for crazy Joe. He, being an alcoholic, commandeered that neighborhood block. Joe knew everyone who lived there; he also had an uncanny sixth sense, when drunk, he would spot people and call them out.

Joe sat on his box when the killer passed him, "Hey, you." Crazy Joe called out. The killer stopped and looked.

"I know who you are," Joe said, he took a swig of whiskey. Reddish liquid ran out the side of his mouth and down his tattered shirt, "Yeah, that's right. I know who you are." Joe pointed his finger toward the killer; he shook it and squinted one of his eyes.

The killer glared at the man; he just stood, he stood like a white statue blistering in the sun, while people swarmed around him like ants. Crazy Joe sensed a killer when he saw one. The liquor freed him of his inhibitions, but that particular instinct grew in him when he fought in the Great War; he killed, he witnessed others killing others, and the smell of death never left a killer. Traumatized by the war; shell-shocked – he never recuperated; alcohol dulled the horror.

Crazy Joe stopped the killer on many occasions; but it amused the killer; after he glared at the drunk, he turned and walked on. Fox and Helen observed and continued to follow the killer. After a few more blocks, the killer made an abrupt turn and walked up to the steps of a dilapidated old home and vanished. Wood slats blocked the windows; faded paint curled upward, some of the broken pieces dangled in mid-air like a ticker-tape machine on Wall Street. The front beams sagged like a sad old battle-ax that had seen better days.

Fox pulled out his revolver and checked the cylinder for bullets; he checked to make sure his knife was there and ready, "Helen, this is dangerous; no more games, I want you to stay here."

"No! I want to stay with you." She retorted.

"Please Helen, I need you out here in case something happens and I don't return."

"But It's dangerous out here too. Just look around Fox; it's dusk, it will be dark soon. Please let me come with you? I'm scared."

Fox listened to Helen and realized she was in part, correct. The slum is no place to be, especially for a woman alone in the dark, he relented, "Fine. Stay behind me and do as I say. Okay." Fox stated with a firm tone.

The steps creaked as they walked up to the front door. They approached the door with caution; with a sense of urgency, Fox pulled out his revolver, he turned the knob, it opened; they were instantly engulfed in darkness. "Rats," Fox said. "No lights." Fox reached in his other pocket and pulled out a flashlight; he pushed a button, it flicked on; a rectangular beam of light flashed, and it illuminated the entrance; dust filled the room from top to bottom, cobwebs hung from the ceilings; motionless, as if time froze, and they entered another time. Fox shined the light toward the floor, footprints materialized, they followed them.

Most of the furniture was gone, except for a few broken chairs. Rats scurried; running alongside the baseboards. They flooded the room with light and noticed an ornate, hand-carved lattice. The ceilings were at least twelve feet high; full, Victorian-style crown molding engulfed each room. Framed oak wood panels rose four feet from the floor; it wrapped around the walls like folding panels; leaving the impression hidden rooms were behind hidden doors.

Fox turned his flashlight back to the floor and followed the footsteps. They passed a grand staircase, down the hall, to the back of the house; the steps led to a closed-door; Fox twisted the nob, the door creaked open; in front, a wooden platform connected to stairs; Fox turned to Helen, "Are you sure you want to go down?" He whispered. She shook her head, yes.

They stepped onto the platform and started to descend; Helen began to panic, her breathing intensified, she gasped for air; she tightened her grip on Fox's arm. He noticed her erratic breathing; Fox tapped Helen's hand with his revolver, to remind her they have protection, "See." He whispered. She regained control, *Thank God*. Helen said to herself. Each board they stepped on creaked; pressure filled the air with each step they made, each step metastasized into a vast swirling pool of fear. They reached the bottom; out of nowhere, noise broke the silence; Helen screamed, Fox shot his pistol in the direction of the commotion; they detected shattered crystal, Fox pointed his flashlight; debris, broken pieces of glass glistened; They heard a squeal, and little feet scurried along the back-side wall. "It was just a mouse, Helen."

She released air from her lungs, relieved, "I can't take much more of this." She said.

"Hang in there," Fox said. He flashed his light across the room. "Nobody is in here."

"What do you mean nobody is in here?" Helen asked. "We followed the footsteps. Could there be another set of footsteps going to another part of the house?"

"I don't think so, Helen. We only saw one set." Fox paused as he examined the room. "There's something strange here, look, Helen." Fox pointed to a row of pews and an altar.

"You're right Fox; strange is the word; this looks like a church – but in a basement? Why would there be a church in an old house, in the basement?" Helen said.

They searched between the pews; "they're short benches." Fox said, "Only four people a pew." The room held four pews on each side of the room; In all, it would seat thirty-two persons. Fox shined his light on the end of a pew, "Helen, take a look at this; engraved on the side is the embossed image found on the candles." Fox kneeled to examine it closer, "Helen, there are words under the image: It says, Keep the LifeStream Pure."

Brass candlelight holders were screwed into the walls; some of them still had candles in them. Fox examined them, "These candles are the same as those left by the killer at the crime scene, Helen." They walked to the front; stepped upon a platform, a tattered curtain hung on the back wall; in the center of the platform stood an altar; elongated, and made of marble, and iron horns protruded out on both sides of the top. Fox stopped; something occurred to him.

"What is it, Fox?" Helen said.

"This alter is no normal altar, it's a sacrificial altar; probably used to sacrifice animals, maybe roosters or goats."

"Oh, my God!" Helen said.

"Look," Fox said, "There's an image on the front."

Fox and Helen kneeled. Along the top; it read, Lucifer the Light Bearer; underneath a grotesque image of a beast hovering over a family – its arms wrapped around two adults and two children. "Everything on this image is the same on the candlesticks, except for the beast; the beast held a staff with a two-headed snake wrapped around it. His feet were hoofs; inscribed underneath the image were the words, Keep the Blood-line Pure; over to its side was a bright star. Fox leaned back; a strange sensation came over him; Helen sensed it too; dread, they felt chains wrapped around their necks and dragging them under; a sense of foreboding controlled their thoughts.

"Helen—" Fox fell silent; his body dropped to the floor, it made a thud sound; his flashlight spun across the room and out of control – light gyrated like a lighthouse.

"Fox! Are you alright?" Helen screamed. "What's wrong?"

Helen, too, lost consciousness; her body fell across Fox's torso.

CHAPTER 22

Helen awoke engulfed in darkness. Confused, she grabbed the back of her throbbing head, "What happened?" She said out loud. Then, reality set in, fear seized her body. *Oh, my God! What am I going to do?* She screamed in her head. *The killer, the killer – why am I alive?* Helen noticed Fox's flashlight pulsating in the corner. In a panic, she jumped up and lurched for it; frantically, she cast light in every direction. *Where's Fox? Please, God, help me!* He's gone.

She froze, unable to think; she clutched the flashlight like a gun, paralyzed — *move, Helen.* She ordered her body. *Move!* Adrenaline pumped through her like morphine; rational thought was impossible; she leaped – Helen didn't know how and where she got the strength, but she did. She raced to the stairs like a clumsy horse gallantly in agony. She reached the top, ran down the hall, and into the low-hanging cobwebs; she screamed as if she was trapped, Helen struggled, pulling and tearing the spider-webs from her face; there, the front door – she dashed, and bolted out like a person on fire.

Helen ran and ran; tears poured from her eyes until they scratched with pain. Panic-stricken, she finally reached her car. *Fox – he,* she couldn't say the unthinkable as she drove her car home. Her thoughts raced, and raced; people, lights, stores, and building were a blur. When she arrived home, she called the police, "Please, this is Miss Helen Carlyle, please connect me with Detective Savage – it's an emergency." She said, with as much force as she could muster.

"Miss Carlyle, he's home and probably in bed."

"You don't understand, Mr. Fox might be dead, he and Detective Savage are good friends, please call him," Helen said.

"You mean Mr. J.P. Fox?"

"Yes, please hurry."

"Please wait, Miss Carlyle, I'll see if I can contact him." The operator said. After a few minutes, the phone clicked, and the officer's voice crackled, "Miss Carlyle, I called him, and he is on his way to your apartment. Just hold on and stay calm."

"Thank you." Helen expressed.

Detective Savage rushed, with sirens blazing, to Helen's apartment; she met him at the front door, "What has he done now?" Savage said, annoyed; stomping through the front room and threw his hat on the table.

"He was taken—"

"Taken? By whom?" Savage blurted mildly, "If he only listened to me – for God, sakes!"

"Please," Helen said, tears flowing, "Please listen."

Savage's mood shifted when he saw Helen's demeanor. He took off his coat, "let's sit." He wrapped his massive arm around her shoulders, "Here, let me help you, please Helen, sit." He said, "Now, start from the beginning."

Detective Savage listened to every word; the more she explained, the more he became concerned. By the time she had finished, she was a bundle of nerves, "We need to go now," She expressed with grave urgency, "We need to hurry, Fox might still be alive!"

With his hand, Savage covered his mouth not knowing exactly what to say, but he knew the answer, "Helen, do you know where the house is located? What street and number?" Savage asked.

Helen stopped crying, I . . . I, well, no." She said, she slammed her hand on the pillow next to her. "But I think I can show you how to get there."

"In the dark?" Savage asked.

"Maybe, I did get home."

"Sure, but that's different; you were in the moment and running for your life. Now that time has lapsed, you might have forgotten how you two got there." Savage said, "Think, can you remember?"

Helen tried to remember; she looked up and pointed her finger in that direction and then another, she realized she forgot, "But we need to try."

"Okay, I need to ask you another question." Savage took out his hanky and blew.

"Helen wiped her eyes, "What?"

"Why weren't you taken?"

Puzzled by the question, "I—I don't know."

"Why aren't you dead?"

"What?" She arched her back, "Why are you asking me questions like this? We need to go and go now?" Helen said, obsequiously.

"Helen, there's a reason why I'm asking these questions. If the killer wanted Fox dead, I believe he would have killed you as well."

"Why?" Helen asked.

"If I'm correct, the killer knew about both of you; he's been following you and Fox. He wanted you to believe he was being tracked, but it was a ruse; it's a hunch of mine, but if he wanted Fox dead, you wouldn't be here, you would be dead as well."

Helen didn't speak; she let Savage's words sink in, "So, you believe Fox is still alive?"

"I do."

"But why?"

"I don't know yet." He said. "Why don't you get some sleep. It's late, too dark to find where the house is, and too dangerous."

"No!" She said with an uptick of emotions. "We need to leave now."

"Do you remember the address?" Savage said, reminding her of her lapse of memory.

"Well, no," she hung her head.

"Then it will be impossible for us to find the house in the dark," Savage said. "Besides, it's almost morning; the daylight will be a guide; you will be able to remember buildings and landmarks. Otherwise, we will lose valuable time."

Helen realized Detective Savage was correct, but still haunted by the thought Fox was out there, in danger, while she was safe at home. Nothing could dispel her tortured thoughts; images of violence, despair, and her overall feeling of guilt.

CHAPTER 23

Fox opened his eyes in a dark room. He tried to move, but he was tied to a chair; his head ached from the blow, "Where am I?" He yelled, there was no answer. He struggled to free himself; he pulled and yanked, no use. Fox continued to fight, but the rope encircled his wrists, wrapped around the back of the chair, and gripped his ankles like a tied hog. The more he exerted energy, the rope tightened, and cut into his flesh; powerless, there was nothing left to do but wait. *Where's Helen? Is she close by, or is she dead?* He thought.

He was at the mercy of the killer. Fox began to meditate and pray to calm his nerves. He listened to every beat of his heart, he took deep breaths; relaxed his arms and legs – his heartbeat began to slow. *Think. Think man.* He told himself.

Time crept by; inch by inch, like a snail crossing a sidewalk; minutes turned into an hour, then another hour passed; all of a sudden, something clicked, it came from the back; medal on medal, something metallic in need of oil; it opened, someone stepped in, the door slammed like a hatch on board of a battleship.

"Who's there?" Fox said, twisting his head trying to see the killer.

The killer remained silent. He lit a candle and placed it in a candle holder attached to the wall. The light illuminated part of the room, leaving the front in shadows.

Fox's heart started to race again; tension built; the individual moved to the other side of the room. "Where's Helen?" Fox demanded.

A guttural utterance broke the silence, "Mr. J. P. Fox," the killer said.

"Where is Helen?" Fox restated.

"You shouldn't concern yourself over Helen."

"What have you done with her? — Please don't hurt her."

"You're weak."

"Fine, I'm weak— so where's Helen, damn you?"

"Helen, Helen, Helen, enough of Helen, she holds you back. You're better than she is."

"What are you talking about?"

"You have a superior intellect; her IQ is below yours."

"What does that have to do with anything? Is she alright?"

"Stop, you're hurting yourself, Mr. Fox. She doesn't belong to our kind."

"Kind? What do you mean?"

"You're from good stock; born of good blood, from a long line of geniuses. Helen is from a churl – low breed stock. Her bloodline is tainted."

"It doesn't matter, she still is a human being, made in God's image. She deserves to live."

"God?" He said, in a petulant tone, "Ah, another weakness of yours. Do you honestly believe in a magic genie in the sky? Not to worry, we'll soon fix that."

Confused and bewildered, Fox lashed out, "You're a psychopath."

"Psychopath, you say?" The killer moved to the other side of the room, but still out of Fox's view, "I'll tell you who psychopaths are, the crazies are people who believe in God, they believe in love; let me tell you something, those things don't exist."

"Then, what is real?" Fox asked, trying to buy more time.

"Strength, Mr. Fox; strength is real. Power controls everyone and everything. The strong will rule the world."

"Survival of the fittest," Fox said, quoting Herbert Spencer.

"That's right. You do understand, only those who are fit will live." The killer said in a smooth crackly way, as if a broken record played in the background, "But you're weak; we will fix that."

"I'm weak? Fix – what does that mean?" Fox said.

"You are my strength and my weakness," The killer said.

Fox's body jerked in pain; his head twisted, hoping he didn't hear what he just heard, "What? What did you say?"

"You are my strength and my weakness." He repeated.

"You!" Fox said, anxiety-filled his thoughts like Noah's flood; Clara's French perfume apprehended his nostrils; he felt her silky-textured strains of hair run through his fingers – he pictured her face, smile, and sensuous touch, "You are the one who broke into my apartment, and you stole my journal; I'll—"

"You'll do nothing." The killer said. "Your journal told me all about you; about your family, where you went to school, your friends, and yes – Clara, she is your weakness; you said so yourself."

Fox struggled to set himself free, but the knots were too tight, "Stay away from Clara— I warn you if you have harmed her . . ."

"Or what?" The killer said scornfully, "Look at yourself, you're a pathetic creature; look how weak she makes you? Don't you understand, you're one of us; you just need some help to make you stronger – like evolution; rise up, take your place among the fit, leave the un-fit behind, supermen are the true gods – not the weak God of the slaves. What kind of god dies? A weak God, that's who." The killer's words vibrated with spite and cruelty.

"If you're so great yourself," Fox said, "Then why do you kill children? Cowards kill the innocent who can't fight back."

Immune, and unmoved, Fox's words didn't penetrate the killer's concentration, "I don't kill just anyone, I fix people. I'm the fixer— now I'm going to fix you. You'll see, you'll be stronger." Said the killer.

Speechless, *is he going to kill me?* Fox thought. *Why mention Clara? Unless –* "No," he screamed. Silence descended like gravity, "Hey," Fox said, "I'm not sure what you have planned, but please don't harm Clara; kill me instead, I beg you."

A clammy stillness hung in the air like faceless pictures on a wall. . . Then, a click broke the brazen silence; artificial light from above flickered on, Fox squinted to see; he blinked his eyes lids, and objects in the room came into focus. In front of him was another altar; a sacrificial altar made of white marble; red-stain marks flowed from the top to the bottom like tributaries etched in the sand. A human body laid stretched out, with her throat cut.

"No! Not Clara!" Fox screamed; tears flowed, like a dam burst; giving way to gallons of emotions, pulverizing his inhibitions; he lost control; shook his head back and forth, "It can't be! No, it can't be! Why did you kill Clara?" Fox said. "There will be no place on earth you can hide— I'll find you." Fox gnashed his teeth as if trying to crunch down on the killer with the only weapon he had. His body and emotions oscillated from pain to hate, and back again; his heart palpitated; it wanted to leap toward Clara; waves of plangent strikes rushed and crashed against his out of control heart, thrashing him into a comatose state.

"All done," The killer said, "I fixed you." Fox heard footsteps; the metal door opened, and slammed shut, sending a vibration through the room. He glared at Clara's body; helpless, ridden with guilt. "If only I listened – if I . . . Clara would be alive." Fox said, and hung his head in shameful resentfulness.

CHAPTER 24

The morning sun broke the nightmare; Detective Savage, Helen, and a few squad cars raced through town until they reached the place Fox and Helen parked her car. By remembering landmarks, Helen was able to guide the police to the house where she and Fox got knocked out.

"Detective Savage turned to another officer, "Take two men and go to the back of the house; these streets are old and winding, do what you have to do to get there." He ordered.

Savage and two other officers took the front. Pistols were drawn; they rushed through the front door. Everything was as Helen described, except for the broken cobwebs, loosely hanging, dancing like thin white threads of silk. Helen followed the officers; she pointed, "That way, past the stairs. There's the door to the basement."

In haste, they ran to the basement door, opened it, and hurried down, flashlights pointed in every direction. As they descended into the dark, the rays from their flashlights appeared to be a many-headed beast with many bright eyes.

"Spread out, men." Detective Savage barked. Within moments, the basement lit up; just as Helen described: candle sconces screwed to walls, pews, the platform, and altar. Savage stood in the middle, "Incredible. Who would have thought such a place existed in an old home?" He shook his head in disbelief.

The basement appeared to have one entrance; no window, no crack to let sunlight in.

"So," Savage said to Helen, "Can you remember anything else? Where could he have hidden? – one way in one way out."

Helen's credulous eyes scanned the room, "I don't know, Savage."

"Men, check to see if there is a hidden door on or around the platform."

After a diligent search; touching and knocking every inch on and around the stage, nothing; no door or compartment found. Savage pointed his flashlight toward the walls, "Men," he charged, "The walls, check the walls."

They seemed thick; lined with wood and brick. Candleholders were screwed in the wood-panels every three feet or so, and right above eye level. Officers moved along the wall, felt every knot, scratch; pulled every brick; nothing left untouched. "Keep searching men," Savage ordered.

"Do you have an extra flashlight?" Helen asked Savage.

"Sure." He handed her one.

While officers scanned and felt the wall up close, Helen stood back; and examined it from a different angle; a birds-eye view, *we're missing something.* She thought. Wood sections separated brick sections; brick and wood, every three feet apart, or, so, Helen observed. If there's a hidden door, it must be part of one of the wood panels, she theorized; and it made sense, and it also made sense the door had to be controlled by a mechanism to allow a person to slip in and out with ease. *Where's the hidden handle?*

One of the candle-wall-sconces, yes, that must be it. Helen tried the first candleholder; felt it, touched it, and tried to turn it – "tight," she said, it wouldn't budge. She did the same to each consecutive holder, until she reached the last one, next to the platform. Nervous, and even a little afraid to try, Helen managed; she stretched out her jittery hand and took hold of the handle; she turned it; something clicked, it moved, ball-bearings rolled across rusty tracks; the wooden panel opened without a glitch; a gush of air rushed out of the hermetically sealed room.

Savage and his officers ran inside waving guns. They found Fox tied to a chair, body limped forward, and Clara's dead body— sacrificed like an animal.

One officer vomited; another turned his head in disgust. Helen ran over and tried to untie Fox, but failed, "Does anyone have a knife?" She yelled.

Savage pulled out a pocket-knife, "Helen, step aside," He said, frantically, and he cut the rope.

Fox fell into Helen's arms. Another officer ran over to help, they escorted him into the other room, away from Clara's body.

Savage stood, transfixed, glaring hopelessly at Clara's dead body. Sadness overwhelmed his tough-guy exterior; then rage smoldered deep, and spread wide throughout; then the guilt set in like concrete. *Why didn't I listen to Fox?* He thought. He looked to his officers, "You," Pointing his thick finger, "Call an ambulance." He looked at another, "You, call the station and have them send the crime team – pronto! I want every inch dusted for fingerprints," He said, "I want this monster caught."

Helen looked at Savage, "What are we going to do?" She expressed desperately.

Speechless, for the first time in Savage's life, "Someone," He said and all he could muster to address Helen's pain, "I want an ambulance, now!"

"I'll do it." A young officer yelled and ran upstairs.

"My God, what kind of devil could do this?" Savage said.

Helen didn't know what to say, she was more devastated than Savage.

"I have seen death before," Savage said, "I've seen mothers, fathers, children killed; but this, this," He pulled out his hanky and turned away.

CHAPTER 25

"He's in shock." Dr. Dudley said. "Mr. Fox experienced emotional and psychological trauma."

"When will he get better?" Helen asked.

"Hard to tell. The closest thing I've ever seen to this, soldiers in the Great War; some pulled out of it, others, well— let's say it didn't go well."

"What can we do to help?" Detective Savage asked.

"Give him time and let him rest." Dr. Dudley reached into his bag and pulled out a bottle of sleeping pills, "Here, give him one to two a day, it will help him sleep. Given the fact he has had very little rest in the past few days, assaulted, and this; he needs his rest."

"Thank you, Dr.," Helen said.

"Call me if there is any change." Dr. Dudley smiled. He took Helen's hand, "I've known Fox for a long time. I'm sure he will be fine."

Dr. Dudley left; Savage and Helen retreated into the living room. Upset and guilt-ridden, Savage looked like a ghost, gaunt – cheeks puffed out, his eyes sunken inward, "I can't help it, Clara is dead – she is, or was a good friend of mine." He placed his face into his large hands, "I did this. It's my fault, it's all my fault." His eyes itched like sandpaper.

"Detective," Helen said, "I can't relate to your pain, but one thing I do know, you and Fox are friends— that hasn't changed."

"But when he comes around, he will hate and blame me for all of this. Can't you understand?"

"He might, but one thing I have learned about Fox, he forgives. Sure, he gets angry, yell and scream, but he's a reasonable man, he'll come to his senses."

"How do you know this? You've only known him for a few days or weeks."

"True. But I know it; I feel it." Helen reached out and took Savage's hand and rubbed it, "I'm a good judge of character; Fox is a good man. Forgive yourself."

Detective Savage left. Fox tossed and turned throughout the night, "Clara! Clara! No, not, Clara!" He shouted. His upper torso arched; his body shook, and sweat emitted from his body, drenching his bedsheets.

Morning finally arrived — the sun lit up the room, Fox's night terrors dissipated, and he appeared to be in a sound sleep. Helen decided to cook some breakfast.

The brewed coffee filled the room with an exotic aroma. Helen cooked eggs and toast. But it was the pungent odor of sizzling bacon, which dominated the apartment and aroused Fox from his slumber; he climbed out of bed, put on his robe, and strolled sleepy-eyed into the kitchen.

"Well, hello, sleepyhead." Helen smiled sparingly. Disheveled and almost comatose, Fox fell into a chair at the kitchen table.

Fox looked dazed as if he was under a spell as if a witch cast a spell and placed him in a sealed transparent bottle for everyone to stare and gawk at. But, perhaps, it was the combination of Helen's presence and the smell of food that grabbed Fox's attention and made him self-aware of his surroundings. He scratched his head, "Helen," He said bewildered, "How long have I been asleep?"

Helen lifted her spatula in the air, "Well, let's see, in total, about twenty hours."

Fox's head jerked backward, "Twenty hours?" He said, surprised. "My God, time is of the essence, we are this close," holding his thumb and forefinger a breath apart, "This close, Helen." His hand shook emphatically.

"Before we go off chasing killers, you want some breakfast?"

"Yes – but Clara," Fox said, looking up at Helen, "I can't eat."

Helen walked over to the table and sat beside him, "Fox," Her voice soft and gentle, "I'm so sorry about Clara, but if we are to continue, you need your strength; please, eat something."

Fox acquiesced; Helen made sense, "You're correct. Besides, I can't think on an empty stomach."

After Fox ate, he regained his strength. Sitting, his coffee cup half full, "What happened last night? I mean, did I say or do anything —?"

"You had a rough night Fox. You were under stress, whatever you did or said helped you." She reached out and took his hand, "Fox, again, I'm sorry."

Tears welled up, filling his eyes with salt water, "Me too. Me too," He muffled, his voice tapered off in the distance like the of the sound of a small squall moving off the shoreline.

They sat in silence. Shoestring-like steam swirled and curled up from their coffee cups and vanished into the incandescent light above the kitchen table. Guilt manifested itself; *Clara was safe; how wrong he was*. He thought.

Helen noticed remorse written all over his face, "Fox, listen, I can't imagine how you feel right now, but one thing I know— you were right about this case. Just look at what you have uncovered?"

"But Clara—"

"Yes, Clara is gone, but it's not your fault."

"What do you mean?" Fox said, "It's not my fault?" His face contorted.

"It was the killer, the killer killed her, not you." Expressed Helen, "I understand my words are of little consolation, but you must know you didn't kill her, the killer did." Helen realized Fox had to face the situation dead on. She looked into his eyes with compassion, clarity, and firmness, "You must finish what you started."

"Why? The killer knows me, personally. What if he decides to go after you?"

"If he wanted me dead, I would be dead; he had the opportunity, but he didn't."

"But why, why did he let you live?"

"All we know at this point, I'm alive, and he wanted me to help you." Helen grinned awkwardly, "I know it sounds, well, weird, but that's all we have to go on, for the moment."

Fox stroked his goatee. He struggled to remember the killer's words; but, in a cloudy haze, there was something the killer said; something eerie, creepy, and familiar; it was something Professor Black, "Helen," Fox addressed Helen, "The killer echoed, well, I felt as though I was listening to one of professor Black's lectures."

"Did you see his face?" Asked Helen.

"No, he was always behind me."

"Did you recognize his voice?"

"No, and it didn't sound like Dr. Black's voice."

"What's the connection?"

"There must be a connection," Fox said; his thoughts drifted to the newspaper article about the eugenic couple giving birth to the first eugenic baby.

"For now," Helen said, tapping his hand, "Savage will be here soon; why don't you get cleaned up."

Detective Savage arrived; he knocked on the front door. Helen answered, "Hi Savage, please, come in."

Savage was carrying a briefcase filled with photos and descriptions of the house they found Fox in. "How is he?" Savage grinned hopefully.

"Fox is awake and doing better." Helen said, "Here, let me take your hat and coat. Would you like some breakfast?"

"No, thank you, Helen. I already had breakfast, but I could use a cup of coffee?"

"Sure. Let's step into the kitchen." Helen said.

Helen fetched a cup of coffee and placed it in front of Savage. She noticed his depression; sunken, dark rings around his eyes; puffy cheeks, and wrinkled clothes; evident to anyone, he had slept in them all night long.

Fox walked in; showered, shaved, and fresh clothes on. Savage looked Fox's way, but couldn't look at him in the eyes; he just looked guilt-ridden. After a few awkward moments, "Hello, Fox," He said uneasily, with a nervous twitch in his eye.

Fox stopped and glared. Every fiber, every part of him wanted to pulverize Savage. Rage rose; like a caged animal, his hot passion leaped into his eyes, flooded his cheeks, "You—"

Helen jumped between them. She grabbed his head and forced him to look into her eyes, "Fox." She said. "Fox, remember what our mission is; he can help us find the killer."

All his anger was instantly diverted into Helen's face; her soft hands, and her sweet voice. His body shook and shook; then the tremors subsided, "Yes, of course, I need to control myself. Thank you, Helen."

"Fox," Said Savage, "Please forgive this old fool." He swung his head down and began to cry. "I'm so, so, sorry."

Deep down, he knew Savage; he knew Savage would not purposely put Clara in danger. Fox sat, "I know, I know Savage. Clara is gone, now we need to work together to find the killer. Now, I see you brought a briefcase, what did you bring?"

"We checked the house out; the owner is dead. We don't know who he was, that might take a while to find out. You know how the city works."

Fox shook his head. "So, what else did you find out?" Fox said.

He opened the folder and placed several pictures on the table in front of Fox. "These are the most important ones. We couldn't make sense of them. What you're looking at are inscriptions on the wall in the room we found you in. They appear to be ancient writings."

"Fox pulled them close, "Ah, yes. The words are ancient Greek."

"Greek?" Helen expressed with surprise.

"Yes. I immediately recognized it, we — I mean every student in college had to be able to read and translate Greek and Latin."

"What does it say?" Savage asked.

"Helen, would you please get me a pen and pad?"

She pulled out a pen and pad from the kitchen drawer. "Here you go."

"Thank you." He said. "Let's see," Fox began to translate. He scribbled down one word after another. After a few minutes, he pushed his body away from the table. "Hmm, makes sense—"

"What makes sense?" Savage expressed with urgency.

"Well, the first inscription is a true story based on ancient history. It tells how Spartan families took their newborn babies to be examined by the Ephors. If they passed the physical examination, then they would be raised to be a soldier."

"What happened if they didn't pass the examination?" Helen asked.

"They would throw them off a cliff."

"My God!" Helen expressed with disdain.

"You said there was another inscription," Asked Savage.

"Yes. That one is from Plato's book, *The Republic*. There is quite a bit taken from Plato."

"Don't tell me he too threw children off a cliff?" Helen said with a scowled look.

"Not exactly." Fox said, "This is far more sophisticated. I remember reading the *Republic* in college. Here is a portion of what's in the book. Plato writes about a well-functioning city. There is a three-layer cast system. Philosophers ruled and made the laws, guardians guarded the city, and the others lived as citizens."

"Interesting, but so what?" Savage and Helen said at the same time.

"More to the point, Plato advanced the notion of engineering families. Good-stock women mated with good-stock men, to give birth to better human beings. They used animals as examples. This is no different than eugenics," Fox said. "The lower breeds were discouraged from marriage and procreating."

"This is all very fascinating, but what does any of this have to do with the killer?" Savage said.

"What this means, is the killer is connected with people who built this place, influenced by Plato, and who believe in eugenics. At the center of all this is the cult, Lucifer the Light Bearer, which is influenced by Nietzsche." Fox said. "Are you beginning to see a pattern?"

Savage was at a loss, "Are you saying Fox, the killer is a scholar, motivated by the Greeks. . .."

"At this point, we can't rule anyone out."

"If that's true, we have our hands full," Savage said.

"One thing we do know for sure, the cult is well-connected and well-financed." Fox said, "The Greek language alone tells us this group is well-educated."

"But who are they?" Savage said. "And where are they?"

"I don't know, but they seemed to have abandoned that house a long time ago." Fox tapped his fingers on the table, "But the killer used it. Why?"

Fox, Helen, and Savage racked their brains.

"So much information, pieces to a larger puzzle – but how do we start making sense of it all?" Helen mused. "We don't know the killer, but what's frightening – the killer knows us."

After a long pause, Fox snapped his fingers, "Our next move, we go to where Clara worked," Fox said, "The Eugenics Record Office."

"Where's that?" Savage asked.

"Cold Spring Harbor, New York. It's on the north shore of Long Island." Fox said.

CHAPTER 26

"What do we know about Cold Spring Harbor?" Fox asked Savage. The train conductor pulled the cord, a puff of smoke erupted from the train's chimney; there was a long toot, then two short blows, then another long toot, as the train came to a screeching stop; compressed steam hissed out from the bottom, flooding the landing with white vapors.

They stepped off the train and walked through the station. "Let's see," Savage said thumbing through his notes, "Cold Spring Harbor Laboratory, in 1904 the Carnegie Institution funded it, establishing the Station for Experimental Evolution and starting in 1910 they started the Eugenic Records Office."

"Carnegie," Helen responded, "Do you mean the Dale Carnegie?" Her eyes animated.

"Yes, that's the one."

"He's one of the wealthiest men in America."

"Indeed, Helen," Fox moaned peevishly.

"No need—" Helen almost retaliated, but she bit her tongue, realizing what Fox has been through.

"Tell me more about the Eugenics Record Office." Fox requested; Clara had already told him about it, but he needed more information.

"They collect data from human beings. For example; human traits, everything from a person's eye color to diseases." Savage stopped reading. "Fox, this is strange;

why would anyone want to collect these things?" Savage said rhetorically. A part of him knew the answer, in part; eugenics permeated society, it was in the newspapers, on the radio, scientist and lawmakers mentioned it at every turn as if it was part of the air people breathed.

"Who's in charge?" Helen said.

"Charles Davenport is the director of the laboratory; Harry Laughlin is the superintendent of the ERO."

Before long, they had rented a car and was on their way to the laboratory. Once a thriving whaling community, Cold Spring Harbor grew into a respite, a place to get away from New York City highways, congestion, and the concrete wilderness.

"Feel that breeze?" Helen said, holding her hands out the door window. "Suck in that air, fresh, isn't?" She inhaled deeply, her nostrils flared out like a dolphin's porthole spewing out oxygen and inhaling fresh air again.

"Yes, Helen," Fox said passively, "It's fresh and clean. Cold Spring Harbor is also known for freshwater, fishing, boating; an idyllic place to raise a family."

Suddenly Helen felt a chill, but it wasn't from the air. Given all that has happened, the laboratory sounded spooky, something remote, like the house they found Clara in. She shivered and looked around, "Strange place to hide evil." She smiled crookedly.

"We don't know if this place is evil, Helen." Fox said, "Keep in mind, Clara worked here, and she wouldn't have knowingly worked for malevolent people."

As they approached the laboratory, the turquoise sky reflected the blue lakes and rivers. They stopped and walked to the home; painted red and white roses swayed in the breeze; a towering Red Oak tree stood to the right of the building in the front, its branches in full bloom with dazzling leaves, tantalizing onlookers to gaze with wonder; and almost daring would-be painters to try to capture its essence.

On the other side, Black Cherry trees lined up like ducks but spaciously separated. Staghorn Sumacs, Black-Eyed Susan, and perennials dotted the grounds. Closer to the front porch, junipers shot straight up like ready-made Christmas trees. A plethora of birds, blue jays, sparrows, and terns, flew from tree to tree, singing and chirping different chords, like one majestic orchestra, and nature being its conductor.

As they approached the laboratory, a flock of black crows, high above, shrieked through the sky like a badly damaged Nieuport 28 – fighter plane, billowing smoke from one of its wings.

Fox, Helen, and Savage couldn't help it, their attention was drawn upwards.

"I hope this is not a bad omen." Savage sighed.

"May we speak to Dr. Charles Davenport or Mr. Harry Laughlin? Please." Fox said to the greeter at the front desk.

"And who might you be?" She asked sternly; her sharp pointy nose flashed reddish on its end. Before Fox could answer, she responded, "Can't you see we are busy?" and shooed them away; her arms were thin and wiry when she waved them, they flapped around like kites. Her hair was short and pulled back into a small fist-shape bun. Her tone, demeanor, and her body, all combine making one clear pugnacious bluenose, a prude; one hard-nosed bureaucrat through and through.

Detective Savage pulled out his badge and flashed it, "I'm Detective Savage."

The greeter didn't change; she flicked her head back-ward like a petulant child, "Fine. Wait here, and I'll see if they're available." She shoved her small-framed body away from the desk, stood, revealing a shapeless form, thinly grotesque; she stomped her feet and marched away militantly.

The laboratory buzzed with life. Women and men, some dressed in white lab jackets, were busy; they moved with ease, back and forth, like bees.

After a long wait, the greeter returned, "They will see you now," She said with her nose turned up, "Follow me."

The moment Fox stepped in the room, Davenport immediately stood and came around to greet them, "Fox, I'm so glad you came. And we heard about Clara," he said with deep sincerity, "You have our sympathies. We are so, so, sorry."

"Thank you," Fox responded controlled and composed.

"Please this way," he pointed to three chairs, "Please sit, can we get you or your colleagues anything to drink?"

"No, thank you. We are here on business."

"Business? What business?" Davenport frowned cheerfully. He reached into his desk, pulled out cigarettes, and lit one.

"This is Miss Carlyle, my associate, and this is Detective Savage."

"A pleasure to meet both of you," Davenport tipped his head in a friendly gesture. A round of smoke rolled off his tongue, covering his face – etched in a ghostly silhouette. He addressed Fox once more, "You mentioned business . . .."

"Well," Fox began to chock, Helen turned and patted his back. "Well, the police have kept this out of the press; Clara was murdered."

Davenport's eyes grew round and strained, "Murdered? Who, what happened?"

"That's why we're here. We are investigating Clara's murder." Fox said.

Harry Laughlin, who sat next to Davenport, and remained silent until now, "Who do you think you are? You stroll in here start pointing fingers—"

"Mr. Laughlin," Detective Savage spoke up, "Nobody is accusing anyone of anything, at this point. We need to cover all our bases," Savage stared intensely, "This is official police business," He said emphatically.

Laughlin clammed up, sat in steamy silence; hands crossed in smoldering anger.

"Excuse my colleague," Said Davenport, he's been under a lot of pressure, "Of course we will assist you in any way we can."

Fox refocused. He reached in his pocket and pulled out a picture of the killer's first victim and placed it on the desk, "Have you ever seen this child before?"

Davenport picked it up and held it in his fingers, "No, never." Shaking his head.

"What about you, Mr. Laughlin?" Savage asked.

"No."

"Why would we know this child?" Davenport said.

"It's routine." Fox explained, "Have you seen a large person; an albino, he usually wears a black cloak, and wears a ring?"

"No," Davenport said, "What about you, Harry?"

Laughlin shook his head, "No." He said indignantly.

"What does this child and an albino have to do with Clara's death?" Davenport asked baffled.

"All we can tell you, at this point, we believe the albino killed both the child and Clara," Savage said.

Davenport wiped his dry lips with his tongue, "I, well, we hope you catch him," Davenport said earnestly, "We loved Clara. She worked hard; she was a real devotee, a real trooper." He leaned slightly back in his chair, "Is there anything else we can help you with?"

"Yes. We would like to briefly discuss eugenics."

"Well," Laughlin said bluntly, he stood, "It sounds like police business is over, "If you will excuse me, Dr. Davenport." He bent his body to say goodbye and left the room.

"Yes, what are your questions?" Davenport said, smoke streaming out of his mouth.

"According to eugenic literature, Sir Frances Galton founded the movement and coined the phrase eugenics, Correct?"

"Yes."

"Why did he develop eugenics?"

"Life evolved by process of strength; the strong survived, and we are the end result. But the birth of the fit, for example, geniuses, are born based on good bloodlines. Mating good blood with good blood continues the evolutionary process, but that is in danger," Davenport said, "Please understand, eugenics is a science, it helps evolution; or I should say we – with the help of eugenics – help evolution along. It's a matter of survival, Mr. Fox."

"What do you mean?"

"Humans have evolved over millions of years, by the process of natural selection. Now that we have modern science, we can speed up the process. At the same time, we can slow the other end down, the unfit, from destroying the fit."

"Speed up the process?" Fox asked.

"Yes. Eugenics develops more advanced human beings."

"You mean, eugenics will help the fit to become supermen and superwomen?" Fox said.

"Indeed."

"Let me see if I understand correctly," Said Fox, "The future is your aim; the future of the human race."

"Yes, by manipulating human breeding, we shape the future."

"This world you envision, will be flawless— it will be perfect?"

"That's the goal."

Fox leaned back in his chair, "So, Plato's theory of breeding and the Spartan's military society influenced Dr. Galton and everyone involved in eugenics?"

Davenport's eyes lit up, "Why, yes!" He said, his face flushed with enthusiasm, "Plato and the Spartans understood the principle of Eugenics. Although their methods were a bit crude, nonetheless."

Of course, Fox had heard this from Dr. Black and read about it in the newspapers, but what he wanted to see was Davenport's reaction.

Fox decided to press him further, "What about sterilization? How do you determine the number of people who will be forced under the knife?"

"That's a moving target. In 1915 some of us argued the number should be 15,000,000 people, but the population has grown. Too many undesirables have been born since."

Helen gasped for air. Savage shuffled his large body; the chair squeaked.

Davenport sensed their dislike, "Society must protect itself." He said, "We have a responsibility to save the human race."

"I can't believe this," Helen said.

"Try to understand Miss Carlyle. Society puts murderers in prison and even kills them; doesn't society put rapist away? And what about thieves, bootleggers, and extortionists? Why? Not just to punish them, but to protect society." Davenport said, blowing the last string of smoke from his nostrils, "Eugenics works the same way. It will aid in creating a healthier, saner society in the future. "Eugenics," Davenport leaned forward, "Eugenics is settled science." He stamped out the last vestiges of his cigarette in the ashtray.

"But we have institutions, charities, churches, synagogues, and philanthropists that help; they give millions to help the poor; we have reform schools for the youth; no, it's not perfect, but goodwill and compassion is a trait we, in society, should never lose," Fox said, knowing his words fell on rocks.

"And where has that got us? Millions of dollars, wasted; all that effort, for nothing – we still have murders, thieves, and the insane. They're not worth it, Fox, miscreants, are a drain on society" He said. "Eugenics, on the other hand, is science; just imagine those millions handed over to eugenicists?"

"Where's your humanity?" Fox said, "Where's the compassion for those who need help?"

"The best we can do is let them die," Davenport said coldly, "It's best for them and us."

Fox ended the meeting with Davenport, he learned nothing new, except the conversation solidified Fox's theory into one unbroken chain, link by link, the killer is not only influenced by eugenics but in some way, he is a part of it.

CHAPTER 27

" Little Frank," His mother called him over to see the dinosaur exhibit. He was named after his father, Frank Pawlak. "Look, little Frank at how large this dinosaur is."

"You know what kind of dinosaur it is, momma?" He said, excitement stuttering from his little body.

"No, why don't you tell me." She smiled like any caring mother.

"It's a T-Rex." He lifted his hand and pointed to the sign.

"Oh, yes, I see it now." Mrs. Pawlak pretended to understand. In reality, she couldn't read or write English. She and her husband spoke broken English, just enough to get around. Mr. Pawlak worked as a janitor at the museum part-time.

The American Museum of Natural History was busy, as usual. Men and women strolled around as if they had nowhere to go. Groups of school children were there from nearby schools like packs of wolves.

Little Frank twirled a stick of cotton candy in his hand. It melted the moment it hit his wet tongue. He stood in front of the towering dinosaur, but he wasn't frightened. Unlike the monsters his grandfather used to tell him about when he was small, to scare him.

The killer was across the room, watching. He observed the boy's movements. Little Frank's left hand involuntarily twitched; they were abrupt, sudden, and short flicks. The more the killer watched, the more he observed he realized the boy couldn't control it. It was a tic. *A sign of poor breeding,* the killer thought. *Something had to be done.*

Little Frank and his mother moved from one exhibition to another. They had never seen such large animals like the Brontosaurus and the Stegosaurus. They passed the dinosaurs exhibit and emerged onto a cultural presentation. A Tahitian culture was on display. Half-dressed mannequins held spears, fished, hunted, and cooked food.

Little Frank pulled on his mother's coat, "Look! Look, Mommy!" He said with enthusiasm, "Look at the man walking on fire. See?" His eyes were wide and flamed out with wonder.

"Yes, dear, I see it." She said, speaking Polish. "He's not real, you understand?"

"I know, Mommy." He said with a burst of sarcasm, "Gee, I'm not little anymore. I know what's real and not real." He shook his head like an ordinary adolescent.

They moved into another part of the museum. Brilliant Murals painted right into the walls shined under the artificial lights. Murals of wildlife; American Bison roaming the Great Plains, another mural has two domesticated Water Buffalo, harnessed, plowing the ground in a four-thousand-year-old Chinese providence. Little Frank stopped in front of another wall; a painting of how mankind evolved; from the caveman, through different stages, then the modern man and woman.

"Frankie," The mother said, "What does that sign say?" She pointed to the plaque.

The boy squinted his eyes, "This is a rep, o, duction." He said, his words fragmented.

"It says—"

"'This is a reproduction of the ape-man Java, of the Heidelberg and the Piltdown man,'" The killer said.

"Thank you, sir." Mrs. Pawlak said, she felt a little embraced she didn't know how to read English.

"It also says the Neanderthal and Cro-Magnon men and women living and thriving with each other." The killer explained.

"What does it all mean?" Little Frank said.

"Evolution." He said. "It shows how we evolved from lower life forms." The killer bent down to the boy's level, "Only the strong will survive," He smiled malevolently.

"Lower life?" Mrs. Pawlak asked, "What does that mean?"

"We came from gorillas."

Mrs. Pawlak jerked her head backward, "Gorillas?" Her face flushed red with anger at the thought, "God made us." She responded. With a clear and unambiguous statement, "We come from God." She proclaimed, "Come along, Little Frank."

The killer watched them turn the corner. He followed, but he kept his distance. The museum was crowded. He darted between exhibit after exhibit; then the boy left his mother, walked out the front entrance, and went across the street into Central Park. The boy had grown tired of the museum, he wanted to play in the park. The killer felt a sensation, he pursued the boy.

Central Park bubbled with life; birds, squirrels, and other animals cohabited among the trees and ponds. But the Park was really developed for people; and it hummed with human traffic like the museum, but it wasn't as dense, people were spread out. With a zoo, an ice rink, and many landmarks and attractions, Central Park was the place to get away from cramped city living— a place to slow down, an oasis for the body, mind, and soul.

Little Frank gazed at the green grass and fulsome trees bending in the wind. To his right was the Lake. He followed a path around it, following the lakes' outer contours until he reached the Bow Bridge. It was made of cast iron and shaped in a Classical Greek motif.

It had a perfect arch that spanned the Lake to the other side. Little Frank walked across the bridge like he had many times before. He knew Central Park well enough to be a tour guide, at least that's what he espoused to his classmates; he crossed the expanse, rowboats were in the water on either side; instantly, an alarm bell went off in his head; his mother warned him to be careful: several years ago, someone found a dead body near the bridge. He registered it and went on.

After crossing, he landed onto solid ground again. To the east was Bethesda Fountain. Within a few clicks, he arrived. His mother ordered him to go to the angel of waters and stay there until she and his father came.

Little Frank played; he skipped around the great fountain, singing a child's song. At the bottom of the basin, coins sparkled and reflected the sun. On occasion, when he felt no one was looking, he would grab a penny or two. After he played, Little Frank skipped over to a bench and sat next to the Birdman. People called him the Birdman because he feeds the birds; he was always there as if he lived somewhere in the park. They chatted, and the old man gave the boy some bird feed to feed the birds with.

Scars crisscrossed the Birdman's face, like a net; his skin darkened by the sun, his eyes grey and pale as if two once-great suns burned till now, they are fading candles. His mind and body perhaps damaged by alcohol or drugs, with nothing left, he just wants to spend what's left of his life in peace. No one knew who he was, he talked very little. After frequent visits, the Birdman and little Frank developed an unspoken bond. They sat together, they fed the birds, and they laughed and smiled.

The killer followed little Frank to Bethesda Fountain. He stood at a distance, watching. The boy's tics increased. *He's unfit to live.* He thought. *The boy must die.* Saliva ran out and down the side of his mouth.

After half an hour, the Birdman left. The boy remained; feeding the birds. *This is my chance.* The killer said. He looked around, the Terrace was empty, except for the boy. Sunlight started to slither away; long shadows began to form; the killer had to act and act fast.

The killer approached the boy. "May I sit?" He said.

Little Frank twisted his head, "It's you. Sure."

"Do you like this place?"

"Sure." The boy tossed out another fist full of feed. Flocks of birds cavorted around, squawked, and poked the ground.

"Have you been here before?"

"Yes. I know every inch of this Park."

"How so?"

"You see, mister, my father works at the museum. Me and my mother have been to the Park many times." The boy said. "I like the Park. My mother lets me go alone, sometimes." Little Frank smiled confidently, "I can take care of myself."

"You're an important person. I mean just look at you. All alone, but strong."

The boy grinned.

The killer smiled back; he methodically lifted his bag, sat it on the bench next to himself; he opened it, reached inside—"

"What's that, mister?" The inquisitive little boy asked.

"Tools."

"What kind of tools?"

"Special tools. They can help you and help the future."

The boy squinted his eyes, "Whatever you say, mister," He said, his legs dangling off the end of the bench.

The killer grasped hold of the knife; he squeezed it tight. His blood rushed through his veins, but before the blade breached the top of the bag, a shadow seized his eyes; it reached out and touched his feet like someone chained him to the bench. His eyes followed the shadow along the ground, to the bottom of the basin; his eyes hit the water – it sparkled with life. The killer felt an extreme and mystifying emotion, but it was more than a feeling, it was an experience – deep, moving, but troubling.

Bethesda Fountain is twenty-six feet high by ninety-six feet wide. Captivated, the killer's eyes couldn't help but notice its neoclassical design; there were three basins; the large one at the bottom, the middle pool, and a smaller one above the others. At the top stood an eight-foot bronze angel. In one hand it held a lily, and in the other hand – nothing. Water flowed from the top, pouring down each consecutive basin, all the way to the bottom. But it was the angel's bronze wings that apprehended the killer.

In the angel's winged shadow, the killer was speechless. *What is this?* He thought. Both frightened and loved; the shadows of light rippled over his white-skin as if a power wanted to change how he saw himself – colorless and devoid of hate.

"Hey, mister, you alright?" The boy said.

The killer didn't hear the boy. He had forgotten him altogether; mesmerized and transfixed, he dropped the knife, glared at the angel of water in a trance-like state.

"Little Frank." A voice called to him in the distance, "Time to go."

The boy turned and saw his mother and father in the distance waving for him to come along. "Goodbye, mister." He got up and left to meet his parents.

The killer didn't notice the boy; dazed to his surrounding, he sat as the angel's shadow almost engulf him. Thoughts flooded his mind like the water in the basin; rippling, churning, and overflowing. The killer re-membered when he murdered the child; when he killed Clara and every evil act he committed. *Why are they evil acts?* He thought. *They were good, but now, they are evil?* He felt a heaviness; it weighed on his conscience like boat anchors. He couldn't move, he cried.

CHAPTER 28

Fox's phone rang, "Hello?" He said.

"This is Savage. Meet me in Central Park."

"Central Park?" Fox asked, stumped by no hello, or how are you. "Where in the Park?"

"At Bethesda Fountain," Savage said. "You know where it is?"

"Of course. I've been there many times. What time?"

"Pronto."

"We'll be there within an hour." Fox hung up the phone. "Helen?"

"Yes?" She responded in her usual chipper way. She slunk amusingly from the bedroom, dressed like a detective; donned by a trench coat, and one of Fox's Fedora Hats. Helen was ready and dressed to kill.

Surprised, "Helen, why are you dressed that way?" Fox asked seriously.

"You like?" She twisted to the right and to the left like she was in a fashion show.

"We don't have time for this, we've got business to attended to." He expressed sternly. "Fox," she said, "No play and all work will make you break. Besides, I'm auditioning to be a detective one day."

"That's all fine, but at the moment we have to meet Savage in Central Park."

"Did he say why?"

"No, but he wants us there now. So, chop, chop, let's go."

Central Park was just a few blocks from Fox's apartment. The morning sun blasted through the sky and landed upon a greenish Park. Grass, trees, and flowers material- ized, breathing life. Like a carpet, dew spread across the ground, wet, and fresh.

Fox and Helen entered the park. By the time they reached Bethesda Fountain Detective Savage was busy and waiting. The fountain's plumbing system pumped clear water through its pipes; like a heart pulsating blood through it's veins, and throughout the body.

"Good morning, Detective," Helen said.

Savage took off his hat and tipped his head forward, "Good morning."

"So, why are we here?" Fox said, "Don't tell me you found another body?"

"Late last night, we received an anonymous tip; some- one spotted an albino, with a briefcase, sitting with a boy, here at the Fountain."

"Where's the body?" Helen asked, frantically.

"That's the odd thing, we didn't find a body, at least not yet."

Helen turned to Fox, "That has to be him." She said.

"Maybe," Fox said, addressing Savage, "Why would anyone call the station with a tip?"

"We placed an ad in the newspapers stating: 'If anyone has seen or spotted a person fitting this description, please call the police right away."

"Okay," Fox said, looking around the terrace, "You believe the caller spotted the killer, then you want us to look around and see if the killer dropped something, or, if the killer did strike again, then we might find the body?"

"Yes, and after we're done here, we also need to visit the American Museum of Natural History," Savage said.

"Why?" Fox said.

"The anonymous caller also said he knew the boy and said the boy's father worked at the museum," Savage said, as the wind flapped his lapel up and down.

"Why didn't the caller leave a name?" Fox asked curiously, "Is that common?"

"People don't want to get involved. So, no, it's not strange; in fact, quite a bit of our cases are solved by anonymous tips."

"Did your men search the area already?" Fox asked.

"Yes and no." Savage said, "I could only bring one man, and we just arrived before the two of you. He's off in another direction at the moment; the surrounding area is fresh. Fox, why don't you start here, search around the Fountain; Helen, you look around the rest of the terrace, and I'll inspect the surrounding trees and bushes."

Fox looked at Savage, "I have a question."

"Yes," Savage said, desperate to shed more light on their search.

Fox took off his hat and scratched his side-burn, "We know the killer kills without remorse and without provocation. Let's assume for the moment the killer was here, why didn't he murder the boy?"

Helen's face lit up, "Good question."

"Yes, Fox, good question," Savage said.

They stood pondering Fox's question – a long silence. Then, Helen's eyes suddenly were drawn to the Fountain's water. It usually had a calming effect, but ripples mysteriously beckoned for attention, it demanded to be heard; the water cascaded off the edges of the basins as though each molecule had a voice, it would not be denied. It dawned on her Bethesda Fountain's source wasn't just the pipes that feed water throughout, making it appear alive. But the angel on the top gave it its mystic, a certain kind of enigma planted on the human spirit, "Could this be the answer," Helen said glowingly, "Could this be it," pointing to the Fountain and especially to the angel?"

Savage and Fox looked at Helen, then at the Fountain.

After a long stare, Savage laughed, "Baloney! Have you been drinking giggle-water?" He said sarcastically, "Have you gone bonkers? We're dealing with a madman."

"But think about it, maybe, just maybe, the killer experienced something, something deep and spiritual. And maybe it stopped him." Helen said, forcefully.

"Nonsense. Nonsense." Savage shook his head in disbelief, "Helen, let's deal with the real world, facts and clues, nothing more – no hocus pocus."

"But—"

Fox grabbed her arm, "Helen, for now, let's search the area, and we'll keep your idea on the backburner." Fox said comfortingly.

The American Museum of Natural History was packed. Swarms of people from all walks of life and backgrounds throttled each exhibit, congestion consumed the hallways; Fox, Savage, and Helen battled their way past the entrance.

"Why is the museum so crowded today?" Helen asked.

Fox looked to his right, "Here's why." And he pointed to a sign.

Dr. Samuel gives a lecture on evolution and eugenics, the sign read.

"The museum always attracts a large mass of people, given their dinosaur and other exhibits, but this is an added feature," Fox said.

"Ladies and gentlemen," a sonorous voice boomed, "Eugenics is science, eugenics is based on evolution, and eugenics is the future." He proclaimed, placing his cuffed hand around his lapel. "We're offering this lecture, along with many others, to help the public understand cutting-edge science. Most scientists worth their salt agree the human race is doomed, but it can be saved by applying eugenics."

The massive crowd swayed to each syllable, word, and sentence as if listening to a prophet.

Helen quipped, "How ironic; everywhere we go, eugenics is there. Strange, very strange, as if eugenics had been hidden in broad daylight until this case exposed it."

"Indeed, Helen. The more we investigate, the more we discover, eugenics is fundamental to this case."

"Fox," Helen said, "I know eugenics pops up everywhere we go, but do you think it's just a coincidence?"

Detective Savage butted in, "No, Helen; given the amount of evidence we have uncovered; the answer is no, eugenics does play a major part in this case." Savage stated, with certainty, "The real question is, just how much eugenics has a part and who are the major players?"

They made their way to one of the help desks. A well-groomed young man sat combing his hair; his hair neatly greased down to shine; he dressed like a stylish dandy, "May I help you?" He said respectfully.

"Yes, we would like to speak with the president of the museum, please," Fox said.

The young man shook his head," Oh, I don't think that's possible."

"Why not?" Savage asked.

"He's a busy man; besides, you need to make an appointment." The young man stiffened his back and straightened his bow tie. "Yes, sir, he's an important person." Then he slightly pulled back on his self-assuredness, "Wait, are you scientists?"

Savage sensed his equivocation, his sudden shift between confidence and self-doubt, "No," Savage said, he pulled out his badge and flashed it, "But I'm the police, and this is official business."

"Oh, good," He said, self-assurance filled his lungs, "Wait, the police? You mean you're not scientists?" As fast as his bravado came, it went. "Please, wait right here." His lanky, thin legs fumbled around the desk and hurried to the office.

"Wait?" Helen said. "Can't you just call him from here?" She pointed to the telephone and smiled at the young man's protean behavior.

He stopped, "Yes, I forgot." He turned around and dialed the office. He told Dr. Osborn's secretary the police were here; he hung up the receiver, "Dr. Osborn is on his way. Please don't let him know I almost turned you away," he said alarmingly, "It's my first day and my first job." He swallowed and gulped a dry, imaginary lump.

"Not to worry young man." Fox padded his shoulder. "Keep up the good work."

The young man's obsequious bravado seemed to tax all three of them. Apparently, he had an impatient father or mother – or both; over-demanding, crotchety, and captious. His mannerisms displayed specimen-like behavior; always under the microscope and under-the-gun.

Henry Fairfield Osborn arrived, "Hello." He said. "May I be of service?"

Detective Savage flashed his badge, "We are investigating a crime."

Osborn recoiled, "A crime? There's been no crime around here. In fact, we are up to date with city permits and licensing."

"No, Dr. Osborn, we are investigating a murder. We need to speak to one of your employees." Savage said.

Fox stepped in, "Before we do, I would like to speak with you first. My name is Mr. Fox, this is my associate, Miss Carlyle, and this is Detective Savage."

Osborn skipped the greeting, "Why me?" Osborn said. "I haven't committed any murder."

"We received a tip the murderer was spotted in Central Park. He might have been in the museum during this time." Fox responded.

"What does he look like?"

"He's a large man, tall, and strong. He has been seen wearing a cloak, carries a briefcase, maybe more like a medical bag, perhaps."

"That describes a third of New Yorkers," Osborn said.

"He's albino. White as rice." Detective responded.

"Albino?" Osborn cringed, "That would make him unfit. Other than that, I haven't seen such a person." Osborn looked at all three of them, "Who do you need to speak to?"

"We're not sure," Fox said.

"Then, I can't help you." Osborn started to turn and walk away.

"Wait," Savage said. "Your employee has a little boy." He looked at Fox and back again towards Osborn, "We believe the boy's parents are poor and foreign-born."

Osborn thought, "Maybe, it might be Frank Pawlak. He is one of the museum's janitors, he also has a child." Osborn looked around, "Come with me to my office. I'll call, and have him meet us there."

Osborn called the custodial supervisor; he instructed him to have Frank Pawlak come to his office. While they waited, Fox took the opportunity to examine Osborn's office. Everyone was a suspect; especially anyone involved in eugenics. Of the many pictures and plaques hanging on the walls, Fox noticed a sketch – it stood out like red paint against a dark background. The drawing was of a large tree; full of branches, and roots showing. Close to the top, a banner stretched across its branches, written in bold letters the word *EUGENICS*.

"Dr. Osborn?" Fox said. "Can you tell me more about that sketch?"

Osborn walked over, "Of course. Take a closer look. See? See what it says?"

"Yes, of course." Fox read out loud . . . *"Eugenics is the self-direction of human evolution."* Fox snapped his fingers. "Of course!" He exclaimed. "That's it in a nutshell. I've been trying to wrap my head around eugenics for days. Don't get me wrong, I understood it, it was explained to me, and I have read up on it, but the sketch and words are dead-on; it's brief, to the point, and brings out its essence."

Osborn smiled, "Look closer. What else do you see?"

Fox moved in closer, "Written on the roots are the words *biology, mental testing, medicine, statistics, politics, law, psychology, genetics, anatomy, history, surgery, medicine, economics, and so on.*" Under the roots is written, "*Like a tree, eugenics draws its materials from many sources and organizes them into a harmonious entity.*" Fox read out loud.

Osborn stepped back, "Now, Mr. Fox, see the big picture?"

"Indeed." Fox said, and looked at Osborn, "Indeed."

There was a knock on the door, "Ah, that must be Frank Pawlak." He expressed. He walked over to the door and opened it, "Mr. Pawlak, come in, come in."

Mr. Pawlak was dirty from cleaning the bathroom stalls. He took his hat off and held it between his hands in a servile position. "You wanted to see me, sir?" He said in broken English; his eyes were plastered to the floor as if he was ready for a lashing or to lose his job.

"Mr. Pawlak, these men wish to speak with you," Osborn said. "By the way, did your son happen to come to the museum today?"

Pawlak looked puzzled, "My son?" His eyes shifted between Osborn, Savage, and Fox. "Do you wish to speak with little Frank?"

"If he's here," Savage said.

"He's not. But what is this about?" Pawlak said. "Is he in trouble? What did he do?"

"No, Mr. Pawlak, your son is not in trouble," Fox said. "We believe he might have seen and spoken to someone the police are looking for. That's all."

Pawlak's lungs exhaled a sigh of relief. His shoulders relaxed. "Thank God." He said. Pawlak looked at Fox, "My son tells me everything. Is this about the man in the park?"

Fox looked at Savage, "Yes, I believe so Mr. Pawlak. What can you tell us?"

"Well, you see, a man was sitting with my son, and they were talking. You know that place? Where the angel is?"

"Yes."

"My wife and I found him there with a stranger, they were talking." Mr. Pawlak said, "My wife warned him never to talk to strangers." He said, his face showed signs of stress. "My son didn't mean nobody harm, honestly." He felt tense; Pawlak squeezed his hat, transferring his tension onto his hat like clothes pressed through a clothes wringer.

"We know Mr. Pawlak, we just want to know about the stranger."

"Well, my wife told me he was in the museum, he talked with them, you see."

"What did they say?"

"My wife only remembers the stranger told them we came from monkeys. Then my son left and went to the park; he plays there a lot. We saw him there with the same stranger."

"Did your son tell you what they spoke about?" Savage asked.

"He didn't remember. What he does remember, the stranger stopped talking after a few minutes. My son said it was like he was sleeping, but with his eyes still open." Mr. Pawlak turned to Dr. Osborn, "Can I go now, I have work to do. That's all I know."

"Yes, of course, Mr. Pawlak. On your way." Osborn said.

Mr. Pawlak walked out and closed the door behind him.

Osborn turned to all three and slapped his hands together, "Well, gentlemen and lady, if that is all— I too am a busy man."

As they started to walk out the door, Fox turned back, "One last thing. I remember reading there was a conference here several years back. Can you briefly tell us what that was about?"

"Yes. That was the Second International Eugenics Congress, conducted in 1921. Scientists, politicians, and philanthropists met here to discuss what could be done with the unfit."

"What was the consensus?" Fox said.

"Major Darwin stated it perfectly. You know who Major Darwin is?" He asked.

"I think he is Charles Darwin's son."

"Correct. Well, Major Darwin advocated in simple terms the elimination of the unfit, to discourage the unfit from procreating, and encourage and promote well-endowed families – fit families – to mate and procreate healthy children. In other words, marriage unions must be controlled." Dr. Osborn expressed, "It's a known fact, race degeneration is due to the breeding-out of the best stock and the rapid increase of the poorer strains. The human race will die if we don't save it— it's settled science. This is the consensus, Mr. Fox."

CHAPTER 29

When Fox, Savage, and Helen walked out of the American Museum of Natural History, they were no closer to knowing who the killer was than before they walked in. Odd, though, they know his beliefs, his connections to eugenics and the cult of Lucifer the Light Bearer. It was as if the killer stood right in front of them, taunting them, laughing at them, and daring them to reach out and touch his face, and feel his pain; but at this point, he was an illusion, a phantom, like a puff of smoke, here for a second, then gone.

Fox looked across the street, "Let's go back to the park," Fox said. "We need to talk."

"I agree, you lead." Detective Savage said.

They crossed the street, but before they stepped into the park, they stopped at a hot-dog-stand and bought three hot dogs and three drinks. They walked and ate. Fox led them to the area in the park called the Mall. They strolled to the south end where statues of William Shakespeare, Robert Burns, and other literary figures loomed.

Helen began to feel depression, even overwhelmed, "Fox," she said, "I never realized detective work was this hard." She looked around, people were walking up and down the Mall. "Just look at them; I was like them just a few days ago, ignorant, and oblivious to the horrors of eugenics, and to death."

Fox wrapped his arm around her shoulders, "Helen. I have a secret to share with you." He said, and smiled unhappily, "Most detective work is boring. We track down leads, but more often than not, they're dead-ends. But this case, well, I too am overwhelmed; especially by Clara's death."

Savage responded, "Me too, Helen. Trust me, I think we are in over our heads."

Helen looked up into Savage's weary eyes, "Then what do we do? Can't we go to the Feds?"

"No, Helen," Savage said. "This would be considered a local matter, to the Feds."

"But what about the eugenics movement? How the killer is connected?" Helen said, with a strained, but a tiny glimmer of hope in her voice.

"Where's the evidence? They would say. Besides, the federal government supports Eugenics. The Supreme Court just upheld eugenics in *Buck v. Bell*."

"Then, what can we do?"

"We find the killer," Fox said. "We know eugenics plays a part, we do it by the book. We follow the clues and evidence." Fox gestured at both of them, "Agreed?"

Helen felt a little better, enough to straighten her back flat as a frying pan, "Agreed." She held out her hand like one of the Three Musketeers. Fox and Savage placed their hands on hers. All of them spoke in unison, "'All for one and one for all, united we stand divided we fall.'"

"Now down to business," Fox said. "Here's what we know: The killer is large, probably strong, he wears a cloak, carries a briefcase or some sort of medical bag, and he's an albino. He is either involved in eugenics or is influenced by it; nonetheless, eugenics appears to be the cardinal motive in the murders. And then there is the cult, Lucifer the Light Bearer."

"Yes, all true." Said Savage. "And the killer kills his victims sacrificially like ancient religions did to appease their gods."

Fox jerked his head, "What did you just say?" He said, as if a Tarpon, in a Florida lake just snagged his fishing line.

"The killer kills his victims like they are sacrifices—"

"No, no, the other part? The part about the gods?"

"Oh, he kills like the ancients did when they killed to appease their gods."

"That's it! By Jove!"

Savage and Helen looked surprised, "What? What is it, Fox?" Helen asked, anxiously.

"Think about it; the killer killed using candles, positioning them in a semi-circle as if the victims were offerings. Clara was murdered on an altar, the room glorified ancient killing practices; and when I was tied to the chair, he told me *I was fixed*," Fox sucked in fresh air into his lungs, "Fixed? What did that mean?" Fox's eyes animated.

"What?" Savage said.

"Our killer is killing for a reason. I don't believe he hates his victims, nor do I believe he gains any pleasure in killing, and I do not believe he's insane, maybe psychologically screwed up, but so are millions of Americans." Fox paused, "He's killing to appease someone— to gain approval from someone or thing. He wants recognition – approval."

"Well, he got that. Half of the police department is hunting him as we speak." Savage said.

"He doesn't care about us, Savage, he doesn't care what the public thinks of him," Fox stroked his goatee, deep in thought, "No, the killer is trying to appease someone very close to him; a person or individuals that know him, and he, them."

"That makes sense," Helen said. "None of this made any sense until now. But who is he trying to appease or gain approval from?"

He reached in his pocket and pulled out the newspaper clipping, "Savage, remember the newspaper clipping found close to the first murder?"

"Yes."

"Here it is. Remember what it said?"

"Not really, but go ahead and reread it."

"I'll just read the relevant parts; *eugenics will produce a super-race free of diseases. . .. [It] will be a healthier, stronger, purer, happier, and wiser race. We have already conducted such a test; a prearranged marriage was conducted this year. They are from excellent stock. The well-fit couple, their offspring will be a superman or woman.*"

Helen snapped her fingers, "Superman, Leopold, Nietzsche." She quipped.

"Right," Fox said.

"Fox, your theory about the killer's motive is sound, and plausible, but we're still not absolutely positive, but we need more evidence," Savage said.

"Indeed," Fox responded. "But let's go with my theory for the moment. And to add to that working thesis, the killer might be the child of this eugenic marriage."

"If so," Savage said, "Where do we go from here? —I mean, how do we find his parents?"

Fox looked at Savage, "My suggestion is this; why don't you put more men on the case; we do have a description of the killer."

"Of course. I'll get right on it."

"In the meantime, Helen and I will follow up on the second scene, you know, where the killer almost killed again in the graveyard."

"You mean where no dead body was found?"

"Yes. We will see if we can run down the names on the tombstone."

They leaned back on the bench, all three exhaled air from their lungs as if letting out built-up steam from a tea kettle.

After Savage refreshed himself, he got up, "I'll be going, now, and I'll get right on it. Goodbye. I'll meet up with you two later." Savage said.

"Will do," Fox said, looking into his eyes as Savage turned and walked away.

Helen and Fox sat for a while longer. Their minds needed the time to relax, just a bit. They knew the next few days would be long and dangerous.

"Fox, the world has gone mad," Helen said.

"Yes, it has," Fox said. Looking up at Shakespeare's statue. He was reminded of a poem,

The expense of spirit in a waste of shame
Is Lust in action; and till action, Lust
Is perjured, murderous, bloody, full of blame,
Savage extreme, rude, cruel, not to trust:
Enjoy'd no sooner but despised straight;
Past reason hated, as a swallow'd bait
On purpose laid to make the taker mad:
Mad in pursuit and in passion so;
Had, having, and in quest to have, extreme;
A bliss in proof, and prov'd, a very woe;
Before, a joy propos'd; behind, a dream.
All this the world well knows, yet none knows well
To SHUN THE HEAVEN THAT LEADS MEN
TO THIS HELL."

"Wow, where did that come from?"

"Shakespeare. It's a poem we had to memorize in college."

"Repeat the last line, Fox."

"*'Yet none knows well To shun the heaven that leads men to this hell.'*"

"Incredible." Helen said, "I feel like the world is in that heaven Shakespeare warns us about." She clasped her arms around her body and leaned her head into Fox's embrace.

CHAPTER 30

The killer hid behind some boxes in a loft. He witnessed blacked robed individuals sitting below on pews. On a platform, a speaker stood speaking, "My fellow brothers," The speaker said, "We are changing the world for the better. Many U.S. State legislatures are in the forefront. Thirteen states have passed eugenic laws, other states are working to that end. The Supreme Court upheld eugenics in *Buck v. Bell,* and the doctrine of eugenics is taught to the public as a religion," The speaker paused and looked around, "Stay strong; stay vigilant, stay focused; we are the generation to save humankind from itself, we are the future."

The room erupted with applause; cult members cheered. The loft the killer was hunkered down in, vibrated. He sat and watched as if he was watching a baseball game; the chamber glowed with excitement. He felt something warm, he felt at home, the speaker's words resonated in his head and heart.

"Eugenic religion will replace traditional religion," The speaker continued, "Christianity must replace Christ and the resurrection with eugenics. It must, or die. The Christian religion stands in the way of progress and saving humanity." He walked to the other side of the stage, "I know what some of you are thinking, it's impossible to snuff out an ancient religion with billions of devotees. I will not lie to you; we have a difficult task ahead, but we have made some inroads. Some denominations have already thrown out their tired-old-doctrine of redemption and replaced it with the science of eugenics. They preach eugenics. They preach eugenics as a religion."

Another round of applause. Then silence.

The speaker raised his hands; long, thick, sleeves hung from his arms like magic in the air, "Remember my fellow brothers, our founder – Sir Francis Galton; remember his own words: 'It must be introduced into the national consciousness, like a new religion.' Through our hard work, it's happening."

The killer continued to listen, he stayed hidden and silent. But the image of the angel forced its way into his mind; he tried to shake it, but it remained. A mental struggle ensued. The more he fought, the more the angel persisted; he grew angry.

The killer watched as the speaker finished, and as each black-hooded cult-member lined up and marched out of the candlelit chamber like ants. The killer knew the place well; it was, in many respects, like an old stomping ground, even a place he felt at home.

Several passageways branched out away from the central chamber, the meeting room was the hub. The speaker went the opposite direction than the others; the killer followed. Lined with trash and debris, the corridor twisted and turned, it diverged until the speaker arrived at another room. He took out a large skeleton key, unlocked the door, and entered. At the other end, a massive desk stood, shoved up against the wall. Erected next to it was a life-size mirror. Robes and different types of clothing hung in a closet. The room came into focus when the speaker lit a lantern.

The speaker sat, the door slowly creaked open, he turned, "You!" He said, with disdain, "Why are you here? You're not allowed in here."

Draped in his cloak, the killer didn't stop, the speaker thought he was a member.

The speaker shot straight up from his chair, "I said, nobody is allowed back here!" He said emphatically.

The hazy blackness protected the killer from full view, but the speaker noticed something familiar to the looming silhouette standing by the door. He stepped closer; then, like an image etched in fog formulated and materialized right in front of him; he pulled back in disgust, "You! I told you never to come here." He said, meaning not just the room they were in, but to the whole meeting place, "Are you out of your mind? What if – what if someone spotted you?"

The killer felt humiliated; mortified, he lowered his head in pure silence.

"Why did you come here? Answer me."

The killer dared not lift his eyes, "I – I" He stuttered.

"I what?" The speaker shouted.

"I'm confused."

"Confused? Confused about what?"

The killer was afraid to speak. He tried, but nothing came out of his mouth.

"Well? I'm waiting."

The killer lost his nerve. He stood there like a little boy who wet his bed.

The speaker raised his hand and slapped the killer across his face, "Shame! Shame on you!" He said. "Don't grow a brain. I do your thinking. Understand?"

The killer shook his head up and down like a trained dog.

"You've made a mess of things; stupid. Don't you understand I'm trying to protect you? You sought and found me years ago, now I'm stuck with you."

The speaker turned, walked toward the mirror; slipped the button out of its loop to unfasten his rob, hung it on a hanger, and placed it in the closet.

"When will you learn?" The speaker said, "I don't know why I protect you. Why, why?" He turned to the killer, "Now get out of here and never come back."

The killer began to walk toward the speaker, his strut was slow and pathetic; he reached out his arms, "Father. Please—"

The speaker snapped, "I told you never to call me, father. I'm a master. Call me, master."

"Yes, master."

"Now lower your arms. As I told you before, you're unfit. You're not fit to have a father or to be a father. That's the reason why we sterilized you when you were a boy. You're alive only by my will and goodness."

"But I'm confused." The killer blurted out once again.

"About what?" The speaker yelled.

"I saw an angel—"

"An angel? That's your problem?" He walked up to the killer, clasped his hands around the killer's cheeks, "You listen to me. Angels aren't real. False religions made them up to scare people." He said, "Trust me. There are no angels, and there is no God. Now, you only feel and think about what I tell you to feel and think." The speaker said, aggressively pushing the killer's head backward as to make his point in a violent display.

The killer backed away and stood in a dark corner.

The speaker sat in the chair and started to take off his makeup. "You're not fit for our society; you're like a person with leprosy." He said, looking at the killer in the mirror, "Just look at yourself, you're an albino." He said nauseatingly. "No good can come from the likes of you! Now leave."

The killer slipped out of the room and went back to the slums. His father's words were apart of who he was; he had heard them a million times before. He believed them. *Why shouldn't he? After all, why would my father lie to me?* He thought.

The darkness swallowed up the day like a dark robe covering a body; it was a blanket, the killer was able to hide; hide his skin, hide his deformity, conceal his shame. The darkness allowed him freedom. His father gave him the ability to force the Angel of Water out of his mind. The killer was back on track; his confusion dissipated like heat drying up the morning dew.

CHAPTER 31

Another tip came in; the killer was spotted going into a slum-apartment-building in the Lower East Side of Manhattan. The police arrived and quickly found the killer's room. Detective Savage called Fox and Helen for them to meet them there, *fast.*

Fox and Helen arrived; squad cars and police barricades blocked the road. Police officers were in full swing; Detective Savage had ordered them to treat this with full priority, "Be careful, don't miss a thing." He ordered his men. Savage was determined to catch the man who killed his best friend's fiancé. Besides, Clara was a close friend, as well. His emotions ramped up, feeling her loss, mixed with anger towards the killer.

A policeman escorted Fox and Helen through piles of garbage; through the entrance, up the squeaky stairs, and to the fourth floor; they made their way to the killer's room. Along the way, people peeked out their doors, then slammed them shut when the police walked by. Babies cried, families argued, drunks smashed bottles and furniture.

The killer's room conveyed a typical slum dwelling; wallpaper displayed yellowish faded surface, seams cracked and peeled out from the wall itself. One chair, one dresser, and one dirty mattress tossed on the floor; and one window – a luxury.

Savage walked up behind them, "Fox, Helen, that was quick," he said, "I'm glad you're both here."

"Good to see you too," Fox said, he looked around, "So, this is the killer's home?"

"Yes, it is."

"Yuck," Helen said, this place stinks; she waved her hand in front of her face.

"Who called in with the tip?" Fox asked.

"A local dry-cleaning service; they noticed the ad and called. One of their delivery boys delivered clothes here."

One of Fox's eyebrows arched upward like a tent, "Have you had a chance to interview the boy?" Fox said.

"We did," Savage said, clearing his throat, "According to the boy, the man who lived here was large and was an albino. . . And there is more; on several occasions when he picked up the man's clothes and took them to be cleaned; his clothes were drenched in blood."

"Incriminating, good," Fox said, "We're getting closer."

"One last thing, Fox." Savage said with heavy breath, "We found Clara's fingerprints."

Fox glared at Savage; speechless, tears welled up in his eyes, "You mean my Clara was in this apartment?" He said, his jaws clenched down. The room started to spin; a torrent of unimaginable thoughts forced its way to the surface . . . He went blind with rage.

Helen grabbed his arm, "Fox! Fox! Are you okay?" She asked, filled with concern.

"No!" He snapped. "I mean, yes," he touched her hand, "I'm fine, sorry for lashing out."

"I understand, Fox, no need to be sorry."

After a few minutes, Fox regained his composure, "Savage," Fox blinked, he wiped the tears from his eyes, "Did you find anything else?"

"We did." He turned and ordered one of his officers to bring him the box. "We found this. It's full of old newspaper clippings and photos."

"May we see the contents of the box?" Fox asked.

"Sure, they've already been dusted for fingerprints."

Fox held the box and ran his fingers through the evidence, "Some of these cutout newspaper clippings feature an orphanage," Fox said, "Strange."

"Do you think he was looking for possible victims?" Helen said.

"Maybe. But wait. Helen, there are two or three pictures in here."

She took them and examined them. "They're kind of blurry and faded. Can you make out who is in this picture?" She handed them back to Fox.

Fox held them up closer to the light streaming through the back window, "They are hard to make out," He said, examining them with a careful eye, "But," silence, "But there is something familiar," He explained, a slight redolent memory wanted to come out, shrouded in a foggy haze as if trying to remember a dream.

Helen picked up another picture, "Fox!" She almost shouted, "Look, look who it is!"

He took the picture; shocked, he did a double-take. He couldn't believe it, "Savage," He called out, "You better take a look at this."

"Savage walked over and took the picture in his fingers. His eyes grew wide and large, "My God!" He said and looked at Fox, "What is the killer doing with this?"

"Your guess is as good as mine, but I have my suspicions."

"You know what this means?" Savage said, "Dr. Black, Dr. Osborn, and Charles Davenport, who are in this picture, may know the killer or worse; might be implicated, one way or the other." He said.

Helen gasped, "Fox, what you said in the park about the killer being of a eugenic marriage— could these three be part of it?"

Fox didn't answer right away, he waited till he thought it through, "Helen, I'm not sure. But what this does is raise more questions."

Savage grabbed the box and called over another officer, "Take this and tag it as evidence."

"Wait," Fox said. "Can I take another look at the first picture?"

"Sure."

Fox reached back into the bag and held the picture up, "I can't make out the face, but there is one thing that stands out like fireworks."

"What's that?" She asked with anticipation.

"Look at the man's hand. See the ring?"

"Yes."

"I've seen that ring before, I just can't place where, but I've seen it." Fox said, "Besides, remember the old lady with her grandson? She noticed a ring on the killer's finger."

"That's right, Fox."

Fox made a note about the ring. "By the way, may we take the picture and a newspaper clipping about the orphanage?" Fox asked. "These may help us find the killer."

"All yours," Savage said.

"Did you find anything else?" Fox asked.

"Just some clothes, nothing out of the ordinary, though."

"What about people who live here or the superintendent?"

"We spoke to everyone in the building, nobody saw, heard, or knows anything, except for the superintendent; he said the man who lived here was queer; he caught him with two call-girls."

"What happened?"

"When the super came to the room, the door was open, the two chippies bolted, and ran like scared jackrabbits."

"Really?"

"Yeah. If you ask me, the super is a weirdo," He chuckled, "I guess it takes one to know one."

Fox interrupted, "Could have been Clara and one of her colleagues?" He said. Deep down Fox sensed it was them, and for some odd reason, he felt relieved, he couldn't explain it – at least at that moment, they got away.

CHAPTER 32

The pressure was on. Fox knew it, Helen felt it; and Savage was on his game like never before, determined; with only one thing on his mind: catch the killer. But more importantly, the killer was on the run. Time was of the essence.

"Helen," Fox said, "The stage we are in right now, is called the *hot zone*, the part where the killer is on the run, we must keep the pressure on until we succeed; if we drop the ball now, the killer may fall through our fingers."

"What's next, Fox." Helen smiled.

"I have been consulting with a friend of mine about this case throughout."

"Who is he?"

"His name is John Simmons—Justice John Simmons. He sits on the United States District Court for the Southern District of New York. I just placed a call in for him to meet us at a restaurant on Park Avenue, right across the street from Central Park."

"You never told me you have a friend who is a judge," Helen said peevishly, although she didn't know why she felt irritated.

Fox reacted a little surprised, "Well, Helen, I have only known you for a short time." Fox cocked his head towards her. A rush of pride covered his face, "Helen," He said, "Are you jealous?"

Helen slapped his shoulder, "Yeah, right." She rolled her eyes. "It's obvious, men are chauvinist. Anyway, why would I be jealous of another man?" She said. "Now, can we move on?"

Judge Simmons was already seated by the time Fox and Helen arrived.

"May I help you?" The headwaiter asked Fox and Helen.

"Yes, we are here to meet someone, his name is Judge Simmons," Fox said, looking around to see if he could spot him.

"Let's see . . .Simmons . . .Simmons," He said out loud, as he ran his finger down the reservation list.

"Oh, yes, Simmons, it's right here," He said, and he picked up two menus, "Right this way, please."

The Silver Spoon was lavish, but not as expensive as Monte's or Angelo. Small circular decorated tables dominated the middle, checkered table clothes covered the tops, and candlelight in the middle; ritzy, but cozy – fit for two, or three. Booths were stationed along the outer walls, creating a sensual ambiance aimed for a comfortable dining experience. The owner had an eye for detail, with his customers in mind.

Judge Simmons saw them approach and stood to greet them, "Hello Fox. Good to see you again." He said, "And who might this be?" He asked and took Helen's hand and kissed the back of it.

Helen blushed, "I'm Miss Helen Carlyle."

"Hi John, Helen is assisting me on this case," Fox said.

"Well, very nice, very nice, indeed." Simmons said, smiling, he noticed Helen was shaking, "What's wrong, Miss Carlyle? You are shivering, are you cold?"

"No, no." She fumbled her words like a gullible young girl. "I'm just a little nervous." She smiled faintheartedly.

"Why?" Judge Simmons asked.

"Well, oh, it'll sound, well, silly, but I have never met a judge before. I mean, judges kind of scare me."

"Ah, my lady, don't be scared, I won't bite." The judge said. "I'm a person." He pinched his skin, "See the red? That hurt. Now, let's sit and chat."

"I called you because there have been some new developments in the case we are working on. I was hoping you can help." Fox said.

"You know my position, Fox. There's not much I can do." He said, "But, as I explained to you before, I'll do whatever I can do to help."

"Remember Clara? My fiancé?"

"Yes."

"The killer killed her."

"What?" The judge said, "I am so, sorry, Fox. If there is anything I can do, please—"

"Yes, you can do something."

"Name it."

Fox pulled out the picture of Dr. Black, Dr. Osborn, and Charles Davenport and placed it on the table. "Take a look at this." He pushed the image in front of the judge.

Judge Simmons took out his glasses and placed them on a deep crevice on his nose marked by years of use. "Hmm."

"Do you know these people?"

"Yes, indirectly. Dr. Osborn is the curator at the American Museum of Natural History. I met him a few times. He has appeared at dinners and other events I've been a guest of. We talked about a range of topics." He tapped the picture, "I know the other one as well. . . Dr. Davenport; yes, I believe he runs the Institute on Long Island, at Cold Spring Harbor." The judge scratched his ear, "As for the other one, I think I've seen him before, but never spoken to him." The judge looked up, "Why? What's this about?"

"We found that picture in a box in the killer's apartment," Fox said.

The judge pushed his body back into the cushion, "Well, that is a game-changer."

"Do you know why the killer would have this picture in his possession?" Fox asked.

"I haven't a clue. Besides, why would I know the mind of a killer?"

"Since these people are high-profile individuals; and so are you, I thought you might know them or at least one of them either on a personal level or on a professional one."

The judge shook his head, "Sorry Fox. I do know of them; and like I said, I've spoken to two of them on occasion, but I don't run with these guys."

"Have you ever had a chance to dine or visit them?"

"Maybe, but I get a bad vibe whenever I'm around them. The group is obsessed with eugenics. That's all they talk about, they're zealots. They believe people ought to be coerced in believing eugenics is a religion." He handed the picture back to Fox.

"I have another question."

"Of course, go ahead."

"Have you heard of Damien Fields?"

"Damien Fields?" He repeated the name, "Let's see," he closed his eyes, straining to see if he knew or heard of him, "I'm not sure, why?"

"Fields was sent to put pressure on Detective Savage for him to stop the investigation."

"Does Savage know who he is?"

"No. But Savage was breathing down my throat to stop, that is, until Clara was murdered," Fox lowered his head, "John, a powerful person or group is protecting the killer, and he or she wants the investigation to end."

Justice Simmons leaned forward, "Let me see, Damien Fields, the name does sound familiar, but I can't place it."

Fox started to feel the meeting was a dead end. "A few days ago, I spotted a man following Helen and I. I confronted him, and he confessed he was hired by Damien Fields to follow me. He swore he was only to keep tabs on us."

"Odd," said judge Simmons, "Your case becomes more dangerous by the day. But the case ballooned from a poor slum child's death, too," he swallowed, "I don't mean to be insensitive, but to Clara's death," his face reeked of serious deep marks of concern for Fox, and now Helen. "Fox, have you thought about just letting this case go? I mean it sounds as though you're in danger, and so is Helen."

"I can't. Clara's killer must be found, or her death will mean nothing."

The judge picked up an empty glass. He twirled it around in his hand. Reflected light lit up his eyes; deep in thought, as if the luster from the glass transported his thoughts to another place. It ushered in an invisible wall of silence, impregnable; Fox and Helen on one side, the judge on the other.

"Fox, I feel cold." She whispered.

"Here, let me give you my coat." He started to take off his jacket and cover her shoulders.

"No, not that kind of cold."

Fox didn't understand Helen's feelings. Nonetheless, he didn't want to disturb the judge, "Please excuse us, we'll be right back. Fox said in a low voice.

The judge ignored them.

They walked to the bathroom hallway, "Helen, what did you mean, you're cold?"

"I'm not sure what I meant; I just felt cold, inside." She said, "I . . .I," She gulped speechlessly, "Oh, I don't know, just a feeling."

"I think I know," Fox said, "Judges go within themselves to examine all the evidence, without bias or prejudice, at least they try to stay neutral. Judges, scholars, and thinkers share the same trait and fate. They are often misunderstood and even laughed at or scorned."

"If you say so," Helen said, her arms wrapped tightly around her body.

"Now, let's go back and hear what the judge has to say," Fox said. "He grabbed her shoulders and looked into her eyes, "Are you okay?"

"Yes. Let's go." She smiled awkwardly.

They arrived back at their table and sat.

"Fox," Judge Simmons said, "Here is what I will do. I will do some digging and see what I can find. Damien Fields is a mysterious person; we need to know who he is and whom he works for. As for those individuals in the picture, I'll see what I can find out."

"Thank you, Judge," Fox said with relief. "The more people we have looking into this case, the better."

"Fox, I can't promise you anything, but I'll try," The judge said, sipping wine.

"Again, thank you for your help," Fox said, thrilled the judge was willing to do more; if anyone could dig into who's high on the totem pole, it would be the judge.

CHAPTER 33

"Where, too, Chum?" The taxi driver asked Fox. His words garbled; he Chewed gum and talked at the same time. Many thought it fashionable or even stylish, but in reality, many people imitated the famous Christy Mathewson, a well-known baseball player. Rumor had it; chewing gum made him imperturbable and unwavering. Or the actress Miss Fay Tincher; the newspapers joked, 'She chews gum for a living, in the movies of course.' But others, chewing gum and talking at the same time was a new shtick.

"To the Old East Side Cemetery," Fox said. "And stop spitting on us." Fox took out his hanky and wiped the side of his face.

The taxi driver rolled his eyes, "On my way." He slammed on the peddle. His jalopy was an older model but still had spunk as it sputtered and burst onto the freeway.

"This is a piece of junk," Helen said to Fox. "And it's filthy."

The taxi driver's beady-eyes flashed in the rear-view mirror at Helen, "Hey, lady, you're talking about my car," He snapped, with a clenched jaw, "This piece of junk, as you call it, is a cash cow, it has fed my family for years."

"Yeah, well it's still dirty." Helen quipped. "It's rubbish, it belongs in a garbage-heap."

"Look, I can let you out right here." He started to pull over.

"No, keep driving," Fox said.

"Then put a muzzle on your dame." His eyes shifted. "I've had many people in that backseat—classy people." He said, fired-up, "Ms. Bluenose, yeah, that's right. I'm talking to you, Ms. clean, the queen of New York, I've had everyone in that seat – from classy to Chippies pleasing their Johns." His eyebrows furled up to see her reaction.

Helen's face turned blood-red. She balled up her fist, bent her arm and elbow ready to strike, "Why you—"

Fox grabbed her hand, "Helen, stop. He's just messing with you; don't let him," He said. Fox turned to the rude driver, "Shut up and drive, Hack."

The driver sped through the streets; his body and facial expressions twitched with pettiness; his eyes shifted back and forth like a snake's tongue.

The taxi drove up to the cemetery, "Here you are Mack."

Fox and Helen got out, and he paid the taxi driver.

"Good luck with that tomato," He said, "That dame has locked-legs."

Helen kicked his car as he sped away; she crossed her arms, defiant, and angry, "Why didn't you let me slug that dolt?"

"Because we were in the slums, it would have been difficult to grab another taxi. Besides, I'll call the company and file a complainant." Fox said. "Isn't that better than being charged with assault and battery?"

"It would have felt good." Helen fumed. "He's a Boob, he deserves one across his kisser," Helen turned to the graveyard. "Fox, why are we at this dark and gloomy place?"

"We believe the killer was here and almost killed again."

"So, he didn't kill at this location?"

"Right."

"So, again, why are we here?" Helen said, stressfully.

"Helen, are you alright? Why are you, acrimonious?" He said.

At that moment Helen realized she was petulant, crotchety, and downright cross, "Oh, I'm sorry Fox. It's just that taxi driver got under my skin." She demurred. "Forgive me?" Helen said, her white teeth flashed.

"We all have bad days," He said, and smiled, "Forgiven, but I do believe there is more to it than just the taxi driver," Fox scratched his goatee; *women are a strange breed,* he thought. "To answer your question, I wanted to take another look; possibly we overlooked something. Also, there was an eyewitness. We never discovered who he or she was. Maybe you and I can find that person, and if so, they might remember more details."

In agreement, Helen shook her head; her bobbed hair bounced around her neck.

Fox was caught off guard. Helen's dress, the way she fit into it; her natural hair, her makeup— all of a sudden, she appeared to be a movie star; a Vamp — slick eyes, and seductive black stockings; raptured in a transcendental moment, her alluring body and charm captured the sunlight. Here, in front of a ghastly graveyard, stood a statuesque Athena, demanding worship.

"Are you all right?" Helen said after she noticed his dream-like state of mind.

"Yes. Yes, of course." Fox said, shaking off the chemistry he experienced. "Come along, no time for lollygagging."

Fox and Helen were lucky; the sun shone bright, but it was getting late. At night, the Old East Side Cemetery was home to roving gangs, drunks, drug addicts, and prostitutes – and of course, the occasional fool who dared ventured in without protection from the cops or bright lights.

The main path was still recognizable, although it was overgrown with weeds; trash and debris hugged the outer parts of the walkway like barnacles clinging to a ship. It twisted, wrapped around, and bent until they reached the back of the graveyard.

They came to a small cul-de-sac. Helen looked around at the dome of the tombstone and noticed something strange, "Fox," She said, "These stones are old."

"What do you mean?"

She kneeled in front of one, "Take a look at this one. The dates date back to the seventeenth century; and look at the artwork, this one is decorated with a skull and bones motif, in the middle is a winged angel." She looked up at Fox, "Don't you think this is strange artwork?"

"It was common years ago," He said, "In fact, take a look around, you'll notice many of the stones have similar etchings, but they are also different from each other, like fingerprints."

Fox walked over to the tombstone where the police found the candles earlier in the investigation, "Helen," He said pointing to Alene Houck' stone, "This is the spot where we suspect the killer was and might have attempted to kill another child."

"Why did he stop?"

"Your guess is as good as mine." He shrugged his shoulders.

"What are we looking for?" Helen asked.

"Anything. Anything out of the ordinary."

The section had been combed through by the police, but people sometimes overlook minute details; a new look and fresh eyes might force the invisible, visible. Besides, Fox didn't have an opportunity to thoroughly search the area earlier. But now, without the police around and Detective Savage breathing down his neck, he had that chance to look closer.

Fox and Helen took their time. They picked through discarded trash; paper bags, bottles, they even checked bubblegum wrappers; nothing was left untouched, but they found nothing. They searched all around the tombstone, the bushes, and trees – still nothing.

Helen became frustrated, she stood in front of Alene Houck's grave, put her hands on her hips, then turned to the other tombstone adjacent to it, "What?" She said out loud.

"What did you say, Helen?"

She walked over and kneeled – facing the tombstone. She brushed the dirt away, and the inscription came into focus. The gravestone was simple, nothing ornate about it, just a name and a date. "Fox," Helen cried out, "What was the name on the other stone?"

"Houck. Alene Houck," He said, "Why?"

"You better take a look at this."

He walked over and kneeled beside her. Fox's eyes widened with disbelief and surprise at the same time. Shocked, "Unbelievable!" He exclaimed. "Helen," he looked into her eyes, you struck gold, this is huge, I mean, this is fantastic, to say the least. How did the police miss this, how did I miss this?" Shaking his head.

"They have the same last name."

"Yes, they do. The name on this stone is *William Houck*."

"Do you think they are related?"

"The odds are great – yes."

"So, you mean I actually found a clue? Not just any clue, but a major one? Wow!" Helen said with pride.

"Take a look at the date Helen: *born January 17, 1902, died May 20, 1902.* Notice anything?"

She paused, "Wait," Helen looked back at Alene's gravestone, then back to William's, then at Fox, "The dates are the same. What does this mean?"

"What it means these two people are related— they are twins." Fox took off his hat and scratched his goatee. *Born January 17* is normal, but both died on the same day? I don't think so. Also, why would the killer come here? Of all the places?"

"Maybe his conscience led him here."

His eyebrows furled and stretched between his eyes. Deep crevices formed across his brow like cracks on the surface of a dried-up desert plateau. "I don't believe this is a coincidence; no, but it's a conundrum, a puzzle to why the killer came here, but whatever the reason, this new evidence will aid in finding the killer."

"In what sense?" Helen asked.

"Well, take a look at the whole picture so far. The murder of a poor child opened Pandora's box. The cult we discovered might have something to do with these graves."

"In what way?"

"It's all beginning to come together." Fox looked at Helen, "Remember the eugenic marriage?"

"Yes."

"I have a hunch," Fox said. "I'm willing to bet there's nobody in this grave, marked William Houck. Don't ask me how I know, I just know, I have that gut feeling, and my hunches usually pan out; but the eugenic marriage gave birth to a set of twins, I believe the girl died young, but William—"

Helen didn't know what to say, she was still a little overwhelmed at the reality of it all, and all of the machinations that made this happen.

"Now," Fox said, "Let's see if we can find the person who called it in, the eyewitness."

"Where do we start?"

"Just look around, pick one," Fox said, pointing to slum dwellers.

People were sleeping; others huddled together in groups of three or four sharing a bottle of liquor, "Fox, do you expect to get a straight answer from this lot?"

"All we can do is try."

"Okay, that one," Helen pointed to a man leaning against a large oak tree. Threadlike strains of moss dangled from its branches like gray hair flowing down the head of an old woman. The slum-dweller was disheveled, holding a liquor bottle in one hand and brandishing a cigarette in the other; sucking and blowing out white smoke as it blended into the hanging moss; middle-aged, wearing a pair of overalls.

"Hi," Fox said.

The man looked at Fox, his eyes were tense, but his matted face relaxed, "Hi." He said, and he belched up a significant hiccup as if a frog jumped from his throat. Helen pulled back; his breath contaminated the immediate air around them.

"I'm Fox this is Helen, may we ask you some questions?"

He looked at them, and took another swig out of his bottle, "Sure," He said, his lips glistened.

"We are looking for a man or woman who called the police the other day, they reported they saw a man with a child," Fox said, pointing to the tombstone, "Would you know such a person?"

"Maybe," The drunk said tightlipped.

"Fox, let's move on," Helen said, "He's drunk, he doesn't know anything."

"I know plenty!" He said as if offended.

"Then, tell us if you overheard a man talking to a little child," Fox said.

"Fine." His body swayed like the wind. "What's in it for me?"

"Hooch." Fox expressed, "I'll give you money so you can buy more liquor."

The drunk held out his palm and wiggled his fingers, "Well?"

Fox pulled out a five-dollar bill, and put it in his palm, "There, now talk."

He grinned, revealing blackened teeth. He shoved the five-dollar bill deep into his pocket, "I can't do you here." He said, his lips puckered.

"What? What was that?" Helen said.

The drunk waved his arm holding the bottle, like a conductor, "He said, 'I can't do you here." He said as he stumbled, "That's what the man said. "Now, blow."

Fox and Helen walked away.

"What did that mean? Really? – We can't entertain the words of a Booze-hound. Let's find another person." Helen said.

"Helen, wait for a moment. I know this may sound crazy, but what if he did hear those words?"

"Okay, if he did, we don't know if he heard it correctly, and if he did— we don't know what it means."

"Think about it. If the killer's twin is buried here, as we discussed, and the other grave is empty, then something in his mind might have stopped him from killing the child."

"Maybe. But how do we know for sure?" Helen said.

"We don't, we follow the evidence and clues we have. Then incorporate new information as we go along and develop theories that will help us find the killer. That's all we can do, but this piece of information, if true, may give us insight into the killer's mind."

Fox and Helen spent another hour asking questions from others, but nobody was willing to offer anything.

CHAPTER 34

After a long and needed sleep, Fox and Helen were rested.

"Helen," Fox said, after taking a sip of coffee sat his cup on the table, "We need to investigate the names on the tombstones, who, if anyone is buried there, and possibly why the dates are the same on both headstones."

"How do we do that?" Helen said as she covered her lips with red lipstick.

"We visit the county records office and search for Alene and William Houck."

"How would that help us find the killer?"

"If we can find their records, that will tell us who their birth parents were unless they have been tampered with." Fox pulled out his pocket watch to see what time it was, "Remember, we discussed the eugenic marriage?"

"Yes."

"Someone has gone to great links to hide not only the child's identity but also themselves and the child's parents. If we can find out at least one of the parent's identity, that will lead us to the killer; a hunch I have."

"Parents? What if they are dead, or disappeared? That could lead us in a different direction." Helen said as she put her pocket mirror in her purse; she pressed her red lips together and released them as if releasing two red balloons, full of buoyancy.

"I don't think so, Helen. We have to follow up on all our clues and hunches. I hope if we find the killer's parents or parent, that will lead us to the killer."

Helen agreed, but she still had some doubts, "I understand, but this is my first case, so I'll take your word for it."

"At this point, it doesn't matter if his parents are alive or dead. What matters is I believe he has a deep connection to them, and as I stated earlier in the Park, he is trying to appease someone or something by killing."

Helen shook her head, "It seems all very strange, Fox. I mean, I have never heard of such a thing. Sure, we have all heard of people killing others for jealousy, for love, and gangs killing over drugs, alcohol, and turf— but this is like, well when John Carter was transported to another world, the novel, *A Princess of Mars.* Remember Fox?"

"Yes, it's like this case has transported us to a world where normalcy is cast to the wind; where morals are turned upside down, where dark figures parade in the open like a marching band."

Vital Statistics was in the basement of the Clerk of the Court. Fox knew the room thoroughly; he had used it on many occasions. Vital statistics gave the name of the person, birth, and birthplace, parents, and when and what the deceased died from.

The room was large; crammed packed with rows and rows of filing cabinets. Three windows were positioned high up, to let sunlight filter in. Added to that, the city installed incandescent lights on the ceilings. Fox flipped the switched, light flickered on, buzzed like artificial hummingbirds. They were more of a nuisance and an annoyance, but most people blocked it out. Others grit their teeth and bear it until they were able to escape modernity's clutches.

"This place needs a good cleaning," Helen said, disgustingly. She sneezed, "This place is dusty."

"I agree, but you'll forget about the dust after we get to work," Fox said. "Besides, it shouldn't take too long." Fox looked around the room, "Helen, try to find the 'H' section for Houck."

She started with the 'A's, moving from one filing cabinet to the next. Helen finished with the 'A's and moved along to the 'B' section. "We could be here all day." She said. "There are so many people."

In the meantime, Fox searched an area where a chaos of files consumed a corner table. "Their filing method is not so great," Fox said, dust erupted in the air.

"You can say that again." Said Helen. "I just opened one cabinet, what a mess. They need a good librarian." She said and giggled.

Fox continued skimming through stacks of unfiled folders. Some started with 'H,' but most of them weren't even labeled. "Some of these files are over twenty years old," Fox said. He picked up one file; he blew the dust off its cover; it was as if an ancient artifact was hidden for millennia and now just uncovered.

"Ah!" Helen expressed, "I found it, the 'H' section."

"Good job, Helen."

Fox met Helen, and they began to search for Houck. "My goodness," Helen said, "There's a lot of Houck's, I would have never guessed. It seems such a rare name. Let's see," She flipped through the files like they were buttons on a typewriter, "Houck . . . Houck . . . Houck, Alene Houck. I found it." She handed the file to Fox.

Fox began examining the file, "The dates correspond with the dates on the tombstone, but," There was a pause, then he began to read again, "This file doesn't show the father or mother, strange."

"Does it show what she died from?"

"Let's see," Fox ran his finger down the page, "Yes, yes it does. She died of Smallpox." Fox looked at Helen, "Why would a child this young die of Smallpox?"

"Many children die of Smallpox Fox."

"This young? — Maybe she had a weak immune system."

"Does her file say anything else?" Helen said.

"Yes, it was the New York Foundling Hospital that buried her."

"Then we need to go there next, right?"

"Right, but there is something else in this file."

"What is it?"

Fox snapped his finger, "Just as I suspected, Alene Houck had a twin brother." They looked at each other, "His name was is William, William Houck."

Helen's emotions jumped like a rabbit, "Could that be the killer?" Helen asked.

"Possibly, Helen, possibly." Fox said, "At least we have our next lead, New York Foundling Hospital."

"Let's find William's file; here, I'll check," Helen said, as she thumbed through the tabs . . . "Fox, this is strange, William has no file, at least not here."

"I didn't think you would find William's file, it never existed."

"But why would someone make a tombstone, put a name on it, buy a spot in the graveyard, and put the marker there and not create a file?"

"Who knows; maybe they ran out of time, or plain sloppy," Fox said, "But at least this wasn't a dead-end."

CHAPTER 35

Since the police found the killer's room, he was home-less, on the run, and hiding. His father would protect him from the police, other than that that is all he could expect from him; besides, going to his father for help is like plunging his hand into hot boiling water.

Night fell on Manhattan like a knife; especially East River, where the killer found himself. Bums and tramps huddled around barrels of fire to keep warm; the liquid blaze flickered, it could be seen for blocks like tongues of fire licking and snapping at the night air; like Dante's Inferno, the dark river reflected ripples of the reddish hue as if looking into oblivion.

The killer walked past the bums. Large buildings stretched far like long-running carpets; then, openings appeared. Clotheslines fastened from each building like ship cables; linen and clothes draped over them; the wind-tossed them about like flags; at first, they startled the killer – it was as if thousands of birds took to flight all at once.

A dark figure came out of nowhere and bumped into the killer, "I'm sorry." He said. His words slurred and were almost incoherent. He spilled liquor on the killer's clothes.

The killer pushed him back and drew his knife, ready to strike.

The drunk didn't realize the killer was about to kill him, "Here," He said, "Let me clean that off for you." He tried to wipe the liquid off with a handkerchief.

The killer was about to plunge his knife into his chest, then a hint of light flickered from the side of his eye. He stopped and looked. Across the street was an old, abandoned church. He looked at the drunk and drew his knife back, ready to thrust, then something stopped him. He relaxed his arm and looked at him, then shoved the bum to the ground, "Scram!" He expressed with disdain.

He followed the faint light across the street. Every step he took, he thought of his father. *My Father is proud of me,* he thought. *How could he not be?* The closer he got to the Church, he shook his head in a torrent of violence, as if there was an internal struggle.

The light that caught in his eye, now morphed into a mission to stop whatever was going on in his head. First, the angel of water, now this. *I'll put a stop to it once and for all.* He said to himself as he rolled his fingers into a tight fist. But he didn't smash through the front door, he went down the side alley of the Church and stopped.

He leaned against the other building; his body slid down the brick wall into filth. He was still angry; his pulse raced, his face turned red, his insides were ready to explode like a volcano. He laid his throbbing head onto his clasped fists. *I must please my father. I must.* He thought. *Nothing must stop me. Nothing!*

"Want some bread?" Spoke a weak and small voice.

The killer's head jerked up. There stood— to his dismay— a young girl holding a piece of bread in her hand, offering it to him. Overwrought, the killer acted like a trapped wildcat. He slapped the girl's hand, and the food flew against the wall. His violence exploded like someone ran a match down the side of a matchbox.

The girl began to cry; the killer grew angrier, he stood, and the haggard little girl ran off. As he fumed, images populated in his retina. He waved his hand as if to brush them aside, but they remained and even intensified. Light bounced off a stain glass window attached to the Church. He stopped the struggle; he focused, then an image came into view as he stepped backward— it was an image of a Shepard holding a staff protecting his sheep.

Stunned.

He walked around to the back of the building; the back door was jammed, he rammed it with his shoulder, it flew open, dozens of doves flew everywhere and out the door.

The killer's eyes were bloodshot, he walked inside, waving his fist around. "God!" He called out with a ruff voice. "You're a monster!" He screamed. He beat his chest like an ape as if challenging God to fight. He stopped. There was silence.

He went on another rampage. He broke pews; thrashed the pulpit to pieces, and threw songbooks against the wall. He stomped and cursed. Then, he stopped, out of breath, he sat in the silent noise of a forgotten old Church. He sat for a long time; ages seemed to pass. Sweat rolled down his forehead as his face hung low as a vagabond lost to civilization.

Time slowed; he felt his heartbeat as if each pump corresponded to each tick of a clock. *Why am I here?* He thought. For a moment, the killer had forgotten his rage. Lights from a passing car lit up the church revealing a ruff looking cross nailed to the back wall. Something struck him in the heart; hot and penetrating. He found a kerosene lamp and lit it.

The killer gawked at the wooden structure. It wasn't made of gold or silver, no jewels were embedded around the edges, it was merely a wooden cross. *Why would some-one leave this behind?* He thought. *It was abandoned. Just like me.*

On the pew next to him, he felt a book – it was a Bible. He picked it up, opened it, and began to read out loud, "'but Jesus said, 'Let the little children come to me and do not hinder them, for to such belongs the king-dom of heaven.'"

With reverence, he closed the book and placed it next to himself. *But my father?* He thought. *But this father?* He thought.

The killer blew out the flame; the darkness engulfed him, he sat for what seemed to be hours, but somehow, a light still burned. He got up and walked out the back entrance. He came in driven by anger, and hate; resent-ment and bitterness were all he knew; now, something changed . . . He didn't understand.

CHAPTER 36

Helen's phone rang, "Fox, is that you?" Detective Savage said in a huff.

"Nice to hear from you too," Fox said.

"No time for decorum Fox, we have another situation on our hands."

Fox felt uneasy as if something was about to pop out of his chest, "No, not another death."

"Not exactly," Savage said, slowing down his speech.

Fox let out an air of relief, "Then what happened?"

"We had a call late last night from a married couple. They claimed their child was taken."

"Abductions happen all the time," Fox said, "What does that have to do with this case?"

"The parents said they saw the abductor." Savage cleared his throat, "They said he was a large man and an albino."

"Did they actually see the child being taken by this person?"

"Well, not exactly. The parents were in the slums waiting in a soup line to get fed. The soup line is located in lower East Side— near Grace Church. The church has been abandoned for years."

"Yes, I think I remember driving by it on several occasions. Now, it is a de-facto landmark, of sorts to the locals."

"We scrambled all the police we could muster. The police teams are searching every alleyway, abandoned building, and graveyard as we speak," Savage said, "It's only a matter of time before we find the child."

"I think it's too early to jump to conclusions, Detective; besides, something doesn't make sense. If the parents didn't see their child abducted by the killer, then how do they know he took the child? Better yet, why are you jumping the gun and assuming it was the killer?"

"Look here, Fox," Savage said bluntly, "A child was abducted. We have the killer's description near where the parents last saw their child." Savage paused and sucked in the fresh air, "It all fits. We have the killer's last location. We will find the killer . . . Now—"

Fox interrupted, "I share your desire to find the killer, Savage, remember, Clara was my fiancé?"

The mention of Clara's name stopped Savage in his tracks, even though his thoughts brewed deep within and his heartbeat with excitement. "Yes, you're correct, Fox," Savage said. "It's just I believe the killer abducted this child," Savage stated his position in a claimer voice.

"As I expressed, I want to catch the killer as much as you, I'm trying to remain calm and think this through so as not to make any grave mistakes – we must be absolutely correct."

"Then, explain your objections a little more," Savage said.

"Well, it's not that I object that this could be the killer, it's that the more we have discovered, this isn't the killer's MO; the killer had always been careful not to be seen abducting children in the open."

"So, you are saying, the killer is cautious?"

"Yes. Everything the killer does is for a purpose and a reason— he doesn't make mistakes."

There was a long pause on the other end of the line, then Savage spoke up, "Maybe. Maybe Fox." It was as if Savage was thinking out loud. "But there is something else, Fox."

"What?"

"When we searched inside the church, we found someone had recently been in there; someone destroyed pews, the pulpit shattered; it was as if two or more people fought each other."

"Bums. It was your local alcoholics and drug addicts," Fox said, "What makes that unusual?"

"That alone doesn't make it unusual. But we found a note nailed to the cross."

"A note?" Fox's left eyebrow arched, "What did it say."

"It said, 'The unfit must die.'"

There was silence. The air stiffened, Fox couldn't even hear his own breath; Savage waited for a response, Fox's face changed, color evaporated as if he turned into a ghost.

Helen was standing by him. She couldn't help but notice his changed complexion, "Fox, what is it?" She said; shaking his arm. He remained silent as if encased in ice, "Fox," She shook him again. Her upper torso limped forward at the thought of another death.

Fox blinked his eyes, "Yes, Helen, I hear you." Fox expressed. "Just one moment."

"I understand, carry on, Detective," He said, "Helen and I will continue on our end, we'll touch base with you shortly," Fox said before he hung up the receiver.

Fox turned to Helen and translated the conversation between himself and Savage.

Helen collapsed in her chair. Her arms fell to the sides like wet spaghetti. Air rushed out of her lungs with the force of an avalanche. The thought of another death broke her heart. She cried, "Not another child!" She closed her eyes as if trying to shut the horror from her mind. She grabbed her throat, started to hyperventilate, "Fox, I don't know if I can take much more of this."

Fox knelt beside her, took her hand, held it tight, "Helen, look at me."

She waved her head back and forth, "No, Fox. No. When will this nightmare end?" She said, desperately.

Fox stroked her arm; he grabbed her body, forced it to his; he embraced her with all the comfort he could muster. "I got you, Helen. I'm here." He felt her heartbeat, her erratic breathing.

Tears gushed – she cried out, "What are we going to do?" She said. Her strained voice sounded like a clutch in an old model-T. The more she cried, the deeper her breathing increased; it was gut-wrenching. Her insides were gnarled and twisted.

Fox held her, he let her cry. No words could soothe or take away her pain. *Perhaps words would make it worse.* Fox thought. *Just let her get it out of her system. She needed this catharsis.* Fox held her for a long while, her outburst slowed to a whimper. She started to fall asleep in his arms, he picked her up and carried her to the bedroom. He changed her clothes into nightclothes and tucked her in.

Helen experienced things most people never go through. Something had to be done and fast. Fox determined.

Fox woke the next morning. His back ached from sleeping on the living room couch. Neither did it help his cracked rib, and his throbbing purple bruises. He let Helen sleep in the bed no matter what apartment they stayed at—his or hers— it was the gentlemanly thing to do; besides, it was the right thing to do. Nonetheless, at times, her beauty and personality drove Fox crazy. It couldn't be helped; he was a normal red-blooded man like any other.

Helen was still in bed; Fox determined it was for the best, she needed more rest. After he showered, he fixed breakfast, and he sat in the living room with a cup of coffee. He looked over his notes and brushed them aside.

Helen needs time to relax, a day off. He said to himself. A killer on the loose, a child murdered, Clara, everything compounded, she simply collapsed under the weight. Everyone has a breaking point; Helen was no different, but Fox marveled at her strength and perseverance, given the fact she had never been in a situation like this.

Fox tried to think of the best place for a getaway. *Maybe take in a silent film and dinner? Ah, Central Park,* but he ruled that out as well, it may remind her of the case. *What Helen needed was a new scenery, she needed to experience fun and relaxation. She needed to get away from murder, cults, intrigue, and danger.* He thought. Fox snapped his fingers; I've got just the thing.

It was around 9:00 in the morning, Fox walked into her bedroom; she tossed and rolled around under the covers; she peeked out, yawned and stretched her arms in the air, "Good morning." She said.

Fox pulled the drapes back, the sun blazed into the room like an angry sun god, "Good morning, sunshine." He said, smiling.

Helen's eyes squinted as if she was caught naked in the shower. "Fox. What are you doing?" She said as she covered her head with a blanket, trying to block out the sun, "I'm not awake yet."

"I've got good news."

"Good news?" She said; happily, her eyes glowed with excitement, "What is it?"

"It's a surprise. Now get up and get ready, we're going for a ride." Fox said mischievously, with a twinkle in his eye.

She felt his tease, "No, tell me now," She demanded teasingly.

"Let's just say we're going for a jaunt, we are taking the day off; in the meantime, I'll fix your breakfast. Now, chop, chop."

The taxi drive refreshed Helen. Air rushed in the open windows, tossed her hair around; the scent of her perfume was like seductive flowers. She still didn't know where they were going, this made her curious and excited.

By the time they drove over the Brooklyn Bridge, she had a pretty good idea where they were headed. She smiled and nudged Fox's arm, "So, let me guess." She said, her tone playful and with slanted eyes.

Fox acted innocent and coy, "Where do you think we are going?"

"Hmm," she tapped his hand, "I think we are going to Coney Island!" She stated gushingly, she couldn't help herself, like she was a schoolgirl on a field trip. She wrapped her arms around Fox's arm. And laid her cheek up against his dress coat.

Fox caved to her bubbly charm, "You figured it out." He smiled. Fox was taken back; magic permeated the taxi like a warm snowy day. He couldn't put his finger on it; but something was taking place—and it was good, even his bones felt good.

They reached Coney Island. Fox paid the taxi driver, and they walked into the park. "So many people," Helen said.

"Yes, it's a bit crowded," Fox said, "Did you know Helen, Coney Island is the largest amusement park in the United States?"

"No, but I bet it's the largest in the world."

The sun was in full force, not a cloud in the sky, but not a scorcher either.

Married couples with their children populated the park; couples on dates also seized the day to experience different rides and different parks Coney Island had to offer.

Most people dressed as if they were at church; older gentlemen wore traditional clothing; suites, an assortment of puff ties or Ascots which wrapped around the neck of upturned collars, topped off by a wave of Bowler hats crisscrossing throughout the Park; they held walking sticks, and canes like kings holding scepters. In many respects, their fashion was declarative statements telling the world of their class and conservatism.

Younger men wore knickers with long socks. Others wore Oxford bags, when they walked, they sounded like tents flapping in a windstorm.

Women, too, expressed this dichotomy. Some adorned themselves in elegant dresses decorated with floral designs. Like men and their canes, women wield parasols like queens. They twirled them like cotton candy, throwing off an array of colors to dazzle and tantalize their husbands, or their boes, and or impress onlookers. Setting aside the fact they protected their delicate white skin from the sun; all in all, parasols added to their overall ensemble.

Younger women wore sheer dresses that revealed more skin than their older counterparts. Instead of large or small brimmed hats, they wore cloche hats, that resembled shower caps, but a bit more stylish.

Younger women, not all, pushed the envelope; morals shifted, mores were challenged; some smoked, they were called flappers.

Helen clapped her hands like a dolphin, "Let's go to the Wonder Wheel." She said. "I've wanted to ride it since they finished it."

"Okay, off to the Wheel."

They bought tickets and got into one of the cars. After a short time, the giant wheel shifted and began to turn like a screw. It slowly lifted them; top of tree-lines came to eye-level view, "My word!" Expressed Helen. "Look, look at the Atlantic. See all blue?"

"It's beautiful," Fox said, his focus only on Helen; as the wind gently lifted her hair, her eyes bright as the ocean; then he made his move, it wasn't calculated, it was spontaneous, natural, like eating or drinking – he wrapped his arm around her shoulders.

"Fox! Can you see it?" She pointed outward.

"You mean the Statue of Liberty?" He said, "Yes, it's grand. Very statuesque." As he drew his eyes back to into Helen's glow.

The wheel inched upwards till they reached the top, then it stopped, leaving the cars swinging in mid-air. Helen wrapped her arms around Fox, "Why have we stopped?"

Other passengers became uneasy; one, then another rider yelled below for clarification, Fox heard a woman cry; anxiety grew from one car to the next until the whole wheel was electrified as if it became one giant human semi-conductor.

Fox looked down and saw a man pulling a seven-foot lever, he shrugged his shoulders to another man standing beside him wearing overalls. It didn't take long before everyone on the ride realized the wheel lost power, and they were stuck. *Panic.* Panic-stricken, one man tried to climb down, people watched in horror as he slipped and fell. Men came out of nowhere, they carried him off, perhaps to ease tension, but it wasn't clear if he was dead or alive.

"Stay calm," A man yelled from the ground holding a hand-held-horn in his hand, "Please, stay calm. We lost power. We will have it fixed shortly. We have everything under control." The man's voice, in some strange way, seemed to calm the passengers.

All of a sudden, Helen's eyes twinkled; she smiled mischievously, "Fox," She said as she snuggled deeper into his embrace, "We're all alone," Her words laced and threaded with seductiveness. Helen was bold, but not so bold to break decorum. She teased, she implied, but it was the man's job to make overt advances. Besides, she was single and had a reputation to protect.

Fox fell for her silent coup. He looked deep into her eyes; her lips shined; they were wet with anticipation; he moved closer, lips close to each other, he gently kissed her. He drew back to see her face; her eyes were focused and wild; then their lips locked – passion erupted around their heads like tiny seeds blown into midair from a dandelion. Their desire for each other was like fire, Fox suddenly stopped and pulled away, "I can't." He said guilt-ridden.

"Why?" Helen said, feeling hurt, her voice trembled, "You don't find me attractive?"

"It's not that."

"Then, what?" She asked, but deep down she knew the reason, she just wanted to hear it for herself.

"It's Clara, well, you know what happened. I still love her, and I feel like I'm betraying her memory."

Helen hung her head, "I know. I do understand Fox. It's just that, well," She bit her tongue and wouldn't let Fox know she fell in love with him.

"Well? go ahead, Helen."

Helen stroked his arm, "It's nothing."

"Helen," Fox said, "I need to finish this case before I can even think about moving on. For now, let's keep this a Platonic relationship." He looked at her, "You do understand, right?"

"Yes, of course." She plastered a smile on her face, to cover her sadness. The wheel started to move, and they were on their way.

The ride came to a halt. Fox and Helen decided to walk along Riegelmann Boardwalk. The wind was crisp and delightful. "Fox, I'm hungry." She said.

Fox looked around and spotted a hot dog stand. "How about a hot dog?"

"Sure."

"That'll be a nickel apiece and a nickel apiece for the drinks," said the vendor.

Fox paid the man, "Helen, let's walk over to the edge and eat over there; we can put our food and drinks on the wide board stretching up and down the walkway; at the same time take in the view." By the time they arrived, Fox had eaten half of his hotdog.

"Nathan's Hot Dog," Helen said. "I've haven't heard of this kind before."

"Me neither. They're new, I think," Fox said, "They will probably be out of business by this time next year."

They laughed and soaked in the park's sights, thrills, and fun.

It was late by the time Fox dropped Helen off at her apartment. Earlier that day, he had arranged to meet up with Savage at his residence to discuss the case and any new developments. Instead of taking a taxi, Fox hopped on the trolley car. Although the trolley was full of people, he managed to find a seat. The trolley car clanked along on the rails like a factory popping out Model-Ts every second. The steel noise became white-noise for people living close to the tracks. Fox glared out the window watched people standing, walking, and talking. They appeared to be moving in slow motion. Others looked like mannequins, in store windows, showing off new fashions from Paris.

The trolley car filled to capacity after a few more stops. People were stacked together like pieces of wood, eager to go home. Others, pockets stuffed with dough, couldn't wait to blow it on booze and dames.

The ride to Detective Savage's apartment took about an hour. Fox stepped off the trolley and walked up to Detective Savage's front door. He rang the bell.

Savage opened the door, "Hello, Fox, come in, come in." He said.

"Hi, Savage. How was your day."

"Fine, just fine," Savage said, "Here, let me take your hat and walking stick." He hung them on the cherry hat and coat rack close to the front door.

"Thanks."

"You're welcome. Come in Fox and sit."

Savage's apartment was small. Cops didn't get paid much, except for higher-ranking officers. What they did have was a decent pension to retire on. After many New York policemen retired, they would leave New York, move to another state where the cost of living was cheaper. Many would even pick-up part-time jobs as security officers, while others became private detectives.

"Since it's late, I'll get right to business," Fox said, "Are there any new developments?"

Savage emerged from his little kitchen holding a glass of ginger ale, "Would you like something to drink Fox?"

"No, thank you. Maybe later."

"Yes. We still haven't located the abducted child. It's unfortunate."

"Maybe not," Fox said.

"What do you mean?"

"Well, if you haven't found the child's body, there might be a chance she's alive, albeit, a slim one at that."

"I hope your right."

"Anything else about the missing child?" Fox asked.

"Yes. We interviewed many people, and a few did corroborate the parent's statement, they spotted an albino in the area. Two drunks even witnessed the albino going into the church. They heard screaming and yelling; glass shattering and wood snapping. The hullabaloo was nothing short of hell-raising, violent, and hurricane-like."

"So, you're confident the child was taken by the killer?"

"Yes," Savage said confidently, "It's only a matter of time before we find the poor child's body." Savage hung his head in despair. "Fox, I have to be honest with you about something."

"Sure, go ahead."

"I hate this case. I hate my job. I have seen so much bloodshed, I'm tired, plain tired," Savage said, wiping his forehead, "Before Clara was murdered, I was able to separate my private life from the murders, from scumbags, and this whole seedy underworld of darkness." He rubbed his eyes, "Now, now I can't; it haunts me day and night, my dreams are soaked with blood and dead bodies." Savage's voice strained as if the strings on a guitar were old and about to break.

"Old friend," Fox said, "Stay the course, you have other friends and me; don't slip backward." Fox understood where Savage was going, he was an alcoholic. It was a way to self-medicate himself and numb his senses from a horrid and wretched world he had to face every day.

Savage eyes opened; thin, stringy-like red-lines fractured around the whites of his eyes. "I'm trying to hold on Fox. I'm trying."

"When was the last time you had a full night of sleep?"

Savage scratched his head, "It's been a while. My mind won't stop. Clara and others— Fox, we have to find him and end this nightmare."

"Yes, and we will, but what you need is a good night's sleep. We can't afford to lose you." Fox looked around the room, "Do you have any tonic, sleeping pills, something that will help you sleep?"

"I think I might have some in the Kitchen Cabinet."

"Good, right after I leave, please take it and go to bed." Fox looked at him, "We need you."

"Will do. Oh, I almost forgot. Your friend Justice John Simmons phoned me this afternoon."

"Why didn't he call me?" Fox responded.

"He tried, but you weren't home."

"Oh, that's right, I took Helen to Coney Island."

"By the way, how was it? I've never been there," Savage said.

"We had a great day. Helen needed it, and to be frank with you, so did I," Fox said, "That's what you need too, you need a day off."

"Not until we find the killer." Savage snapped.

Fox felt his ears clobbered. Detective Savage's response was brusque, weighted down with an underlining force of fortitude. In one respect, it could be taken as insulting. On the other hand, Fox knew it wasn't directed towards himself; it was towards the killer and the overall case.

Fox had known Savage long enough to understand what he meant and how he expresses himself. "I understand. I do." Fox said. "Now, what did the judge tell you?"

"He said, Damion Fields is an attorney. He works for the state attorney's office. Mr. Fields has a reputation for attacking and bringing down businesses. Most of his cases have been overturned by the state Supreme Court and even the Supreme Court of the United States. He is never reprimanded or punished for his actions. In fact, his power has grown over the years."

"Did the judge say why Damien has this level of power, given the fact of his lousy track record? I mean, most people would have been fired long ago."

"He doesn't know why. All I know, Damien is a blue-nose, a little bug, a pencil pusher." Savage laughed, "One day when he was in my office, I scared him so bad he pissed on the floor." Savage burst out loud laughing. His full belly rolled like logs spinning in water.

Fox laughed along with Savage. . .. "Did the judge say anything else?"

"That's about it. The judge believes Fields is a dead-end."

"Extraordinary a man can do so much harm and get away with it."

"Yes, it is, Fox. I did a little snooping myself on Mr. Fields. The word is, he's dirty."

"In what way?"

"He's bought and paid for. If larger businesses want to squash competition, they hire Fields to go after them. Money talks."

"But why is he interested in me and this case?" Fox said, "Why is he butting into a homicide investigation? Why would any business be interested in a murder case?"

"Maybe there's no business behind Damien." Said Savage. "Maybe he is a gun for hire, to the highest bidder."

Fox fell silent. He thought about what Savage had just related to him, "This case has strangely drawn attention from every angle," Fox said, "Perhaps you might be onto something. If, in fact, he is a hired gun, who hired him and why?"

"That's for another night. I'm tired, Fox."

Fox got up and walked towards the door. He retrieved his hat and walking stick. "Yes, for another night," Fox said. "Now, remember to take your tonic and get a good night's sleep."

A broad smile filled Savage's face like a half-moon. "Fine, I will. Have a good night."

"Goodnight."

After Fox left, Savage went to the bedroom and opened the bottom drawer to his dresser. He pulled out a brand-new bottle of whiskey and walked back into the living room and sat back down. Every fiber in his being longed for its taste. His heart palpitated at the thought of feeling its moist texture run down his throat. He held the bottle up to the light, sweat broke out on his brow, his eyes widened. He pulled the bottle close to his body as if he was holding a child.

Just one swig. One taste and it will calm my nerves, Savage said to himself. *One small glass. I can handle it.* He wrapped his thick fingers around the cap. He tightened down on it like a vice grip, then he released it from his grasp. *What am I doing? I must be crazy. Fox is right. I can do this. I don't need liquor to get me through the night.*

Savage placed the bottle in his lap. He exerted his will over his desire. His last thoughts betrayed his first thoughts. The struggle inside of him continued for hours. Back and forth, like two wrestlers were competing for a prize. He had been here many times.

Fox took the trolley home. After it turned and disappeared down the street, two goons, hiding in an alleyway, stepped out of the fog. They wore blue pinstriped suits, black ties, and white derby hats. One of them had a sharp sword-like nose, the other had baggy cheeks and a double chin. They glared in silence; they had been dogging Fox and Helen all day.

CHAPTER 37

Fox and Helen's short vacation paid off. Helen felt like a dayflower, refreshed, and new. There was a spring in her step. But back to reality. Several murders and now a missing child. A killer was on the loose. Skullduggery surrounded the whole case like a moat-encircled around a medieval castle. It stunk. The entire case stunk. Fox was more determined than ever to solve the case and expose the mystery. Their next step was to investigate the orphanage that buried Alene and William Houck.

The taxi ride to 175 East 68th Street didn't take long. The Foundling Asylum was founded in 1869 by the Sisters of Charity to take in abandoned children for adoption.

Fox and Helen walked through the front doors, the help desk buzzed with life, "Can you help us please?" Fox said to one of the sisters.

A young nun looked up. She wore the usual habit; black tunic, form-fitting coif that fitted all around her face, covering her head, a white wimple draped over her shoulders like curtains, "Yes, how may I help you?" She said, her eyes peering through thick-rimmed glasses.

"May we speak to someone in charge?"

"Yes, what are your names?"

"This is Miss Helen Carlyle, and I'm James P. Fox, a private investigator."

"Wait, right here." She left. Nuns and children floated in and out of rooms like fish in the water. To outsiders, it was strange, bazar, and even a little unsettling to see so many children without parents. Respectable parents struggled to understand why any parent would give birth to a child only to abandon them. But nuns and other Christian charity workers understood full well human plight and depravity.

Within a few minutes the nun returned, "Mr. Fox, Sister Janice will see you now. Take the hallway to my right, and it's a few offices down on the left. You'll see her name on the door."

Fox knocked, "Come in," Sister Janice said.

Fox opened the door, and they walked in. Her office wasn't large or fancy. No lush chairs or plush couches; an office-appropriate for a charity. A picture of Pope Pius XI hung on the wall behind her desk.

"Hello, Sister Janice," Fox said, "I'm Mr. Fox—a private detective, and this is my assistant, Miss Helen Carlyle."

"Oh, yes. I have heard of you, Mr. Fox." She said as she stood to her feet. Her face was animated. "I have read many of your cases in the newspapers," They shook hands, "Please, sit."

"Nice to meet a fan," Fox said and smiled feeling flattered.

Sister Janice was a short, round woman. She had a bubbly personality. A happy tension came across her face, she clasped her hands together like a person ready to watch a silent film. All she needed was popcorn. "Indeed, I'm one of your fans, but I'm not the only one," she said as she chuckled, "A number of the sisters here follow your excursions and have read every case you've been involved in."

Fox was a little taken back, "Impressive, you flatter me, Sister Janice. I didn't realize I had such a fan base among Roman Catholic nuns."

"Just one moment please." Sister Janice said.

She picked up her phone and dialed, "Hello, Sister Plum, this is Sister Janice. You're not going to believe who's in my office?" There was silence, "It's Mr. Fox." Fox and Helen heard an incoherent crackle come from the receiver, Sister Janice shook her head up and down, then hung up the phone. Turning back to Fox and Helen, "Now what can I do for you?"

Fox didn't waste time, he got right to the point, "What can you tell us about two twins: Alene and William Houck?"

Sister Janice's face swelled into shock; stunned and shaken her bubbly personality suddenly evaporated like dew – caught off guard, she was speechless. She closed her eyes as if trying to forget; she shook her head as if trying to jostle William's memory from her mind, but it was no use, the nightmare persisted, "Why do you ask?" She said calmly, reserved, but her lips trembled.

Fox immediately sensed her apprehension, "I didn't mean to cause you any discomfort. You see, we are working on a case, and we have reason to believe William Houck might be involved."

"Didn't you see his tombstone?" Protested Sister Janice, she stiffened her back. "This institution paid for their burials."

"Yes, I did. And so, did the police. But I believe William Houck isn't buried there. If anyone is buried there, it's not William."

Her affected protest changed. She felt caught, trapped, and she knew the lie was over. In a fright, she collapsed her hands together; tears poured from her eyes, she sobbed.

Fox reached into his pocket; pulled out a hanky, and offered it to her.

"Sister Janice, are you alright?" Helen asked.

She dried her eyes, "Yes, I'm sorry, please forgive my outburst." She regained her composure. "Mr. Fox, there's not much I can tell you about William. All of our records are sealed. I'm sorry."

"I understand the asylum has a policy. But since William is thought to be dead, can you at least share with us some information?"

"You don't understand. We didn't really pay for the burial; a sizable donation was given to the institution to not only place the tombstone there but also seal whatever information we had about the child."

Fox wasn't getting anywhere, he had to use another approach. "Sister Janice. You are a devoted Roman Catholic and a Christian. You wouldn't be working here if you didn't care about children." Fox looked into her eyes with compassion, "We need more people like you, who will help others in need. So, let me tell you why we are asking about William. The case we are working on involves the murder of a child, the murder of my fiancé, and the recent abduction of another child." He scooted on the edge of his seat, "The investigation has led us here, to you, to this institution. We need your help. Please."

Fox's words stung her heart; more tears, and more sobbing. She wailed. "I thought, I thought he wouldn't harm anyone." Her face turned upward. "Dear God, what have we done?" Her words were sharp and poignant. Burning passion gushed from her gut like a volcano. "No! No! No!"

Helen shot up from her chair and ran around the desk and put her arm around Sister Janice, "What can we do to help?" She said.

"Nothing." She said as her head waved back and forth. "Nothing. This great sin is our fault."

"How so?" Fox asked.

"The asylum needs food, milk, and blankets – we are always in need of money," Her hands quaked, "Please understand Mr. Fox, we have to take care of so many children; well, out of nowhere, a person showed up with a sizable donation, it was supposed to be simple – but it was a ruse."

"Ruse?" Fox asked.

"Yes, a ruse. Pretend William died along with his sister and fake his burial."

"Who was this person?" Fox asked.

"I can't. We agreed. A promise is a promise."

"But we need to know, lives are at stake."

She pushed herself away from the desk and dried her eyes once again. "Fine, but you have to promise me something."

"What?"

"Promise you will keep the institution's name out of it."

"I promise."

Sister Janice hesitated. Her breath skipped a few beats like a child playing hopscotch. She rolled her eyes back into their sockets. She was trying to find the nerve to speak his name. "His name, his name was Fields, Damien Fields."

Fox and Helen looked at each other in disbelief, "Did you say, Damien Fields?" Fox asked to make sure he heard her correctly.

"Yes. We asked Mr. Fields why he wanted the charity to do this, but he gave us no reasons. He gave us the money with strict instructions to seal the whole matter." Her face distorted, "At the time we accepted the money and his terms, we had no idea what this child would do and grow into."

"Do?" Fox asked, "What do you mean, do?"

"William was a baby when he came to us. Our main purpose here is to find good Catholic homes for abandoned children. And we tried to adopt him out, but there were no takers."

"Why?" Helen said.

"Mind you, most families never tell us why they choose one child over the other. At first, when William was a baby, it was his appearance—his albinism. We were forced to raise William as our own." Sister Janice's lips cracked; a pasty yellowish hue glistened; some teeth were missing, "We did what we could, but no matter what we did, he just got worse."

"Can you give us some examples?" Fox said.

"Well, one day, he tried to run away. He came across a dog with a broken leg. He killed it with a rock."

"Did he say why?"

"He said the dog needed to be fixed. He fixed him."

Those words hit Fox right in his heart. Clara flashed through his mind.

"What's wrong, Mr. Fox?"

Fox lifted his head, "Those are the words he used when he told me I needed to be fixed when he killed my fiancé."

"Oh, my," Sister Janice covered her mouth as if she felt responsible.

"Please, Sister Janice, go on."

"Well," She stuttered, still afraid to utter words and stories that if spoken out loud another crime would ensue, "Well, this all started when one of our adopted children— Henry J. King—came back after he was an adult demanding to know who his real parents were. We couldn't tell him, we didn't know. Most of our children are left here without any reference to the parents, they just leave the child and disappear. One day he showed up as usual and killed two of our charity sisters and then killed himself. But before he shot himself, he shouted, 'there's no use living without a father or mother and without knowing who they were.'" Sister Janice looked Fox squarely in the eyes, "William heard those words. After that, he wanted to know the same thing. He obsessed day in and day out."

Fox looked at Helen, "This coincides with my earlier theory about the killer, in that he was killing to appease someone. This is the root of his motives."

"William was relentless. Every day he would annoy the sisters, he didn't accept our answers. William resisted; and turned increasingly more and more antagonistic. He refused to attend chapel and behave. William treated the other children with contempt. He would even go as far as to beat other children to a pulp. The more we punished him, the more he hated; he hated the sisters and everyone around him. He felt alone and betrayed by his family and society."

"What happened to him? Did the sister raise him till he was an adult?" Fox said.

"No. William was about fourteen years old when he ran away. We looked for him, but to no avail."

"Did he show any signs of accepting any of the Christian' teachings he was exposed to?"

"William rejected them all. He would rail against God, he couldn't entertain God in his mind," Sister Janice hung her head, "The vile words he would use against Christ; I can't even repeat them." She looked back up, "We tried Mr. Fox, we tried. We showed him compassion, we tried to teach him between right and wrong. He grew worse. One day, one of our orderlies found magazines and newspapers in his room about atheism and eugenics."

"Eugenics?" Helen said. Anticipating Fox's next question, "Was one of the magazines called *Lucifer the Light Bearer*?"

Sister Janice jerked her head in surprise, "Yes, how did you know?"

"We didn't," Fox said, "We came across that magazine in our research. In fact, they seem to be a nefarious and a clandestine group of atheists who embrace eugenics, abortion, and other toxic ideas. They want to radically transform American society."

"What do you mean?" Sister Janice said.

"For one, they want to rewrite the first amendment to the U.S. Constitution to say, 'separation of church and state,' not 'Congress shall make no law respecting an establishment of religion or prohibiting the free exercise thereof.' In other words, they hate religion; they want to banish it from public life, if not eliminate it altogether."

"I had no idea this material poisoned William's mind," Sister Janice said. "Poor, William."

"I believe so. When hate motivates a person, then they are susceptible to all kinds of twisted notions, and actions," Fox shifted in the chair, "You see, the groundwork was already laid. His family abandoned him. He hated them for it. He took that hate out on you and the sisters – then out on God. His hate grew when reading hateful material. Yet, at the same time, he still wanted to be accepted by his father. This is the longing of every boy. This amalgam of hate and longing creates a psychopath."

Fox felt sister Janice's guilt and her compassion for William. He came to realize she and others did their best. They tried to love him and help him. "Sister Janice, you have nothing to feel guilty over nor feel any shame. I can see you loved William. He rejected that love. It's not your fault or anyone here."

Sister Janice's cheeks turned red and round. She tried to muster a smile; the pain was too deep. "Yes, we love him." She exclaimed, "I'm sorry about your fiancé, and the harm William has brought to others, but I still love him. Please forgive me."

Fox smiled, "Is there anything you can tell us about Alene Houck? Why did she die so young?"

"Unfortunately, Alene was born with a weak immune system, she died of smallpox."

"Thank you, Sister Janice. The information you supplied will help the investigation."

Sister Janice smiled, "No, thank you."

Fox understood Sister Janice's last words. They dripped with pathos; no more words were needed.

"Here's my card, if you think of anything else, please call me."

"I will. And I look forward to reading your future cases, except this one—as I'm sure you understand."

They shook hands and parted.

Fox and Helen walked away feeling enlightened with new information about the killer and the case, but, at the same token, a sense of foreboding crept in like dark clouds forcing itself like narcissists controlling everything and everyone around itself.

CHAPTER 38

Fox and Helen left the orphanage. They flagged down the nearest taxi and gave the driver instructions to drive to Fox's apartment. They were consumed by what they had just learned from Sister Janice. It was mid-day. People were out in full force.

Fox deep in thought, he glanced out the window, "A sea of hats," He said.

"What did you say?" Helen asked.

"Look. Look at all the hats bobbing and weaving, it reminds me of the sea."

Helen looked out the window and crossed her eyes, "Okay, sure, whatever you say," her tone a little snarky, she slipped back into her seat, "Fox, now, back to reality. What do you think about what we just learned? I mean, isn't it sad about those poor children, Alene and William?"

"Yes, it is. Very." Fox grabbed her hand, "It's disturbing on many different levels."

"I think it's obvious William and Alene were eugenic babies. What do you think?"

"It is looking that way, Helen. The irony of it all; their parents were a eugenic match, the perfect match, good genes, good bloodlines; but their children were born with serious health issues."

The taxi suddenly leaped forward, "What the—!" Said the taxi driver as his head slammed against the steering wheel.

The crash threw Fox and Helen forward as well. Fox looked back; two black-Ford-sedans were chasing them. One sedan slammed down on the accelerator again, Fox yelled, "Faster! To the driver."

"You got it!" The driver hit the gas pedal hard, he shifted the vehicle into high gear. All three flew backward as if caught in a windstorm; their bodies sunk deep into the faux-leather-upholstery, "Hold on!" Screamed the driver.

Fox looked back again. The sedans were gaining on them. The taxi weaved in and out of car lanes. Running through red lights. Helen screamed, "Lookout," Ahead of them, a truck jumped out of nowhere. It stalled in the middle of the road, blocking the way. The taxi driver jerked the wheel and swerved, he squeezed between the truck and a telephone pole.

Fox and Helen were tossed around like corks in a rainstorm. The driver drove as fast as he could, but he couldn't shake the sedans. The taxi was rammed again. "Why are they after you guys?" The driver asked, angry, and irritated.

Fox shrugged his shoulders. He looked ahead, "Make a left here." He ordered the driver.

He made the turn, so did the sedans. Fox looked back again and noticed a man reaching out of the passenger side with a Thompson Sub-Machine. He grabbed Helen's head, "Get down!" A rattling sound ensued, bullets showered into the back of the taxi, glass flew everywhere like buckshot.

The taxi drivers' eyes grew belligerent, "My car!" He bellowed, "The goon has a chopper! Bastard!" He said. "Hold on tight!" The driver made a sharp right turn, but he was forced to jerk the wheel to his left to avoid hitting a woman pushing a child in a baby carriage. The taxi hit the curve hard, careening past the sidewalk and pedestrians, and crashed into a store— destroying mannequins and displays.

Helen was knocked unconscious. The taxi driver opened his door, fell to the ground bleeding, and ran away. Fox leaped from the car, hurt, rib hurting, but before he was able to take out his gun and take a strategic position, two men were right upon him. One of them, large man, swung and hit Fox in his mouth; blood spurted from his lower lip like squeezed juice. Fox hit back; the man staggered and fell to the ground. The other goon came around the car, lurched, and swung at Fox. Fox ducked and came back up with an uppercut, lifting him off the ground and clear onto his back. Before he knew it, two other men grabbed him, and Fox was knocked unconscious. Fox and Helen were thrown into the backseat of one of the sedans; they sped away.

Helen awoke. She was gagged and tied to a chair. The room was dark except for a flicker of light buzzing from the ceiling. She blinked her eyes to focus. The room was empty; she noticed Fox was next to her, gagged, and tied to a chair as well. She muffled, to try to wake Fox and get his attention. He was out cold. Fear gripped her thoughts. *We are going to die like Clara and the child. Oh, God, help us.* She began to panic. She struggled, but the rope was too tight.

Calm down. Calm down, she told herself. *Calm down, pray, and focus.* Her fear never left her, but after a while, she was able to control it and channel her negative emotions into more productive use. At least that was her hope. Her eyes started to adjust to the sparsely lit room. She felt damp. The chard walls displayed a thick layer of black soot. The room had been on fire at one time. It reminded Helen of the small town she and her family lived near when it caught on fire when she was a little girl at the time, but she never forgot it. It left the same soot appearance on the brick-walls of the local bank.

The room had a few old chairs and dusty pews. *Church pews.*

Church pews similar to the ones when they were knocked unconscious by the killer. She looked over at Fox. He was still unconscious. She muffled more sounds. She was able to scoot her chair, legs of the chair scratching the floor.

Fox started to wake up. He struggled, but the rope was too tight. Fox looked around and noticed Helen tied up. He tried to talk, but couldn't; like Helen, his mouth gagged shut. Fox took the opportunity to look around to see if there was an exit. There, a closed-door on the other end of the room.

After scanning the room more, he closed his eyes to try to hear a noise, any noise. To the back of them, drops of water dripped on a tin cup. It reminded Fox of the Chinese water torture devise where they would tie people down lying on their backs. Tiny and slow continuous drops of water would drip on their forehead until they went insane. But this wasn't a Chinese water torture device, they were tied to chairs.

They sat for hours. Hunger set in; their stomachs ached, it grew and grew. Then, clanking; shoes, it got louder; the door flew open; five men walked in, and one woman. They dressed alike. The men wore suits and ties. Clean-cut look. No beards or mustaches. The woman was a Vamp. Straight black hair cut, shoulder-length. Her lips red-thin like beets.

They approached, Fox and Helen tensed up, not knowing what was about to transpire. The men surrounded them, the woman stood in the middle, looking down at Fox and Helen, watching them squirm. At first, they said nothing. She stared. Her eyes glared, empty, cold, like a shark. She crossed her arms and tapped her shoe on the ground. "You were warned. We could have killed you, you know, on several occasions." She said, pacing back and forth. "We didn't. We told you we would be watching."

She took off both of their gags, "Before we kill you, we will allow you to say goodbye to each other and make peace with your maker if you believe in such mumbo-jumbo."

Fox coughed, "Why don't you just kill us?" His eyes sharpened and focused intently, "You can't, can you? at least not right away – you have your orders."

"Take my advice, take the little time you have Mr. Fox," She turned her head and motioned to the men, two took out pistols. "You don't have much time."

"Before you kill us, can you at least tell us who you are?" Fox said.

"Fine, I see no harm in that. We are members of Lucifer the Light Bearer."

"What's your mission, your goal?"

"We are trained to bring about the destruction of America and radically change it."

"Why?"

"Perfection. Perfection Mr. Fox; it will be a glorious utopia; traditional religion will end; religious slaves aren't fit to rule. Rulers are to be free of any absolute morality. Private property will be abolished." Her words were like shallow headlines, they flowed from her lips without any thought or reflection, "You see Mr. Fox. We're the future, we're building the future."

"You mean only a select few?" Fox said sarcastically, "The fit, and only the engineered fit. The unfit will be eliminated; eugenics is the method you are using to usher in your sterilized world of misfits."

She slapped Fox in the face, "How dare you call us misfits. We are fit. We have been chosen. Our bloodlines are pure." She said. She looked down at Fox with disgust like he was a cockroach. "You had your chance, Mr. Fox.

You have rejected a chance to be a part of something greater than yourself."

The two men placed their guns on Fox and Helen's heads.

"You may kill us, but you haven't won. You and your ilk will never win," Fox said, "And you know why?"

A smirk came across her face, "Why?"

"Because God can't be exterminated; justice can't be expunged, love wins over hate in the end. Your utopia needs people like yourself to do its dirty work. The foundations of your world will be built on death, hate, and evil. It won't last. Eventually, your kind will turn on each other and destroy itself."

"Fool!" She said, tilting her head back in condemnation. She turned to the men holding the guns and gave the signal to shoot.

Helen screamed; she closed her eyes.

"Stop! Police!" A loud voice yelled from the door entrance. Police officers flooded the room like linebackers, "Stop, or we'll be forced to shoot!"

The goons turned. They started to shoot at the police; the police returned fire, one after the other, each thug fell to the floor dead. The woman pulled her pistol, but before she got off a shot, a bullet hit her between the eyes, killing her instantly.

The smoke-filled room cleared, "All clear, they're all dead." One officer said.

Savage stepped in, "Untie them." He ordered his officers.

"I thought we were dead, Savage," Fox said, "That was close."

"Yes, it was." Helen said, "I almost had a heart attack."

"How did you know we were here?" Fox said.

"I put a man on your tail. He's been following you ever since you got beat up."

"What? Why didn't you say anything?"

"It wasn't necessary. Besides, I was trying to catch one of the pursuers so we can pump him for information." Savage said. He looked around at the dead bodies, "It didn't work. Too bad, I wanted to know more about what we are dealing with."

"Thank you for saving us," Helen said, sweat rolling down her forehead, panting from the excitement.

Helen got up but collapsed after she saw all the blood and mayhem, and her hunger caught up with her too. She cried and sobbed; this was the first time she faced death. "Are we going to die?" She said, desperately looking into Fox's eyes.

"Helen," Fox said. "Everything will be alright."

She sobbed, "What are we going to do Fox?"

"Trust me." He grabbed her, "Do you trust me?"

"Yes, but—"

"No buts, I believe this will end soon."

"Really?" She said, almost hyperventilating.

"Yes."

"How, I mean, how can you know?"

Detective Savage was standing and listening, "Yes, Fox, share with us what you think?" He said.

"It's a hunch. But my hunches are usually right."

"Go on," Savage said. "We're all ears."

"Well, right before we were about to be shot, the killer removed our gags. She gave us time to make peace with God if we believed in God. That's strange, very strange. Why didn't they just kill us on the spot?" Fox looked at Savage, "Don't you think that's odd?"

"Maybe she still had a glimmer of kindness beating in her breasts," Savage said.

"I don't think so. When I mentioned to the leader, somebody ordered her to allow us time to prepare for our deaths, she didn't flinch. This meant I was correct in my assessment. Someone was pulling her strings."

"Who?"

"That led me to my next clue." Fox stooped down next to the woman's dead body and lifted her arm, "See this ring?"

"Sure," Savage said.

"Remember the photos you found in the killer's room? Remember, one of the photos was a picture of a person, but his image was blurry?"

"Yes."

"Remember what I said? Even though we couldn't make out the face, I noticed the ring on the person's finger. I saw that ring somewhere before, but I couldn't remember where?" Fox looked at the ring on the dead woman and turned his head upward to Savage's and Helen's, "Notice anything?"

Both Helen and Savage eyes widen and focused; surprised, "Yes." Savage said, "But what does it mean? What's the connection?"

"Are you suggesting there's more than one killer?" Helen said.

"No. I believe the killer is acting alone. What I'm suggesting is this cult is hiding something. The cult knows the killer and the killer knows the cult." Fox said. His thoughts drifted into a meditative state. "There is something else," Fox said after he thought long and hard.

"What is it," Savage said.

"According to an eye-witness, the killer was wearing a ring. The man in the photo was wearing a ring. And now this woman is wearing an identical ring found in the photo. Coincidental?" He looked at Savage and Helen. "Maybe, but not likely. In fact, now that I've had a chance to see this ring up close, now I know where I've seen it before."

"Where?" Helen asked.

"College. When I attended Harvard, there was a small group of young men who formed a secret society; so secret, its name was known only to its members. But what distinguished them in public was this exact ring."

"Do you know who they are?" Savage said.

"I remember one, just one."

"Who is it?" Helen said.

"I can't tell you yet. But now I know why this case is complex and sinister." Fox said. "If I'm correct, all is lost if we don't act quickly." He stood and faced Savage and Helen, "I can't tell you anything more—at least for the moment."

"Fox, you need to tell me who this person is; I need to know. Period." Savage said.

"You're a police officer, that I understand. But what we don't need at this moment are guns-blazing; that'll gum-up the works. For this to hold up in court, you need to have some sort of confession or at least revealed in such a way it can't be refuted by legalese, mumbo jumbo." Fox rested his arm on Savage's shoulder. "If I'm wrong, no harm is done. If you're wrong, it could cost you your lively hood and pension."

Savage measured Fox's words carefully, "Well, you never have let me down before, then what do we do?"

"I think we need to have a meeting of the minds. You call Cold Springs Harbor Institute and have Charles Davenport, Harry Laughlin, and professor Black meet us at Central Park, at the Bethesda Fountain tomorrow around 10:00 AM. And also call Damien Fields, have him meet us there as well. In the meantime, I'll call my friend Judge John Simmons to meet us there too."

"What if they refuse?" Savage said, wondering what Fox was up to.

"You're a police officer. You know how to persuade people to do things against their will."

"But what about the missing child?" Helen said.

"I hope after tomorrow that will be solved," Fox said, "Savage, you need to prepare your men for tomorrow. Have them comb the area two hours before we meet and position them in key locations. I prefer some of them to be in plain clothes so as not to frighten the killer if he shows up."

"I'm not sure what your plan is, Fox, but I'm trusting you," Savage said.

"You can always blame me if things go south."

"Will do."

"In the meantime, we all need a good night sleep," Fox said. "Can you have one of your men drive us home?"

Savage barked out an order. A rookie police officer appeared. "Take these two wherever they want. Understand?"

The rookie tipped his head forward in compliance, and he drove them home.

CHAPTER 39

The morning dew covered the ground as if a blanket of water-pellets clung to each blade of grass for dear life before the sun called them back up to the atmosphere. Bright yellow shafts cut through the Park, the trees, and bushes like giant crystal ice columns holding up the sky. Wildlife thrived; ponds teamed with fish, birds sang, squirrels played; magic and vitality consumed Central Park, but death was coming.

Fox and Helen arrived early at Bethesda Fountain – the Angel of Water. The bronze angelic figure stood lifelike, but motionless as if frozen, if thawed, thousands of years spoke. The pumps were turned on and water rushed up into the top basin, then it cascaded back down. The effects were another added feature to give off the appearance of a heavenly being with the power to change a natural substance into a healing quality; similar to Ponce De Leon's fountain of youth— but far more potent.

Savage stepped out from behind some trees, "Good morning, Fox and Helen."

"Good morning," Fox said.

"It's a good day to catch a killer," Savage said hopefully, with excitement in his words.

"That's the plan," Fox said, "Did you convince our guests to show up?"

"Yes. At first, each one refused. But then I told them you solved the case."

"What did they say and what were their expressions?" Fox asked.

"Charles Davenport and Harry Laughlin instantly changed their minds upon the news. 'They want Clara's killer caught,' they said. As for Damien Fields, he didn't believe you solved the case. He said he would show up for the show. He wants us to make fools out of ourselves. I told him to bring a lot of popcorn. He sneered."

Fox smiled, "Will Professor Black show?"

"He declined," Savage said, "What about your friend, Judge Simmons?"

"Done. Judge Simmons will be here."

"Good. I have men all around. Most of them are undercover." Savage pointed to a haggard-looking man sitting reading a newspaper, "He's one of ours." He looked at several others. Some of them posed as visitors, innocuous, and average looking. "Overall Fox, we have this placed covered like a tin-roof; the Park is sealed, every entrance is guarded," Savage explained.

"Good."

"I still haven't figured out what you have planned, but I'm following your lead. When the circus shows up, my men and I will be close by. I'll stay next to you and Helen just in case." He patted his side pocket, "Not to worry, old Betsy is right here." His cheeks rolled back like soft waves, revealing his jagged teeth.

"Swell. By the way, did you find out who attacked Helen and me yesterday?"

"Yes, and no. All your kidnappers had the name (Ubermensch and a number) tattooed on their arms.

We couldn't trace who the men were, but we were able to trace the woman's identity. Her name was Julia Houck."

Fox's face flinched, "What did you say?"

"The men—"

"No, no, what did you say about the woman?"

"Oh, her name was Julia Houck."

Fox snapped his fingers, "Of course. It all makes sense now."

"What does?"

"All in good time, all in good time."

"Fox," Helen said, "I'm afraid."

"I know, but if I'm correct, it will be over soon."

"But what if something goes wrong?" Helen said dreadfully.

Fox sensed her palpitating fear; it was extreme and intense. Her heavy heartbeat was manifested by every palpable breath. "Helen, you don't have to be here. Would you like a police officer to escort you home?" Fox said.

"No! Not on your life. I've come this far, I have to see it through, no matter how I feel."

"Okay, then," Fox said. He placed his arm around her and pulled her in tight. She needed his touch and reassurance; in some mysterious way, she not only wanted it, she expected it.

Charles Davenport and Harry Laughlin arrived, "Hello Mr. Fox, Miss Helen Carlyle, and Detective Savage." Davenport said.

Harry Laughlin remained silent.

"Good morning." Fox replied, looking at all of them, "Good morning to all of you."

"So, Mr. Fox," Davenport said, "We were told you solved the case. Now, who killed Clara?"

"In good time. We are still waiting for others to arrive."

"Oh?" A surprised look formed around Davenport's eyes, "Who are we to expect?"

"Soon, you'll know soon enough."

At that moment Damien Field's popped from around the corner. He approached. His face twisted in disgust the moment he saw Detective Savage; Savage returned the look. Then he looked at Fox. A grin fell across his face like a cutout jack o' lantern. "You think you solved the case?" He chuckled out loud. "You fool." He looked at Savage and Helen, "You're all fools." His laugh grew deep, piercing, and penetrating.

"What in blazes, are you laughing at?" Someone said. Everyone turned, it was Judge John Simmons, "Pipe down," He barked like he was in the court ordering an attorney to sit and shut up, "You're the fool, fool."

"Judge, good morning," Fox said, "I'm glad you were able to come."

"Of course, I wouldn't miss this for the world." Judge Simmons said, "I wish I could have been more helpful."

"Now that you are all here, you are probably wondering why I invited each and every one of you. Let me begin." Fox turned away from them and faced the angel. "Isn't it beautiful?" He said. He stood for a long while. Then, he started to walk around the basin.

Baffled, each looked at one other.

"Odd behavior," Davenport whispered to Laughlin.

"He's mad; stark mad," Laughlin said.

Fox took his time; step after step, tension mounted. Even Detective Savage wondered if Fox was off his rocker. But he remained silent. Birds chirped nearby. A brisk breeze came out of nowhere. The men had to grab and hold down their hats.

Fox walked around the basin, completing a full circle.

"See, I told you so. Fool. What a clown." Damien shouted, "Just look at him. I got my money's worth so far." He laughed uncontrollably.

Fox stopped in front of Damien, "So, I'm a fool?" Fox looked into his eyes; he glared deeper and deeper; Damien stopped laughing. His bravado shrunk into feelings of intimidation and feeling small. He coughed awkwardly, then he started to choke, clasping his fist over his mouth as if to cover his feelings of inadequacy.

"I'll cut to the chase," Fox said, "Damien Fields you are a scoundrel. You've been one most of your life."

"If you think I'm the killer—"

"No, you're not the killer." Fox said, "But you know who the killer is."

Damien's eyes widened. His nostrils flared out like a wild boar, "Why you. . ." His words sputtered, "I'll have you arrested for defamation!" He exclaimed. His cheeks puckered like two balloons on the verge of popping, "You have no idea who you're messing with, I'll have your head—"

"William Houck," Fox blurted out.

Damien's cheeks deflated; his eyes dropped to the ground knowing the gig's up; he was caught. "What?"

Damien said, his voice stammered and stuttered like he was speaking in tongues, "How?" His whole body shriveled and dried up like a prune.

"Your involvement was the easy part. The hard part is yet to come."

Damien looked around for an escape.

"Don't you dare," Savage barked, we have this whole park covered.

Fox faced the whole group, "We know about the cult called Lucifer the Light Bearer." He said. Fox watched each of their reactions; each expressed a different look, but no one appeared surprised or shocked.

Harry Laughlin finally spoke, "Yes, Mr. Fox, Mr. Davenport, and myself are well aware of this group. But, so what?"

"I will spare you the details of how they have broken the law at every turn in this investigation, but I will say this, Damien Fields is part of the cult. He was the one who paid a Catholic orphanage to hide, raise, and cover-up William Houck's identity. William Houck is the killer."

"Who's William Houck?" Davenport said, "And how do you know he's the killer?"

Fox was running out of time, he had to act quickly; a child was missing, and he still hoped the child was alive. "Now that I have your attention, all of you," Fox said, as he turned to Judge Simmons, "Judge, would you be so kind as to tell us why your son is the killer?"

Judge Simmons face tightened, his lips clenched, bags formed around his eye sockets like a puff of white powder, "He's not my son!" He said despondently. "No, you're wrong," he shook his head, violently, "Fox, are you out of your mind?"

Fox moved closer, "No, John, you're the killer's father – it took a while, but it all came to me yesterday. The goons who tried to kill us gave us time to make peace with God. Why? I thought. Then it hit me. Only some-one close to me would be so gracious to give us time be-fore we were killed; but that only made me curious," Fox turned to Savage, "Did you bring it?"

"Yes." Savage pulled the ring from his coat pocket and handed it to Fox.

Fox held the ring out in front of himself, "Hold out your hand, judge."

He started to back away, "You're crazy." He stuffed his hands in the pockets, "You know who I am? Touch me, and you'll spend the rest of your life in prison." He looked a Savage, "And that goes for you too. Just think about it Fuzz, you're a cop, spending the rest of your life in the Big House with hardened criminals, some of whom you put there." The judge laughed nervously, "You can't frame me; I'm untouchable."

Detective Savage wanted to arrest him, but he knew the judge was right. All he had to go on was Fox's word, and that wasn't good enough. Savage needed something more. It had to be concrete before he could lay a hand on the judge. His anger mounted and grew every minute, but he was powerless to act.

"Don't show us your ring—" Fox was suddenly interrupted.

Out of nowhere, the killer stepped out of the dark underbrush, holding the abducted child in his arms. Police officers sprang to life; guns were drawn; hammers clicked back and ready, "Stop!" Shouted Savage, "Stop!"

The killer let the child go.

"Over here," Helen cried out, waved the child over. The child ran to Helen instinctively.

When Fox saw the killer, a deluge of rage pumped through his blood-veins like fire. Clara's image flashed before his eyes; all his hate surfaced; ready to pull out his pistol – something stopped him, something mysterious.

Oblivious to the police officers, to Fox, and everyone except for Judge Simmons, the killer held out his arms towards the judge, "Father," He cried, "Father." He stepped forward, inch by inch, as if he was slowly dragging chains – heavy chains; the link of being abandoned, the reality of being shunned, another link of hate, eugenics; but he wanted to please his father, he wanted his father's love and approval – all formed and shaped a child into a killer.

The judge jumped back, "Fool," He screamed, "What are you doing here? Do you know what you have done?"

The killer cried out, "Father, please."

"Please what? We have tried to help you since you were born. We placed you with people that would take care of you; allowed you to keep your mother's last name; just look at you." The judge said wrathfully. He became blind to his surroundings; his arrogance and hate exposed, "We covered up your murders."

"I killed for you, father," William said, "I was wrong, we were wrong."

"Get away from me, you, you, filthy animal. You repulse me. You're a freak of nature. Pathetic— unfit to live in society."

"I killed. You killed. I saw you kill children and others. I saw you plunge a knife into their chest after you yelled, 'unfit to live,'"

"I should have killed you when you were born, but your mother, she showed weakness." The judge's voice was shrill and brusque. His face cavorted into demonic shapes.

The killer moved closer. BANG! A shot went off. The bullet hit the killer's temple. He fell.

"Stop! Stop shooting!" Savage barked.

The little girl screamed, "Stop, please. He saved my life."

Miraculously, the killer was still alive. Blood seeping from his head. Fox's rage dissipated, he reached down and placed his hand on the back of the killer's head, holding it up and firmly. William's eyes flickered, then opened, "Fox, I'm sorry." The angel's bronze shape filled the killer's eyes; his tears matched the water of the fountain. He gasped for air; his throat made a guttural sound – then he died, his eyes still open. Fox stared into the eyes of a killer, into the eyes of an albino, into the eyes of William – who all he wanted was the love of his father and mother.

Fox, Helen, and Savage sat on the edge of Bethesda Fountain; the angel stood tall behind them as the water swirled and churned with life. The city had taken William Houck's body, but his bloodstain remained. Judge John Simmons's words were his undoing, that's all Detective Savage needed to arrest him. But he had questions, "Fox," Savage said, "how did you know this would go down this way?"

Fox smiled, "I didn't. I had no idea the killer would even show up."

"Then, this was a longshot?"

"In part. I knew enough that some fireworks would take place. But I didn't expect the judge spilling his guts and showing his true nature," Fox said, "By the way, did you get any useful information out of Damien Fields?"

Savage grinned, "We did, and more. He squealed like a pig. According to his confession, Judge John Simmons is the ringleader of the cult Lucifer the Light Bearer. They have been performing live sacrifices for years. They took eugenics to its logical conclusion."

"Of course," Fox said, "The eugenic laws, the recent Supreme Court ruling in *Buck v. Bell*, and forced sterilized inmates." Fox took off his hat and stroked his hair, "By the way, who shot the gun that killed William, and why?"

"A rookie cop thought the killer was about to lurch forward, and he nervously pulled the trigger."

"A rookie; you mean a rookie took down the killer? – go figure."

"Yes, but back to Damien, he did all the heavy lifting for the cult. He was Judge Simon's lackey." Savage said. "One last thing, Fox. Damien Fields implicated Professor Black as being a member of the cult. But he has disappeared. No one knows where he went."

"What about the child? Who kidnapped the child that the killer brought with him?" Helen asked.

"Cult members. They were not only following you two but the killer as well. According to Damien, they were going to sacrifice the child."

"And the killer saved his life? Why?" Helen expressed.

"I'm not sure," Fox said, "But that is the reason I wanted us to meet here. It was here, this location the killer was spotted with a child; he didn't kill that child. Why? I asked myself. That was my final hunch." Fox stopped and looked up at the Angel of Water, "Perhaps the answer is found elsewhere. But that died with the killer."

ACKNOWLEDGMENTS

I wish to thank my wife, Brenda, for her patience, proof-reading, and feedback in the production of this book. And there are others. I thank Leona Chance, Greg Sutton, Reon Hillegass, Brenda Bricken, and Chris Goldthorpe for their overall help and contributions. Without God, family, and friends, success is unattainable. If by chance, success comes without the support of friends and loved ones, it's a hollow victory – at best.